A GRAVEYARD OF FIRST CHAPTERS

A GRAVEYARD OF FIRST CHAPTERS

JOHNNY PAYNE

ISBNs: 979-8-9990422-0-0 (paperback); 979-8-9990422-1-7 (ebook)

Library of Congress Control Number: 2025940092

First Printing: 2025

Printed in the United States of America

PRAISE FOR JOHNNY PAYNE

Johnny Payne's new novel is intelligent, skillful, inventive, and moving. It begins in a North American junkyard and ends at a Peruvian hacienda, tracking the struggles of a confused young writer to find the woman who raised him, who may or may not be his biological mother. Surprisingly enough, despite the turbulence of the journey, the book has a happy ending, and even more surprising, the happy ending is earned, and richly satisfying. Payne is such a master of fictive techniques that he can do almost anything he wants on the page and make it work. The text is often insanely funny, yet confronts the unavoidable disturbance at the core of human experience. This is a book that everyone should read.

— STEPHEN-PAUL MARTIN, AUTHOR OF *TWENTYTWENTY* AND *THE ACE OF LIGHTNING*

What a crazy and confounding contraption from the toy-box of a Macedonio Fernandez or a Julio Cortazar have we in our hands when we open this graveyard of first chapters. But an American, rough-n-tumble Macedonio or Gregory Samsonite awakening from one dream into multifarious landscapes of dead-end jobs, alien abductions, Medieval moors, six packs, tow trucks, conquistador battles, and arctic explorers, scurvy-ridden, and surviving on pemmican hash. It's a wild whirlwind, pure fun and a turbine of energy and shrapnel. You won't be able to put this novel down.

— ANTHONY SEIDMAN, AUTHOR OF
THAT BEAST IN THE MIRROR

To Juana whose steadfast love has sustained me through many trials and has been the greater part of what happiness this mercurial world offers. Your genius for the art of living has lighted up my days. I cherish you.

CONTENTS

Foreword   xi
J. Bradley Minnick

1. Junkyard Zombies   1
2. Stroking the Cat   6
3. Antarctic Knob   11
4. Homeric   17
5. Kowalski   21
6. La Plata   25
7. Sunroom   28
8. In the Warehouse   32
9. Outside the Warehouse   37
10. The North Wind   42
11. Breaking the Lease   46
12. All About Shiva   50
13. Graveyard of First Chapters   53
14. The Invisible Man   59
15. The Letter   64
16. A Linen Suit and a Boater   68
17. The Cruise Ship   70
18. Guano   76
19. Flaco and Kinky   81
20. Landing the Marlin   86
21. Hummingbird   91
22. Jasper's Origin Story   96
23. The Naked Stepmother   100
24. Vanishing Point   107
25. The Spanish Flotilla   110
26. Sin Cashed   115
27. Bentley Bentayga   118
28. The Candy Bar   123

29. At the Monastery Hotel Bar   139
30. Jasper and Gaspar   143
31. Ayahuasca   148
32. Coup de Foudre   152
33. The Saints Come Marching In   156
34. Switch Hitter   160
35. Frankie and Johnny   164
36. Edema   169
37. Nighthawks   173
38. Not a Graveyard of First Chapters   177
39. The She-Calf   183
40. Ghazal of the Betrayed Woman   197
41. Zombies   199
42. Antuka Starts Her Day   208
43. The Red Sail   212
44. Ayar Manco and Mama Oqllo   216
45. The Black Virgin   218
46. Lily   226
47. A Close Encounter   231
48. In the Campo Santo   235
49. Banish Misfortune   239
50. The Dinner Party   247
51. I Smoke To the Rhythm of the Stars   255
52. The World and Myself   260
53. The Hacienda Owner's Daughter   267

    About the Author   287
    A Note from the Publisher   289

FOREWORD

J. BRADLEY MINNICK

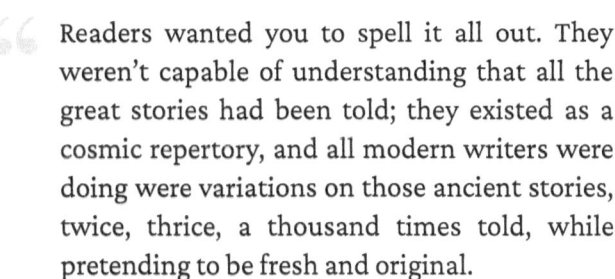 Readers wanted you to spell it all out. They weren't capable of understanding that all the great stories had been told; they existed as a cosmic repertory, and all modern writers were doing were variations on those ancient stories, twice, thrice, a thousand times told, while pretending to be fresh and original.

From the chapter "Graveyard of First Chapters" in *A Graveyard of First Chapters* by Johnny Payne

First Chapters:

In the beginning, a story may take any form with infinite possibilities, but as we read on, those forms limit and delimit—choices become fewer, defined. First chapters serve as road maps, guides, primers on how to read the rest of a book.

In Johnny Payne's first chapter in *A Graveyard of First Chapters*, we meet Jasper Delgado—his car on the blink, standing amidst junkyard wreckage: "Headlights were missing, hunks of plasticine skin ripped away, windshields smashed, roofs caved in as if a meteor shower had hit this exact patch of earth, broken taillights leering, seats stood on end, hubcaps scattered like the giant dropped dimes of forgetful aliens." Without his own zombie model car, without his home, without his ex-girlfriends Vanessa and Geeta: "all he had left to his name was a graveyard of first chapters," which he hadn't even backed up to the cloud. "But he already lived in a cloud, so wherever he took the laptop, it would remain in that cloud by being attached to him." And we ask, will he [Jasper] "suffer the same fate [as his nondescript zombie Corolla], doomed to be stripped for parts until only the naked chassis remained"? Or will he rise up, begin anew amidst infinite possibilities?

Like its precursors, B.S. Johnson's *Alberto Angelo;* Sherwood Anderson's *Winesburg, Ohio,* Giovanni Boccaccio's *The Decameron,* and Ralph Elison's *Invisible Man, A Graveyard of First Chapters* takes the shape of a crystal—many faceted, diamond-like, Payne polishes each side—and Jasper Delgado, his protagonist, is a ragged gemstone—a former community college adjunct professor, a writer of ten books (three best sellers), whose few possessions include a beater laptop within which lie "a cemetery of first chapters, novels that would never be, which were either witness to his recent inability to finish things, or proof of his prudence, of knowing when to quit." And herein we are introduced to Jasper's story and some of these first chapters, kaleidoscopic, interweaving that pile on top of one another—whose facets reflect and whose surface needs other surfaces.

The school teacher, Alberto, in B.S. Johnson's experimental novel *Alberto Angelo* wants to be an architect. He draws buildings whose designs may never be built until after he is dead. His friend Luke asks.

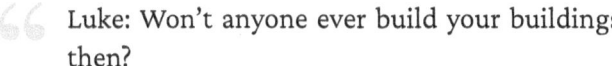

>   Luke: Won't anyone ever build your buildings then?
>   Alberto: Oh—yes one day they'll all be built, I know.

Johnny Payne has constructed promised-imagined first chapters, now entirely built—and in that building, he has sustained a delicate architecture that asks what if? And, Jasper is in process—remaking himself along the way, falling in and out with other characters: the store clerk Travis, his ex-girlfriend Vanessa, and later Butch Cassidy Kowalski Fisher—"My friends call me Butch."

A Graveyard:

When I visit graveyards, especially old graveyards like the one in Marion, Virginia with Sherwood Anderson's tombstone—a sturdy stone inkpot, a delicate sculpted feather pointing to the sky—I think of shapes. And, like Anderson's masterful 1919 cycle-story collection *Winesburg, Ohio*, *A Graveyard of First Chapters* breaks new ground—not once but like a duty-bound grave digger again and again, disrupting different places (a carwash, a warehouse filled with stuff, a cruise ship, Homer Alaska, Cusco Peru) and it erects monuments—carefully constructed chapters that call to each other across vast genres and forms (artifacts, linguistic foreplay, ethnography, oral history, post-modern realism, philosophic comedy, poetics, and folktales) like tombstones calling out for a reader to stand in front of them, remembering what has become of Jasper's life.

A graveyard is where we and our stories ulti-
    mately end up—in a recursive search for
    what?
The fabulous sentence?
The perfect form?
The right word at the right time?
Philosophic insight?
Comic relief?
The perfect chapter?
A small moment of meaning in a world that
    often doesn't make sense?

Yet, as we look at the tombstones that emerge from the improbable beginnings that have made up Jasper's life—these first chapters, this series of beginnings are recast as we find our way through them; individual (everyone gets a chapter) and collective stories in Jasper's monumental efforts to set things right—and through happy accidents to sustain our souls. Jasper, a lovable loser, has made mistakes, many, having gambled away thirty thousand dollars of what he had so easily won "day trading." Now, abandoned like his car on the side of the road, he is propped up again first by a tow truck operator and later by Vivian, Butch, and Inés in an effort to find in his way between this and that; like Dasein's (meaning existence) world of horizons and shaping possibilities of the past, present and future, Jasper says, "that's why he didn't worry. He'd always told himself that even if he lost everything, he could begin over. He'd always weirdly trusted in fate to deliver him."

Graveyard of First Chapters:
    A Graveyard of First Chapters has a chapter called

"Graveyard of First Chapters," which brings to mind the metatextual, the 100 stories in the Decameron—that 14th century novel thematically centered around The Black Plague. But, never fear, this novel is also a love story— Jasper draws on Lady Fortune as he spins the wheel. Vanessa encourages him to turn his first chapters into a novel: "Of course, the notion was ridiculous, so much so that he [Jasper] never mentioned the idea to anyone. Editors would have laughed themselves silly. Readers wanted you to spell it all out. They weren't capable of understanding that all the great stories had been told; they existed as a cosmic repertory..."

Vanessa introduces Jasper to Geeta at a baseball game to be rid of him and pass him off into Geeta's hands, which is similar to the 6th and 7th deception tales in *The Decameron*. (On the day three, when Ricciardo falls into love with the wife of Filippello and leads him to believe that his wife is to meet Filippello at a Turkish Bathhouse.) Furthermore, Vanessa is understanding of Jasper's relationship with Geeta, and before Jasper decides "to move immediately into Geeta's warm bed in her one-bedroom apartment," he tosses his laptop into the trash. He later recovers the laptop under many Hefty garbage bags and finds Geeta, loses Geeta, and recognizes "he'd lost everything, been reduced to nothing. He'd lived briefly in a car wash, then a warehouse, then a dreadful efficiency, believing, as he always had in the back of his mind, that he would become the Invisible Man..." which Jasper "sometimes claimed to be the greatest novel ever written. ...The ultimate universal existential statement" filled with America's everything, including a string of different shapes (mock essays, sermons) and sudden violence.

Will Jasper reconnect with Vanessa? Will he make his

way out of the naked human wreckage he has become? Will he write a novel of first chapters? Will he become visible? Will the novel Jasper's writing end up becoming a graveyard of first chapters or will it move up and out of the graveyard once and for all?

> At least in that instance, he'd had the good sense to write the ending first and make it the opening chapter, the reader then journeying back to see how the debacle had begun.

And how do beginnings end and endings begin?

J. Bradley Minnick
Professor of English
University of Arkansas at Little Rock

1

JUNKYARD ZOMBIES

Wreckage of smashed and crippled cars lay around Jasper. Headlights were missing, hunks of plasticine skin ripped away, windshields smashed, roofs caved in as if a meteor shower had hit this exact patch of earth, broken taillights leering, seats stood on end, hubcaps scattered like the giant dropped dimes of forgetful aliens. He'd called the nearest junkyard from the shoulder of the road rather than leaving the defeated beast there, which had been his first instinct. A winch soon attached itself to haul his nondescript Corolla, the same zombie model he saw all over the road, into the flatbed and he sat next to the driver—which was illegal, but the driver looked at Jasper's face and let him do a ride-along, as Jasper didn't yet have the heart to call an Uber to take him home, for he had no home. He'd given it up in the recent separation, not because he was legally bound to, but because he had no will left. The modest ranch home carried a second mortgage on it anyway, one that Geeta had agreed to take over, in effect setting him free.

Now, the car had died, and he was left almost without

possessions, being too stubborn to keep anything, instead giving his meager, unsentimental trove of personal effects away to Goodwill. All that remained was the laptop under his arm. His car, whose tow bill was the same as its total worth, giving Jasper a profit of zero, had suffered the same fate, too tired to keep running, doomed to be stripped for parts until only the naked chassis remained.

Perhaps that destiny was a purifying gesture, getting reduced to nothing except the skeleton. It was easier to see the rust on the chassis, which he had ignored until it started invading the whole underside and, from there, crept into the engine. Jasper wasn't at all sure that was how it worked in terms of mechanical physics, but it was a great metaphor for his life, and he didn't have to hold himself to some bogus philosophical strictness wherein each analogy gets broken down into its constituents, exactly like him and the car—take that, analogy! Hoisted by your own petard! Jasper had always wanted to give a course called Bullshit Logic, except he hadn't actually taken any philosophy courses.

All he'd kept was one carry-on sized suitcase of clothes and his beater laptop, one that had to keep getting updated every few days and seemed to have about one gigabyte of memory left, less than his grandmother possessed in her final days in the senior home—rest home, nursing home, there were so many euphemisms. Why didn't they call that place what it was: a pre-mausoleum? He should have backed everything up into the cloud. But he already lived in a cloud, so wherever he took the laptop, it would remain in that cloud by being attached to him.

In his laptop lay a cemetery of first chapters, novels that would never be, which were either witnesses to his recent inability to finish things, or proofs of his prudence, of knowing when to quit. He'd published ten novels in eight years, three of them bestsellers, others nobody read, the latter much better written than the bestsellers. His favorite review of all time was a savage newspaper takedown of his thriller *Antarctic Knob,* about a South Pole expedition led by a man so offensive that his men and dogs abandoned him there to die. That review was the only sign that anyone had read the book. It was, paradoxically, like a skier's radio beacon under the snow, the signal that allows him to get rescued after the avalanche dumps three tons of snow on top of him, a sign of life. The review, as the sole witness to that book's death, was also like the solitary penguin watching his hero's death in silence, the sole witness to the end of his existence. At least in that instance, he'd had the good sense to write the ending first and make it the opening chapter, the reader then journeying back to see how the debacle had begun. In celebration, he saved that first chapter in its own file, where it would live in ignominious glory, as an example for the rest.

Jasper knew he'd get by. He was that scrappy. His freelance career and adjunct gigs got him within hailing distance of his now ex-girlfriend Geeta agreeing to have a child together—she was at that borderline age where she had to procreate or not, and under her constant pressure for him to produce income in addition to the paycheck from her low-level troubleshooting tech position, and his jobbing, caused him to get into day trading, for which he turned out to have an unexpected talent. The initial surge netted thirty thousand dollars within six months.

She asked him to stop trading, count that as a nest egg, or pay off the second mortgage. As evidence, she recited to him one of her Indian proverbs, "There are three uncertainties: woman, wind, and wealth"—which felt odd advice, as she was simultaneously indicting her gender and firing a warning shot about the fragility of their relationship. That was her motivational speech? Even weirder, the couple was standing on the back patio of their house at that moment, wind beating the table umbrella he'd neglected to wind down, so that it flapped like an angry Hindu Garuda backing her up with its monstrous wings.

Regrettably, Jasper was addicted to his betting success by then. Nothing had ever come so easy except the best days of his writing. The art of trading felt as artless as when he entered a white heat of fictional composition wherein he could knock out twenty good pages in a day. He did it guided by mere feels, it was not a rational process. You trusted your gut, not a set of rules; the only logic was your inner logic, and thus he got caught in the hypnotic, harlot's betrayal rhythm of investing until he increased their hypo-thetical nest egg to sixty thousand, then eighty, then ninety.

He lost it all in a frenzied three weeks when the supply chain, inflation or Russia—whatever the hell determinants the pundits couldn't agree on—wiped it all out except $217, and he held on to the bitter end as his fortunes plummeted like a suicidal bridge jumper. Even the bit-coin people did better than him. Jasper knew the answer to his sudden reversal of fortune. It was angry gods, savage pre-Christian ones, the gods he could feel inside effigies of Jesus and Moses pulsing to get out when he was a young teenager in Bible school. He knew, even then, that when you ended up getting nailed to a cross, your judgment had been severely impaired from the beginning. And while you were busy being nice to sinners, the earth-demons were consolidating their power the way Latin American dictators do, rewriting the constitution and paying off the Army generals who back them with villas and mineral concessions while everybody in Congress argues politely about preserving ten acres of wetlands.

Jasper was screwed. All he had left to his name was a graveyard of first chapters, also known as aborted novels and no inspiration to draw on as he stood before his defunct and loveless sedan, a lone man encroached upon by hundreds of maimed cars that, in the gloaming, suddenly looked to him like deformed, once-human zombies who encircled him, staggering slowly in the half-life of their half-bodies, holding out the stumps of their arms to ask for an embrace, a final gesture of the affection they'd never gotten from the shocked, lost human who had wandered into their precinct by sheer accident and who they were about to collectively devour with their iron incisors, after asking him for a saint's blessing.

2

STROKING THE CAT

Vanessa lit the votive candle at the altar. Its beeswax smell combined with wintergreen soothed her senses. Jasper was on her mind. He was the guy she'd stayed with the longest, the one who had infuriated her the most, the most eccentric and seemingly destined to failure, endowed with an inexplicable negative charisma. The one who could be pitiless in his scorn for any pieties about state, religion, race, gender, family, all the things that she'd grown up on with certainty and had believed in fervently, the very things he'd take apart with relentless humor, sometimes gently, sometimes trenchantly, ferreting his way to her inner doubt, not wanting to damage her but to free her. And he was the one she thought about the most in retrospect, even though he was the one who she introduced to Geeta, to get him off her back, really, to pass him on to another customer, to keep her from having to break up with him, afraid of failure being her fault. Then she had second thoughts, but the couple already seemed happy; they'd even bought a house, Geeta was closer to his age, and she gave as good as she got with the sarcasm. Vanessa had joked, in front of them both, that maybe Geeta was a fetish, that's what she'd called it, so unlike her, wanting to hurt him, just for a moment, right when she'd set him free and there was no reason for her to wound. She couldn't stomach the bilious taste of her own malice, it was so unlike her to needle someone she loved, or had loved, or still loved.

Truth told, she was worried it was a sign she was going to become like him, the way somebody shows the first signs of dementia: one day they're doing algebra sums, and before you know it, they get lost driving and soon don't know their cat's name, or that it's even their cat, or what a cat is, it's just a thing with fur that they keep stroking out of habit until it scratches their arm because they're holding it too hard, then it jumps off their lap and runs away yowling into a dark corner to pee out of spite.

No, she didn't want to be that person. She was in the church saying a prayer for Jasper because she'd heard that he and Geeta had broken up. Vanessa put a slip of paper on the screen beneath the candle. The paper was blank. She would think of a prayer later and transmit it mentally once she made up her mind about what she wanted to say to God. Yes, she still loved Jasper. But she'd seen him a couple of months ago, they ran into each other when he was picking up Japanese takeout. She liked that about him; he was crazy about ethnic food, and his palate craved it. Vanessa had turned him on to soul food, the real stuff, not this foodie crap. He was even excited when he found out that her ancestors likely came from Senegambia, and he found a Senegalese restaurant in town where you could get thieboudienne and went crazy over the broken rice and sweet potatoes and nétounétou. When she saw him at the checkout, he looked too thin, as if he hadn't eaten in days.

He was at least twenty pounds underweight, still hand-some in a sickly way, and Vanessa wanted to take him home, take him right off Geeta's hands, and her conscience wouldn't have even bothered her. If you let your man get into that shape, you don't necessarily deserve to keep him, but she also didn't want a project, and he definitely looked like a case for emotional rehab.

That's what stopped her from calling him even now that he was free. Geeta and she had stopped being friends by silent mutual agreement. Neither had exactly dropped the other, they simply stopped talking with the excuse that a new man means you're going to be busy for a while getting the planets in alignment, and suddenly you're in bed a lot more and going out to plays and concerts, all the new romance stuff. But Geeta had called her out of the blue after she practically shoved Jasper out the door, that's what came through all her bawling and raging. It seemed self-pitying, and though she offered a legitimate reason—he ran through their savings, she said—there had to be more to it than that. Geeta was keeping the house, and she didn't even seem to know where Jasper was going to live or how he would make ends meet.

Vanessa kept her counsel. She said she was sorry for both of them, dialed Jasper immediately to offer condo-lences, and was about to hang up when she got an auto-mated voice saying the line had been disconnected and was no longer in service. It stung her that he had changed his number, as she suspected it was so she wouldn't call him with regrets, which she never had. Always it stayed stuck in her mind, something Jasper had once said as they ice skated together, casually talking—she was surprised how graceful he was on skates and he said he learned on a frozen lake, so a Zamboni rink was easy—he said that each person was a novel and everybody who mattered got their own chapter in your novel. The rest passed in and out of the book but didn't merit a chapter, and you were both a major character in your novel and a minor character in multiple other novels. And it was important to remember that everybody can influence your story, but only you get to tell it, in the end, and assign its ultimate meaning. Vanessa wondered whether she would ever figure in Jasper's novel again.

Bach's Partita in G Major was resonating on the pipe organ, a slurry mid-afternoon version, almost like happy hour; somebody from the university was probably practicing, as Father Watkins was liberal about loaning the organ out, seeing the church as a sort of community center, sometimes to the consternation of the parishioners. Sure enough, the organ stopped in mid-throb, leaving Bach's glorious piece dead and gone. Once upon a time, Vanessa herself had served as the church organist for funerals, until her mother died and she played that final gig in order to shelter, to avoid the direct and immediate grief among her relatives. At that point, she lost any desire to be around death unless she was compelled to do so.

Yes, Jasper had reminded her of walking death that day, not just a project. It was easy to figure his scarecrow self as that because he was into slasher films and even got her hooked on them for a while. He had this theory that an alien cemetery was located outside their city, half kidding and half serious about it, and he talked about his great-grandparents and other ancestors as if he could commune with them casually, without even having ceremonies, which she, with her New Orleans roots, could believe in. Bring in some candles, spill a little chicken or goat's blood, bring out a cracked photo or two, bring out the Saint Suaire devotional, and Vanessa could jump right in and cock her

ear for the inchoate howls and sobs of those gone to glory
or damnation. The metaphysical realm was real and immediate. But Jasper was either arrogant or crazy to think you
could have the dead on speed dial.

On their first date, he took her to a cemetery, which, as
he pointed out, was really just a lush and beautiful botan-
ical garden with monuments and headstones added. They
picnicked fried chicken and coleslaw with doughy biscuits
under blossoming cherry trees, the tallest she'd ever seen,
petals drifting down after warm gusts of wind, as ducks
skated along the pond, stopping for a toddler who was
hurling handfuls of bread pieces and almost fell in, but was
caught by her mother by the jacket collar.

3
ANTARCTIC KNOB

One too many times, Captain Loghairian had fed his men pemmican hash, day after day of the endless trek, and butchered sled dogs who had pooped out. He'd compared his followers to those same dogs on numerous occasions. Behind them, the ice lay so hard that the sled didn't even make tracks. An eighty kph wind had blown up when he'd predicted clear skies, and all the Cap had answered was, "When life gives you lemons, make pemmican hash." Not the best joke, as some of the men seemed to be suffering from scurvy, and he could easily have chosen a better simile, at least a non-citrus fruit. Instead, he'd corrected it to "limes."

A chunk of ice flew at his head, somehow dislodged from one of his men's sled runners. He didn't even ask who; in a sense, it was all of them, and he knew it. That night, in the tent, as they sat glumly rehashing the pemmican hash they hadn't been able to stomach the night before, he tried to rehash the day's events, ones they clearly didn't want to talk about, least of all the fact that the supply cairn had not been where he estimated. Loghairian attempted to break the ice by saying, "I know I've been skating on thin ice with you men," once again choosing the least apt of all metaphors in the universe he could have landed on. But what else was there to talk about? They were surrounded by ice and sometimes snowstorms. Women had stopped being interesting, even as a fantasy. No one dared speculate which of their thinning team of dogs would be next to drop. Speaking of the future was to invite instant mockery. All that remained was the ever-present ice, the only real fact.

One of the men, as if in rebuke, or possibly it was coincidence, rolled up his pant leg, rolled down his wool sock, and showed the blackening of his foot that indicated serious frostbite. "Maybe it will get better," Loghairian opined, merely trying to be optimistic. Again, not the right words. "What a knob," muttered Adler to Jenkins. At first, the Cap thought Adler was merely commenting on Whitaker's ankle bone, which, to be sure, was such a protuberance one could have guessed that it had been dislocated by walking behind his sledge.

Only upon reflection did Loghairian realize that the epithet had been appended to his person. The rest of the meal took place in silence, as Whitaker faintly moaned in the corner, after which he rose up and ventured out into the wind, possibly to lose himself forever. After twenty minutes, Jenkins called upon the Captain to go look for the missing team member. Loghairian refused, ordering Adler to go instead. Adler refused, a direct contradiction to the expedition leader's order. No one said anything, glumly and severely watching the Captain's face, scrutinizing its intent, as he put on his best bluffing mask before getting up and walking out into the bitter wind, only to find Whitaker softly crying just beyond the entryway, the tears immediately freezing to his face, which, illuminated by the Cap's lamp, showed as especially gaunt and spectral. He gave him the same fondly mechanical pat he administered to each dog before they shot it, ensuring Whitaker everything would be fine, well knowing that within 48 hours, it would fall to him to amputate that rotting foot with a hacksaw, given that the others neither knew how to do it without utterly butchering the poor man, nor would dare to try even if they knew.

To be fair, Adler had tried salving one man's ulcerated leg as Loghairian watched with his intent, inquisitive, doubting, almost daring stare, until Adler flung the pus-soaked rags to the floor, saying, "You're so good at everything. You do it." Loghairian couldn't help it that he was generally a capable sort. He'd saw off Whitaker's foot. The man would probably die, as they had all become malnourished, but either way it turned out, the Captain would get no love, no credit; on the contrary, he'd be blamed. All because his coordinates seem to have been off, although he'd calculated and recalculated many times. It made no sense. It was as if the continent had drifted under his feet.

He should have said, "I've made a mistake," when it first occurred and invited the team to help refigure their course. But he was too proud for such insignificant matters as maintaining communal harmony. He was used to giving orders and having them obeyed without question. The men said nothing then, as their bellies were still full, and the dog supply hadn't yet been diminished.

Hindsight. It was worth nothing. If he tried to sincerely apologize now, if he were even able to unharden his heart enough to admit all his multiplying errors and squint hard to see the speck of divinity like a freckle on the face of each man in the tent, bent over his respective dented mug of weak tea, it would only make him seem weak as well. He'd already acclimated them to unquestioning obedience. But when that obedience cracked, it would turn out to be a crevasse covered with light snow, into which he would fall.

As a result, Loghairian said nothing. The next day, they advanced against a headwind, everyone listening to the runnels going over the ice in the calm spots when the wind deadened. Then, there it was. A promontory in the distance, by all accounts just one more accretion of ice into a geographical formation of indeterminate duration and cancerously approximate shape. Desperate for any sense of accomplishment and banking on the men's increasing delirium, the Captain made a gamble. "Ahoy!" he shouted, as if they were pirates nearing land, rather than Antarctic explorers.

"What do ye spy, Cap?" in a tone that could have been interpreted as faintly mocking.

"It's the South Pole. I'm sure of it."

"Didn't you say we were at least two days from it?"

"I overestimated the distance."

"But it's not an actual pole, is it?" There was general laughter all around, the kind that had been missing for the past two weeks.

Rather than take the witticism for what it was, Loghairian heard himself arguing pedantically that there would only have been an actual pole if another team had gotten there first and planted it with their standard attached. As the laughter grew quiet, leaving an uncomfortable silence, the Captain lurched forward, rushing toward the promontory as if one of the other exhausted men might try to beat him to it. They watched him crazily slip and trip as he doggedly made his way up, their country's standard in hand, half banner, half walking stick, until his sweaty figure under a parka reached the top. Nowhere did the ice want to give way, but somehow, he managed to wedge the pole at a cockeyed angle between two lumps of ice, the flag dangling. "Ta da!" he couldn't resist singing out, like a children's magician.

Perhaps he'd expected the men to clap or sing "For He's a Jolly Good Fellow." Instead, he was met with dead quiet—contemplative, he hoped. Finally, Jenkins cried, "What a knob!" It could be that he was referring to the promontory itself, which did look like a knob of sorts if you thought about it.

There was no celebration. Whitaker was running a high fever. They set up camp, and Loghairian had to set about amputating Jenkins' foot while the other men watched with morbid close attention, as if waiting for him to make a mistake so they could justifiably use the same saw blade to cut his throat. The wound was cauterized, and with a dose of opium the Captain had been saving possibly for himself, Jenkins entered a twilight state.

The men began to make their beds. Loghairian, concerned that they might murder him in his sleep despite all, told them that he was going to pitch the small tent off to one side and sleep there by himself. He was glad the team had been successful, but before they began the return trip, where he was sure he'd be able to locate the supply cairn if the weather held off a bit, at which point they'd be refreshed, he wanted to gather himself in solitude, reflect on his errors, and try to be a better leader to the group on the voyage back. He realized he'd been highhanded at times, all in the interest of efficiency, but they could work together on establishing a real dialogue, a sharing of responsibility, and make real the meaning of teamwork.

In his tent, under a heavy blanket, he fell into a deep and dreamless slumber, one destined to be cleansing, purging the dictatorial badness from his soul. In the morning, he awoke fresh, all things considered. Opening the flap to his tent and crawling out, he was greeted with a pristine morning, no wind, an eggshell sky, and the temperature felt to have raised 30 degrees at least. There was the sun, finally out of hiding. Standing tall and stretching his arms to the heavens in salutation, feeling every inch of his six feet three inches, yet as light in his boots as a newborn babe, he turned to direct himself to the main tent.

There was no tent, only the bare, frozen patch of earth where it had stood the night before. Nor were there dogs or sleds or anything, except the knob he'd dared to name falsely as the South Pole. His men, it appeared, had packed up in the middle of his sleep and left Loghairian behind.

In the distance, a lone penguin watched.

4
HOMERIC

During his early twenties, after he dropped out of college with one semester to go on his anthropology degree, Jasper found himself in Alaska, working on a fishing boat out of Homer. Each morning, after downing a quick coffee, he'd set the net, leave it open for half an hour while it filled, loading itself full of mackerel and halibut onto the deck, spilling them into the hold. After that, he and his mates cleaned the deck.

During the breaks, he ate spam, bacon, hash, cartons of milk, chips, and canned soup. Also, fish straight from the hold, mostly salmon, sometimes halibut for variety. They'd finish at nine p.m. and get in line to off-load the fish. They'd anchor up, prep for the next day, stuff a little more food into their tired, famished bodies, and get to sleep as fast as they could. They stayed at sea for as long as one month at a time. Sometimes, in the nets, they caught harbor seals, skates, puffer fish, and salmon sharks. Harbor seals would gorge themselves on the trapped fish until the crew brought the net on board, where seals ended up on the deck and jumped back into the water. Orcas and humpbacks occasionally sailed through the nets, ripping them as if they were spider webs. In one summer, he made $20,000.

That's why he didn't worry. He'd always told himself that even if he lost everything, he could begin over. He'd always weirdly trusted in fate to deliver him. Seriously, he kept waiting for aliens to abduct him—ones he imagined as being sleek, attractive, eight-foot foxes with yellow eyes who wouldn't arrive on a ship but simply glide in, wingless yet perfectly aerodynamic. And one would flip Jasper onto its back with a giant, fluffy paw, and off they'd sail. So far, this had not come to pass.

Meanwhile, he found himself walking along the hot pavement, rather aimlessly. Abutting the parking lot of a car wash, he strayed onto its unblemished blacktop, soothed and drawn by the hissing of the machines spraying water in the tunnel, hitting the surface of a red pickup that had just entered. These days, it seemed like being a man involved owning a pickup. Those jets were like fingertips pinging his soul, akin to the music of the spheres that the ancients believed in. So hypnotized was Jasper that he walked toward the opening, ready to follow the red pickup into the enchanted passage, get a vigorous and refreshing spray down to bring him to his senses, only peripherally aware that he would also expose himself to possibly scalding water strong enough to knock him to the ground, as well as industrial strength detergents, bleaches, and anti-corrosives that would provide a skin scrub that might end in an emergency room.

Subtly, and as if by prior agreement with the universe, Jasper's footpath shifted up the sidewalk and into the air-conditioned waiting area, where pine and tropical scents hung from a pegboard, along with cell phone cases, steering wheel sheaths and many other items Jasper had thought about buying on impulse when he took his own car to be washed. Still, somehow, he'd never fully succumbed to their enchantments.

The bored yet mechanically alert attendant watched Jasper's every movement, as if he expected him to shoplift and make a sudden break for the door. Did Jasper look that homeless, that delinquent? Eager to vindicate himself, despite his not possessing an automobile, the one prerequisite for legitimately sitting in one of the molded plastic orange chairs without being accused of loitering, Jasper marched straight up to the Doubting Thomas (his name tag actually did read THOMAS), unblinking.

"I want a job."

"I'm not the manager."

"Where is he?"

"He'll be back around 3."

"May I fill out an application?"

"Look, Heathcliff. We're not officially hiring. But it so happens I just got accepted to community college."

"Diablo Heights?"

"That's the one."

"Congratulations. Your parents must be proud."

"Not really."

"Well, I'm proud."

"Hey, thanks."

"I taught there. The Romantics and freshman comp. Sometimes poetry."

"Maybe you'll be my teacher."

"Doubtful. I got fired for teaching *Doctor Faustus* and telling the students it was an allegory of the administration at Diablo Heights. And many other witticisms which, unbeknownst to me, accumulated until the Dean was satisfied that he had sufficient evidence of my insubordination."

"Aw, cool. Sucks you can't teach us that. I'll definitely put in a good word with Walt, the owner. If you want, you can fill in the application."

"I must tell you in advance that I have neither a home address nor a telephone. Nor a car."

"You rely on Providence?"

"More or less."

"It's cool. I grew up Baptist, so I understand. Listen, just fill it in and put an old phone number and address. I'm the one who runs the applications, so Walt will be none the wiser." Thomas motioned for Jasper to lean in closer, and he whispered. "There's a tiny room behind the register. It's got a cot in there and a mini fridge. I stay there sometimes. You can pretty much live in there as long as you return after dark, and you'll have a key if you're a manager. You can wash up in the lavatory after hours."

Jasper brightened up. "I'll be a manager?"

"Of course. We wouldn't put a college professor out there on the line. It would be disrespectful. But don't put on the application that you have higher learning. Walt won't like it. Just make up some job stuff. I mean, you teach English, so that should be easy."

"I did work one summer on an Alaskan salmon boat."

"Awesome! Put that. Only say it was this past summer."

On this day, Jasper's faith in Providence was warranted.

5
KOWALSKI

The insistent honk of a horn had woken him from a dream in which he wore a breastplate and helmet and was fighting his way through a crowd of unarmed Inca slaves dressed in crimson and cream, earth brown and forest green, stabbing them as he tried to push past their sheer numbers to reach Atahualpa, whom he could see one hundred yards away, being carried on a litter, feathers extending from the crown of his head like plumes of multicolored and obedient smoke. Half of him wanted to jump up from the mattress and cuss out the owner of the car, and the other half wished to return to slumber so that he could apologize to the Inca for springing a nasty surprise with sixty soldiers bearing rifles and swords, mounted on horses, men who had pretended to come for a peaceful parley and feast, and instead were lunging and galloping as they eviscerated this or that trusting soul who had gotten all dressed up in alpaca wool and gold and silver bracelets and necklaces just to die. His horse was slipping around in blood when he was jolted awake. It was a dirty trick for Jasper to pull, sneaking up on Atahualpa, even if histori-

cally accurate, and possibly it would have been mere crappy
revisionist history to have a second dream in which the
Inca, who let it be said was a bloodthirsty imperial ruler
himself, got to win, by anachronistically mowing down the
15th-century Spaniards with machine guns.

Truth be told, Jasper had nearly sold a spec script to
Amazon for a similar series, *Inca Armageddon*, with
androids and busty, sexy maidens shrieking in terror while
their cleavage bounced to the beat of the drums, but he'd
balked at the producers wanting to have alien ships float
down onto the boulder-flanked plain of Sacsayhuaman,
Jasper protesting that his concept was more historical
fantasy than sci-fi, at which point they'd told him to wank
off and ended up making their own version of it anyway,
Bizarro Pizarro, a conceit which died after four episodes, yet
he felt no schadenfreude. It wasn't even worth a lawsuit;
not that he could afford one. Now Jasper had to relive his
failure as a writer in this recurring dream, one about which
his therapist had said he was slaying his own father, which
was passé Freudianism as well as pushing it to compare his
long-absent if creative father with the tragically supreme
leader of the greatest Mesoamerican empire.

Arising from the cot, Jasper realized that the car was his
first customer of the day, and he was late opening up.
Perhaps whatever young employee was supposed to man
the line had been a no-show or had walked away when he
saw the business was closed. Slipping on the Washadoodle!
shirt, Jasper scurried outside, hitting the start button that
set the brushes swirling and nozzles spraying, and removed
the traffic cone. A bewhiskered man in a Ford F-250
rumbled up and, through his still-open driver's side
window, growled, "'Bout fuckin' time!" Jasper knew that
Pizarro would have gutted the man, but he only smiled

insincerely, letting all things pass, as the Ford disappeared into the artificial rainstorm, where his truck would no doubt break down, whereupon Whiskers would find himself on the doorstep of a decrepit house, and when he knocked, zombies would pile out and devour him.

As Jasper brought out fresh stacks of hand towels and bottles of degreaser to set around on trays, he watched Whiskers go to work throwing garbage out of his truck bed, vacuuming the cab and rubbing the windshield furiously as if he were getting the truck ready to sell. Then Jasper went back into the micro-building, where he stocked the pegs with hanging trees of air freshener, USB cables, and other overpriced impulse-buy knick-knacks. He was squatting at the bottom row when he felt a shadow loom behind him.

"I'll take one of them pine fresheners."

Jasper turned, and it was Whiskers. "Certainly." He handed one over mechanically. "Anything else?"

"Sorry, I was an asshole back there. My old lady threw me out. I ran two red lights coming here, I was so pissed off."

"Been there. Recently. Freshener is on the house."

"What's a dude like you doing here working as a clerk?"

"What do you mean?"

"You look more like—I don't know, a professor. Or a drug dealer or a weatherman. Anything but this. Are you a tormented artist fresh out of rehab?"

"No drug or alcohol problems. I got separated recently. Lost my house, car. Used to consider myself a writer, a pretty good one, but it's been a string of misses."

"Bad luck, man. You seem okay. I was in *West Side Story* in high school. Couldn't sing for shit, but my dancing was all right."

"What did you say your name was?"

"Butch Cassidy Kowalski Fischer."

"Didn't see that coming."

"My dad's two favorite movies were *Butch and Sundance* and *Vanishing Point.* The Fischer, just my last name. Jewish, not observant, but I do like me a good seder."

"There's more to you than meets the eye, Butch."

"What say you close the store and let's go find a bar."

"Is there even one open at 9 a.m.?"

"If not, we'll get a six-pack and sip it in my truck cab. Seriously, I can offer you a better job than this, one worthy of your talents."

"Such as?"

"I buy all kinds of stuff discount or second hand. Keep it in a warehouse and resell, some online, some in-person. Rebuilt cars, antiques, sports equipment. My own little eBay. I need somebody with a good head to keep track of things, deal with customers when I can't. It's starting to take off. Need a jack-of-all-trades who wants to learn the business. You'd get a base salary plus commission."

"I'm intrigued. What kind of base?"

"Look, it will be more than you're making now. But I'm going to say with incentives, you could make fifty, sixty thousand your first year."

"Is it legal?"

"Mostly."

"Why me?"

"You're down on your luck. You look kind of desperate, especially with that stupid Washadoodle! shirt on."

Jasper shrugged off the shirt and flung it behind the counter. Bare-chested, he took the keys from his pants pocket and tossed them on the counter. "Let's go get that six-pack."

6

LA PLATA

W hen Gregory Samsonite, the world traveler, awoke from his dream in which he'd been suspended upside down in a giant, heavy-fibered cocoon—with strands as if made of synthetic rope slicked over with a noxious chemical coating—a cocoon in which an indeterminate arthropod who reminded him of his seventh-grade biology teacher had trapped him, it turned out he had not in fact been injected with deadly poison for which the only antidote was eating a large amount of stale, crumbly guano, even were he able to escape and find a stash. Rather, Gregory was seated in a kayak, his upper torso surrounded by a waterproof skirt secured to the kayak's body. He'd slumped into one of his infrequent bouts of narcolepsy at precisely the wrong moment, and the cold spray of the Class 5 waterfall, on the lip of which he was perched, had awakened him barely in time to negotiate the impossible flume. From the rubber trees on each bank, scores of capuchin monkeys chittered, like tiny hoodlums at a basketball game, pretending to cheer him on while actually hoping that the athlete would sprain his ankle, or better yet, break a bone after a hard foul sends him crashing to the hardwood floor, and a fibula fragment pierces the flesh.

But Gregory was fine, adept even while semi-groggy. With a few flicks of his wrist, he dexterously descended the decline, literally whistling "Dixie," a song that had apparently meant something to his Confederate forebears but which to him meant nothing more than a merry dance hall tune, one that should never have been conscripted into political service. It was probably born on the strings of some sweet dulcimer deep in a mountain hollow by a peaceable musician who dreamed it would bring harmony and amusement to all mankind, irrespective of race or creed. Politicians who hated music on principle had turned it into a hymn of hatred and cotton-picking misplaced white pride.

He couldn't whistle the melody for long, though, because despite being surrounded by water, Gregory's mouth was as dry as old sandpaper tossed from a car window onto salt flats on a triple-digit August late afternoon. But why would someone be tossing sandpaper from a car window? Was the thrower a hostage tied with ropes in a back seat, holding a square she had secreted away in her shoe, trying to sand away the bonds that held her? But how would she have had such foresight? Did she habitually carry sandpaper in her shoe because she had enemies and was perpetually on the lookout to be abducted? No matter.

Gregory had landed in heavy foam, and boulders rushed by as he bounced like a rodeo rider atop an enraged bull that had been released from the pen after some prankster had placed a jalapeño inside its anus. Yet Gregory held on, in spite of the kayak skirt having been half-ripped from its stays, as pygmies began peppering the boat's sides with blow darts. If he stayed in the middle, he could barely evade the darts' range from either bank. Luckily for him, this particular tribe of pygmies was known to have weak lungs from eating the canned goods that the missionaries from the Summer Language Institute brought as offerings, goods whose chemical additives rendered the pygmies mildly tubercular, thus the weak lungs and darts falling short of the mark.

All the same, their buzzing provoked in Gregory a memory of his grandfather keeping bees on his Tennessee farm and how the swarm hovered when he went down to the hives in a mesh mask alongside his Papaw. Their collective drone unnerved him. Now, as Gregory Samsonite paddled the last stretch of the fiercest water, leaving the tubercular pygmies behind, he tried to suppress that sonic memory, lest he begin to veer and lurch. The scent of purple foxglove and fire-star orchid wafted on the air, as if inviting him to steer to shore into a harem of waiting maidens who would usher him to a hammock and spread balm on muscles cramped from too many days searching for the lost city that his mad poet uncle, Bob, who went by the nom de plume Rodrigo Flamingo (so people wouldn't give Gregory wedgies and shout out "Bob's your uncle!") had supposedly stumbled upon, recorded in epic alexandrines for three hundred pages, but upon returning to these jungles with his girlfriend to inhabit together, he had disappeared without a trace.

7
SUNROOM

Vanessa's sunroom had turned into a jungle, the kind where pygmies with blow darts hide. She was known among her friends for her green thumb, and as a result, no birthday, Valentine's Day or first day of spring came around without somebody gifting her one potted plant or another. Likewise, if a friend moved to a less temperate zone, the departing person would leave behind with her a spider plant, an orchid or a bonsai they didn't think would make it in the new clime. Likewise, when she had to travel for an extended period, she would take the plants to the house of someone trusted, who would care for them until her return. The same way she'd left Jasper in Geeta's care. Now, she could barely sit in her sunroom, which had slowly turned into a greenhouse, with pots even taking up space on the wicker furniture. She'd never meant for things to turn out this way, with a houseful of greenery and living alone. At this point, she couldn't even think about adopting a pet, because it was too tiring to imagine nurturing one more living creature. Unless it were Jasper, again. In relative terms, he'd been the best bet. Which in itself was a comment on the state of mankind. But she hailed from the land of floods and levees and knew all about reclamation projects.

She'd made the rounds of Jasper's old friends and even broken down and called Geeta. Nobody knew where he was. He wasn't answering phone calls, wasn't on social media, and none of the spy sites revealed any personal info on him she didn't already have and wasn't outdated. He didn't seem to have a street address. Vanessa had cruised the grocery stores, pharmacy, and coffee shops they used to frequent, feeling suspect as she walked up and down the aisles. She did not even bother to shop, yet she walked out with the cold-heartedness of an experienced shoplifter.

Meanwhile, a guy she'd dated a couple of times showed up out of nowhere with a bouquet of sunflowers and daisies, which she felt obliged to arrange in a vase she had to scrounge and plump up with greenery before letting this interloper down easy and lying, so uncharacteristic of her, that she was getting back with her ex.

"What's his name?" the guy challenged, as if sensing he was about to catch her in a lie.

"Jasper Delgado. Why? You know him?"

"Yeah. We played basketball in a pickup league at the Y. Chancy three-point shot, but he's a great defender, like his life depends on it."

"What a coincidence. Have you seen him lately?"

"Have you?"

"No, actually. And I've looked."

"Oh, it's one of those. Like you're kind of the stalker."

"That's harsh."

"I don't mean to be. It makes me feel a little bit better about showing up with these flowers. I was afraid you'd get angry. But you know how it feels. Being irrationally lovesick."

"I'm afraid I do. I'm sorry it's not you. That would make everything easier."

"We give our love where we want, not where it's deserved."

"What a beautiful meme. I don't suppose you've seen him."

"I did. Last night, we crossed paths at the liquor store down in Five Points."

Vanessa grabbed the guy, whose name she kept trying to remember, by the shirt and sat him down in the sunroom between two poinsettias, the leaves of which had turned unaccountably red in the middle of summer, in broad daylight. "What did he say? Do you know where he's living?"

"Honestly, it was bro talk mostly. He only told me he's in charge of an import warehouse."

"Where?"

"No clue. But he was coming from there to Sneaky Pete's on a beer run, so it's probably close to there. That's all I got."

"I could kiss you."

"Please don't, unless it's going to lead to sex or love."

She brought him close and hugged him instead. "Thank you—"

"My name is Travis."

"Yes, I was about to speak your name. You've been kind, and I hope you find what you're looking for."

"That's what they say at the grocery store checkout."

"You know what I mean."

"Yeah, I'm cool. If you get really depressed and need a

booty call, I'm your guy. Meanwhile, good luck with your search."

8

IN THE WAREHOUSE

"Women are like hubcaps."

"How so, Butch?"

"Call me Kowalski. My closest friends call me Kowalski."

"How so, Kowalski?"

"You think you need four, but really, you don't need any."

"I'd say you need one."

"What in hell good does one hubcap do? That would just look stupid. It's like an invitation for somebody to smash your windshield."

"I'm talking about women."

"Oh, them. Yeah, Becky and I get along great when she's not reaming me out. She's got like this trip wire. And you never know when you're going to hit it. You can be going, I mean let's say we're getting it on, and I mention in passing that I love her mashed potatoes, she'll jump up off the bed and lay into me that I spoiled the mood."

"Maybe she thinks that's bad sex talk."

"How so?"

"That you mean something else by mashed potatoes."

"Hellfire, I never thought of that. I get peckish, that's all. But if it's what you say, why would she get mad if I said the mashed potatoes are good?"

"Because no woman wants her body, or any part of it, compared to mashed potatoes."

"I never thought of that neither. But why does she get to call me beef jerky and that's supposed to be a compliment?"

"She gets to, that's all. Different rules for him and her. My ex-girlfriend Vanessa, she's a good Catholic girl, but she loved for me to talk dirty in bed. Except one time, I over-stepped, called her a whore and she slapped me. Later, over supper, she corrected me that it was okay as long as I said *my whore.*"

"Personal possessive. Words to ponder. Give me a hit off of that weed." Jasper passed it to where Kowalski sat cross-legged atop a stack of boxed sleds, and Kowalski took a long, pensive hit. "This is why I want you in charge of my inventory. Life wisdom. I sensed you had it."

"You're wrong. I'm a fuck-up."

"Maybe in applying the wisdom, yes. You lost your car, woman, house. You have got yourself in a fix. Maybe I was fated to come along. Maybe I'm your anal retention."

"What?"

"Sorry, your angel of redemption. I'm pretty high right now. I've made something of myself, considering how I started. Used to make saltpeter with my uncle, as a kid, to have a little income. Mix cow manure with ash from burned thistles and wormwood, throw in some tater leaves, a big high pile, throw a tarp on it, pour cow piss over it, and when crystals form on top, you scrape it off. That's your saltpeter."

"What did you do with it?"

"Hell if I know. He said he sold it to the Russian army and the soldiers ate it so they wouldn't fuck so much. But he was full of tall tales."

"And look at you now." Jasper waved his arm at the scores of pallets surrounding them, visible in the high-hung safety lights. "King of the manure pile."

"It's true. Most of this merchandise is the equivalent of cow shit. A step below Walmart. But you haven't seen the real stuff yet. The chop shop sports cars and motorcycles. The appliances of questionable origins and the antiques and art objects of questionable virtue."

"You're saying you're a fence?"

"I'm saying you're on the fence. I have you figured for the clean side of my business. To be honest, that's only going to get you pay of about 35K. The other side is the big money."

"The incentives you mentioned."

"Exactly."

"I have mild criminal tendencies," Jasper replied.

"Only in your dirty mind. Name one really bad thing you've done."

"Stole a box of jelly donuts."

"That don't even count."

"Gambled away my marriage's savings."

"Were you truly married?"

"Not legally."

"So, it was your money."

"Technically."

"You went to a casino?"

"It was my savings, through a stockbroker."

"High-risk commodities?"

"I got caught in a bad market cycle."

"So did everybody. You were a victim of the capitalist squeeze on the collective nut sack. Don't make yourself out to be a ruined bandido. Could you run afoul of the law if necessary?"

"Depends, Kowalski."

"Call me Butch. My friends call me Butch."

"Depends, Butch."

"You were going to be a big-time college professor, had the goods, but you couldn't hold it together. You were too many things at once. It's worse when you have all the potential and know it. The lucky ones are the mediocre shits who know that Whataburger was their destiny, and they slip right into it like a duck to a low-flow toilet."

"Sometimes I wish I was back in the old country. My father was Peruvian."

"That's where Butch and Sundance went to start over, when there was nowhere else left to go, and Joe Lefors was tracking them down."

"You mean Bolivia."

"Ah hell, I always get them mixed up. All's I want to know is, do you want to get involved in the car side of the business? I need somebody who knows how to talk to people. And won't rip me off. I can get the product, but I'm having to resell way too cheap because it's their middleman instead of mine."

"I don't want to go to jail."

"Nobody does. Look, just try it out. See how you like it. You could pull in 80K a year, discreetly. We give you a fake sales name, fake ID, your name goes on no paperwork, because there is none. You don't sell to anybody you know. I line up the prospective clients and you talk to them, that's all. It's just a conversation between two car-loving dudes. And if they agree, you direct them to a certain address, and you never see them again. I have a good system, just needing that closer."

"It sounds too good to be true."

"80K a year. What were you making at Washadoodle?"

"Twelve fifty an hour."

"Think about it, Jasper."

9
OUTSIDE THE WAREHOUSE

With the stack of fifties Butch Kowalski had paid him, so far for merely logging in and out merchandise and familiarizing himself with the facility, as rented Ryder trucks came and went, Jasper walked along the cracked sidewalk with weeds sprouting plentifully, as if from a medium-fresh grave, one from which a zombie would soon be lurching forth. He planned to walk to a used car lot a couple of blocks away, one he'd spotted while riding the bus to work, from his brand-new efficiency, secured only yesterday, a place Butch had put a deposit down on for him. Butch wanted to give Jasper a big loan, so he could set himself up in one of the apartment complexes with granite-countered units, and a swimming pool and jacuzzi outside populated by hot twenty-something babes, overlooking the fact that Jasper needed to gain twenty pounds of muscle and de-age five to seven years to even be qualified for that sort of flirtation. And Kowalski wanted his new employee to drive a shiny, oversized truck like his, preferably the same make and model, different color, so they would be total bros.

But Jasper, hardened by years of pitiless adjunct work, knew all too well that an employee is ultimately an employee, not a bro, and that a corporation, legal or not, academic or philistine, is a corporation. It will gut you when its moment of self-preservation comes. It will sacrifice you to the gods of continuous improvement after ritually burning a copy of *The Toyota Way*. It will shed you the way a salamander does its skin, and scuttle off, wet and slippery, to start life anew, while you, the rejected epidermis, dry up on the sidewalk, right next to the sprouting weeds under which the zombies lie buried, ready to devour humanity.

Therefore, Jasper said no to the big loan. He'd buy one of the ugly, generic, identical white vehicles that used to be rental cars for Avis and are now sold with no guarantee for their reliability or longevity, only the faint glamor that they once belonged to Avis, as a mistress belongs to a mafioso until she outlives her usefulness and goes to turn tricks on the street. You can buy her outright for nine hundred dollars, 137,645 miles on her, and she comes with a cigarette lighter, molded plastic cup holders and retread tires but no Bluetooth. But she's yours, god damn it, and there's no note to pay off. This seemed a safer course of action. As the danger of Kowalski's proposed ventures loomed, Jasper, at a minimum, wished to be surrounded by a familiar low-rent situation which, for his depleted soul, offset the epic instability of his possibly becoming an anti-hero, or if not that, a jailbird.

Possibly a day would come when a Jasper who'd packed on thirty pounds of Cross-Fit muscle from pushing giant tires uphill on hot pavement would half-submerge himself in the company of two nubile babes, one blonde, one brunette, half-suspended on each side of him in the erotic roil of the jacuzzi, where they laughingly drink bottled margaritas together, as he explains to them, as per Hegel, that human beings are not mere accidents of nature; they are reason itself—the reason inherent in nature—that has come to life and come to consciousness of itself. After which, he'd experience the first threesome of his life.

Until that day arrived, he'd be driving the superannuated Avis, off-white like an old dirty sheet where you can never wash all the grime out, not even with bleach, so you slide in, trying not to think about all the butts that had sat in the driver's seat before yours, the same way you rationalize it's okay to sleep in a hotel bed, where lots of bodies have lain, some having sex there, some with infirmities, some who merely smelled bad, and the disinfectant did its work as best it could, but ultimately, the human stain can never be expunged. A bed, and a semi-retired Avis sedan, both are palimpsests, bearing marks that cannot be entirely erased. Derrida may have been an overrated French poser, but he was dead right about that shit.

In this anxious reverie, Jasper looked up and there stood Vanessa, blocking his path, presumably on her way somewhere in the opposite direction. She was wince-smiling in the sun's glare, and he tried to do the same.

"Well, this is a coincidence," said Jasper, feeling that he'd somehow been caught with a stack of counterfeit hundred-dollar bills in his hand.

"Hello to you too."

"I'm sorry." He pocketed the bills and hugged Vanessa, whose body felt warm, supple, and inviting, though he didn't want to think about those qualities. "It's wonderful to see you. But you do have to admit, this is a remarkable coincidence, since neither of us is known to have been habitués of this somewhat sordid part of town."

"It would only be considered a coincidence if this meeting happened in a book," she replied instantly. "Like one of those novels you kept starting, then throwing away or archiving or whatever it is you did with them. Put them in a graveyard, I think you said. But in life itself, coincidences happen all the time, and we don't consider them implausible. We move right on to the next action."

"I accept your logic. You, the intuitive one, the eternal feminine, were always, in truth, the better logician of the two of us."

"Thank you."

"But if I were writing this chapter as a story, you'd be stalking me. You'd have ferreted my approximate whereabouts from some old lover or current would-be lover, whose appearance on your doorstep would represent an even bigger coincidence than this one, and by yet another coincidence, he would have happened upon my person a few days before, after years of not seeing me, an old bar buddy of mine with whom I played spirited games of darts, and he caught sight of me in the natural foods store."

"Or even better," she countered, "a pick-up basketball buddy who saw you shortly after you emerged from this very warehouse and whom I'd briefly and platonically dated, then he brought me a bunch of flowers to try to kindle the libidinal fire that hadn't yet sparked."

Jasper put his hand under his chin in his best thoughtful Rodin pose. "Do you mean Travis?"

"Could be."

"You've been stalking me."

"Don't flatter yourself."

"It's hard to come to a different conclusion."

"Do you know how much like a three-day-old, unbuttered toast you look, Jasper? How underfed and runty? On top of that, you're counting out hundreds like you just hocked your barely functioning car."

"Au contraire. I got paid and I am, conversely, about to buy a car. Anyway, I know how bad I must look, but you do have a strong nurturing, maternal side."

"That has nothing to do with me accidentally stalking you. I have weird taste in men."

"Thank you?"

"Fuck you."

"Said the nice Catholic girl."

"Raised on New Orleans voodoo and dirty rice."

"You're one of Walker Percy's sparrows."

"I am *the sparrow*. I know Binx Bolling said beautiful young women are legion in Elysian Fields, but that wasn't a compliment. I have no equals. Let me go with you to the lot so you don't end up buying a nondescript used Hertz sedan, out of sheer self-hatred."

"Avis. As if I would ever."

"I know you better than you know yourself, professor. After you purchase it on the spot, we're going to drive in it to the grocery store, where I will buy ingredients for jambalaya and said dirty rice, and from there, we'll proceed to whatever hellhole efficiency you recently rented for yourself in the last 24 hours, to further self-punish over your breakup with Geeta, which I don't know the details but doubtless you blame it all on yourself and like a non-Catholic Catholic, you have to do penance."

"You really have a low opinion of me."

"I am merely the medium, not the Eight Ball."

10
THE NORTH WIND

Hoarfrost on the moors. Why is the toot of hens unnerving? They're small creatures, and I am quite sure I could best one in a fight, despite the swooning of my soul. Worst case, I know how to lose. At the least, I'd make feathers fly, leaving the impression of struggle. This cartridge rifle is heavy as a blunderbuss, the antique one sitting over the mantelpiece that my grandfather was said to have fired at an oaken door, believing that a ghost haunting his manse was about to pass through. Instead, he winged his wife. She never rebuked him. Instead, for years, she continued to serve him tea and pork chops, boil his sheets, black his boots, even whisk soap into foam in his shaving mug, and shake the drops of water from it after she'd cleaned it.

All this she accomplished with one strong arm, the other lying lifeless at her side. It was a torture he endured for thirty more years until, at last, he passed quietly in his sleep, avoiding any more of her relentless devotion. I have no such considerations. I am a confirmed bachelor. I never unhang the blunderbuss, and I don't believe in ghosts. Except for hers. Magda, my beloved. The one they called the madwoman of the moors, whose sensual gait upset the matrons and animated the bachelors to improbable feats, such as scaling the belfry without the aid of ropes or ladders, when the church roof shone slippery with ice, to declaim love for her to the north wind; or stage risky horse races among themselves across the marshy plain, under the beat of summer's sodden heat, all while she, without a glance out her upstairs window, read verses from the *Roman de la Rose*.

> *And I had risen from my bed,*
> *Dressed, laved my hand and head,*
> *Drawn a needle of silver, in haste,*
> *From a fine little needle-case,*
> *And threaded the needle, for I*
> *Longed from the town to fly,*
> *To hear the little birds singing,*
> *Setting all the branches ringing,*
> *In the freshness of the season.*
> *I stitched my sleeves in fashion,*
> *And went wandering, quite alone,*
> *Listening to the sweet birds' tone,*
> *For they full-throated did sing*
> *Among the gardens flourishing.*

Fly she did, to Normandy, where I gradually made my way as well, unbeknownst, while I worked as a jongleur, having renounced my patrimony—the estates left to me when my mother left my father's bequeathed vast lands and innumerable sheep to follow him into Hell. Where she doubtless mops his brow with her one good arm. The manse sat, massive and untended. I had a good hand with a lay, especially the ancient ones.

> *Rouen Richard's sole surviving child,*
> *The heiress of his wealth,*
> *By crafty kinsmen and allies*
> *Was borne away by stealth;*
>
> *Was borne away from Normandy,*
> *Where, secretly confined,*
> *She heard no voice of those she loved,*
> *But sighed to the north wind.*
>
> *Haply from some lone castle's tower*
> *Or solitary strand,*
> *Even now she gazes o'er the deep,*
> *That laves her father's land!*

As I sat on a stool among the sawdust, crouching villagers nodding their heads to help me keep time, in floated my Magdalene. Never in Scotland had I pursued her directly, like the many gallants. Instead, I had quietly turned the pages of her beloved romance epic, nestled together, yet decorously, in her family's manse. I had encouraged her to flee, when she read those words aloud to me, lest she be trapped by the love of another, as my haunted father had. Her eyes begged me to tell her otherwise, to assure her that a woman's place was beside her mate. Rather than pursue her, I took my lute, absorbed my silent heartbreak, and wandered to France, not knowing where she'd fled, so I could forget Scotland's forbidding pitches and frigid bluster. I could see my continued life there as naught but a prelude to madness.

But in letting Magda go, I caught her. She came to me, unbidden, that starry evening, whether by accident or fate. And spying me in the tavern, among hard but honest customers, dressed in simple jongleur's clothes, a baize shirt and rough cloth pants, she didn't turn away. Rather, bedecked in a sylphlike green gown of the most delicate rose embroidery, falling off her shoulders as water falls from a precipice to splash upon a stone ledge, she drifted yet toward me, until she sat at my side, picking up the hand-sewn songbook I almost never opened, preferring to rely upon the inventory of my memory. Turning her head to me with a familiar smile, she said, "Play something new, Magnus, one whose notes you don't know well, so I can turn the pages for you, as you once did for me."

How I passed from that blessed moment to holding a rifle as my father once did, waiting for a new ghost to pass through the long-repaired door, I can hardly fathom. But whether in song or story, that haunting is my tale to tell.

11

BREAKING THE LEASE

Vanessa spoke not a word of our three years of mutual absence. Instead, she talked me out of the Avis and into a used Jeep Cherokee, one with 40,000 miles but in excellent condition. I financed through the dealer what I didn't have in hand. Soon, we'd removed the side panels and were humming along the bypass, taking a detour to climb the high mountain road that split the city, sharing a bag of Doritos and a single bottle of root beer as the smell of creosote and prickly pear cactus whipped through the car, and our hair got tossed around in the welcome wind.

When we pulled in front of the efficiency, I was embarrassed, as in those dreams where you stand at a checkout counter in your underwear, groping your skin for the nonexistent wallet in your nonexistent pockets, while the line behind you grows and irate customers begin to hurl insults. That's the kind of recurring nightmare I have, along with being called out of class by the dean to be informed I never finished my PhD and will have to give up my job, when I had just been awarded tenure.

Vanessa said nothing about the threadbare furnishings, the lack of a table to eat at, or the single straight-backed chair to sit in, or the futon couch and the lack of an actual bed. She shut the blinds so we wouldn't have to look out on the gas station next door. "I've only been here 24 hours," I said. "I was sleeping in a car wash, then I was sleeping in the warehouse."

"Shut up," she replied, contemplating the bottom sheet and top sheet, inspecting whether they were clean (they were), and the lack of a blanket or bedspread. Upon which she disrobed, discovering her tawny body, small, compact breasts and tiny feet that somehow perfectly offset the mass of dreadlocks sprouting from her skull. She undressed me as well, as if I were a child. For a moment, we stood looking at each other's bodies, as though seeing them for the first time. Then we embraced, and all the rest happened that we sum up inexactly with the single word *love*.

Afterward, we lay under the top sheet, while she perused the bare white walls, bereft of any picture, or even a nail where a picture used to be. "Is this a new mattress?"

"It came with the furnished futon."

She let out a small grunt. "I wonder how many butts have lain in this bed."

"It does cross one's mind, doesn't it?"

"This shit is going to change."

"I can get a new mattress. And an actual bed frame."

"Damn right, you will."

"And, of course, dishes, which I have none, a dresser, table and chairs, caddy for the shower, a fire extinguisher, a candle for mood lighting, bamboo shades instead of those crappy blinds. Butch has probably got some of that stuff in the warehouse."

"I'm sure it's all poor quality."

"Probably."

"Fuck all that. You're going to move in with me."

"Okay."

"At least I'll know who has slept on my mattress."

"And who has?"

"I just bought a new mattress. Straight from the factory. So, nobody besides me."

"And before that?"

"You don't get to ask me that question. You'd best hush your mouth and count your blessings."

"I'm counting them."

"Jasper, you're so much more than what you've been."

"Maybe."

"You have to become that man."

"I see. You're beginning a campaign to improve me, then?"

"No. You're going to improve yourself. Not because I said so. Because deep down, you want to be that man."

"Very deep down."

"What's holding you back? The suicidal, controlling mother? A chemical imbalance? An inborn self-destructive mechanism?"

"All of the above?"

"Seriously, you either have to figure it out or just not care and move on. It's that simple."

"Is it?"

"Yes. You know, my daddy used to beat me. He was a mean, no-account, awful drunk. He used to summon up the Iwa—Oshun, Ezili la Flambo, Erzuli Freda, Ogo, Mara, and Legba, all at once. Like it was a fantastic, phantasmal family reunion. He'd do all this crazy-ass praying, said he was a Babalawo, you know, a priest, but all I ever knew was he was a barber. And he'd have us kids be setting out a bunch of food, and it would turn out we didn't set the voodoo picnic up right, or else he'd bought the wrong kind of cola and off-brand potato chips, and these gods would get angry and instruct him to whup us. And he'd be shouting out for Legba, 'Open the gate!' And I would pray, too, for Legba to open the gate and haul my daddy's ass to wherever."

"You never told me any of this."

"Because it's not important. It's only what was."

"My boss, Butch, there's something about him. A little crazy but in a good way. He's like those renegades who end up in the Fortune 500. He's trying to teach me the business."

"Why you?"

"He likes me. He sees something in me that nobody else does."

Vanessa's eyes softened, as if we really were in candle-light instead of the naked bulb of the lamp with no shade that had been left by the previous tenant. "Nobody except me. I'm going down to the office manager of this stink hole first thing in the morning and break your lease for you."

"I'm on month to month."

"In that case, gather whatever objects you want out of here, and let's go to my place."

12

ALL ABOUT SHIVA

Lord Shiva was so depressed after his wife Sati died, he gave up smoking Dominican cigars and playing baccarat. Seeing that the sheriff was off the scene for all intents and purposes, the local thug Tharkarusa took to hot-wiring cars with impunity and built up quite a business. Some people started calling him Kruiser. Shiva's son, the lawman apparent, should have stepped in to set things to rights on the streets, been his dad's muscle, but he was off at boarding school in Switzerland, supposedly taking business classes but mainly chasing tail like his dad used to. The devas (by which I mean divine beings in the Vedic period, not a misspelling of *divas*), sent Kama over to get Shiva back in the mood, because a hot-blooded sheriff is a wide-awake sheriff. Kama went to Mount Kailash and shot off a quiver of love arrows into Shiva's ass and perked him right up. His eye fell on Parvati née Sati, who had killed herself but revived, as you may recall. Damn if Shiva, who was an undiagnosed schizophrenic, didn't accidentally char Kama with his third eye. That's the kind of shit he would do when a mood fell over him.

Natch, Rati went crazy when she copped that her man Kama had been offed. What did she do? She smeared her naked skin with his ashes. Crazy widow stuff. Went to church, said rosaries or whatever they do there at the altar, cried her damn head off, made idle threats, but pretty much threw herself on divine pity because sometimes that's all you've got. Parvati Devi, the goddess, the one who cock teases all the boys, but in the end, it's gonna be platonic with her, promised the weeping widow that Kama would be reborn as Krishna's son Pradiyumna.

What did Rati do? Forgot about the carnal stuff, the cold widow's bed, she wiped the crust off her nose, went to the house of the demon Sambara, as instructed, to pretend to be a kitchen maid named Mayvati. Stay with me. These telenovelas are always complicated. The names keep changing, half of them get reincarnated, there are assumed identities, the plot keeps multiplying, and it's worse than a god damned Russian novel. But Sambara is no idiot. He knew ahead of time that Kama planned to off him, he had a devil-dream about it or something. Sambara kidnapped the baby and hurled him into the ocean, which is exactly what I'd have done under similar circumstances. A big old fish gulped the li'l tadpole down. A fisherman caught it, and where did this seafaring tyke go? You guessed it, right back to Sambara's kitchen. Out of the frying pan and into the fire.

Fish got sliced open, as they do, and boom! Mayavati, the fake maid, discovered the newborn Kama, got a jones for the kid and decided to raise him. Proud mama! That's right when Narada, you know, the divine sage, everybody's seen her around the bodega, told her, "You're actually Rati. Deal with it." Complicated feelings! You're raising this kid, but he used to be your boyfriend, so, paging Dr. Freud! And the kid was like, "No way! You're grossing me out, adoptive mom." And she was like, "Well, you were inside a fish, and that doesn't bother me."

She explained he wasn't actually her biological son, and then he said, "Well, in that case, despite the apparent age difference between us, you are kind of attractive, and let's face it, we're mythological beings. We can ultimately do whatever the hell we want. There are only the laws of the heart and Divine Destiny." Natch, she gets right to work teaching him the art of magic and war, as there are demons to be slain. Sure enough, Pradyumna—that's Lord Kama, in case you've forgotten—kicks the demon's asura. Everybody went back to their original form, because, you know, it's a shape-shifting people, and Kama and Rati lived 63,000 years in peace. Don't you love a happy ending?

13
GRAVEYARD OF FIRST CHAPTERS

J asper didn't have the sense of an ending. If he'd been able, he'd have begun by writing all the final chapters. Even if they didn't exactly fit the retroactive stories he'd then imagine, they would have rough closure. He'd never been able to make an outline. Ideas, fiction, plots...came to him spontaneously, even easily. He loved the early pages of a novel, the hot mind, as he did the early days of a love affair, when the universe was boundless and heady optimism and erotic passion overrode common sense, when you never asked yourself or the other person where the thing was going. Perhaps you possessed an intuitive sense of the matter, in his case, how the following weeks or months might play out, enough to where you might plan a summer vacation together while still in the middle of winter. With Jasper, that's as far as his sense of the future extended. The same with the stories he wrote. If he could have made a novel of first chapters, wherein the overall story was implied, not dependent on an overarching plot, that would have been his preference.

Of course, the notion was ridiculous, so much so that he

never mentioned the idea to anyone. Editors would have laughed themselves silly. Readers wanted you to spell it all out. They weren't capable of understanding that all the great stories had been told; they existed as a cosmic repertory, and all modern writers were doing were variations on those ancient stories, twice, thrice, a thousand times told, while pretending to be fresh and original. They couldn't see that, with the requisite attention, anyone could extrapolate an entire story from its first chapter, the same way you whistle a few bars of a familiar song, even a really old one the person hasn't heard in years, and they can sing the rest of it for you. And you and the whistler laugh together in the comfortable recognition that you share a musical knowledge, one that feels like it belongs personally, even uniquely, to you and even evokes specific moments of your life—your first date, your wedding, the birth of your child, or simply that day you went out for pistachio ice cream in the middle of a snowstorm, and that's why your face always lights up when that song comes on the radio. Almost any person can compile a playlist pegged to different phases of their life, which when taken together suggest the whole and complete story of that first life.

Instead, Jasper ended up with a graveyard of first chapters. Vanessa had kept telling him how promising each one was, how this one, then that one, was destined to become the greatest novel of the year. They had *potential.* When he stopped working on each of them, she would go around the house making up new scenes out loud or plot summaries she'd worked out in her spare time, "Just as examples, it doesn't have to be this." She thought she was encouraging him, but the effect was the opposite. She was trying to get him out of his writer's block, but *he didn't suffer from writer's block.* He could easily sit down and come up with a new chapter, in a matter of hours, almost effortlessly. No, rather, Jasper didn't have any sense of closure—that was the problem if there were one.

All the same, he had finished multiple novels and several screenplays, and had his share of early success, even getting on the *NYT* bestseller list. But neither his life nor his art followed the arc that had been described by the mythology of the culture: one immediate big score, followed by a sophomore novel that got panned, after that, a third effort showing a mature, resilient writer, sales more modest but critically well reviewed, and which put him permanently in the arena as a novelist to be watched, no matter what, and who would continue to pile up novels, for better or worse, for decades, alternating between starred reviews and punishing neglect. By the time he was middle-aged, he'd have an "oeuvre." By the time he was old, a fest-schrift. Meanwhile, he'd either become a professor with tenure, teaching in a "good" MFA program, or else a rene-gade, a slightly misanthropic and reclusive free-lancer, who experienced streaks of co-writing screenplays that would be made into movies in the sixty to two hundred million dollar range, while at other times, he'd stretch the meager fees from giving readings into enough to make car payments on his rapidly aging vehicle. Or perhaps he'd land higher and marry an actress, kind of like what Arthur Miller did, and everybody would be secretly thrilled that a nerd and a princess could pair up like that.

When Vanessa casually introduced Jasper to Geeta at a minor league baseball game, he knew right away, although the whole thing was passed off as a spontaneous meeting, that Vanessa was introducing them because she knew they'd spark and she'd get him off her hands. He went along, to be nice, and it so happened that he was immediately attracted physically to Geeta. Vanessa knew his type, which she'd once self-described as "exotic All-American." Geeta was in on the handoff too; they were positively excited, exchanging girlish glances, that they were negotiating a commodity between them—someone who, at that time, was buff from weight training and still collecting significant royalties. Perhaps he should have felt excited and macho, but instead, he felt used.

He did what the women wanted, making it easier on everyone. Going to Geeta's house and hooking up with her for sex was instantly exciting because dirty and taboo, although tacitly permitted, as if they were all secret swingers. He immediately went back to the apartment and told Vanessa, who, to his dismay, was super understanding about his lapse. She then went into adult mode, saying how there had been a distance growing between them— meaning she was growing away from him—and that she wasn't even mad, because maybe this was meant to happen. She'd felt the sexual spark between Jasper and Geeta as soon as she introduced them and had thought about sitting between them at the game, to keep anything further from happening, but she decided to be generous and seat Jasper next to Geeta and look what happened. Vanessa stated calmly that it was her fault as much as it was his, for aiding and abetting them without meaning to. But maybe that was the hand of destiny.

That was the day Jasper's collection of first chapters turned into a graveyard of first chapters. While packing his things to move immediately into Geeta's warm bed in her one-bedroom apartment, with no shot fired between the women, no ugly words exchanged, on the contrary, possibly a finder's fee had been paid, Jasper took one look at the laptop that needed badly to be replaced (like him) after so many updates, knowing that it contained the only existing files of all those neglected first chapters, ones he hadn't bothered to back up on a drive, fatalistically perhaps, as if daring the writing gods to make them irretrievable.

But the gods, in the prevailing spirit of perversity, were going to make him do the dirty work himself, so that he couldn't chalk the outcome up to the accidental whims of the cosmos. He walked around to the side of the duplex he shared with Vanessa and threw the laptop into her recycling bin. As far as he knew, the garbage men would compact it that very week into splinters. Thinking upon that prospect, he felt a great relief to be freed of all that prose and to start life anew, all thanks to the Divine Handoff between his ex and his new steady, soon to be his wife.

But it turns out there was a garbage strike that week. Of all weeks! Who even knew the municipal workers had a union? The gods were mocking Jasper, it seemed. Three days passed, with him barely sleeping, conscious that the laptop was there getting covered over with Hefty bags. At last, he went out, dug around under the faintly disgusting bags, bulging as with human viscera, and retrieved the laptop, minutes before the garbage truck came up the street, rumbling and clanking like a deus ex machina. Because somehow the strike was canceled after three days, as the city and the workers had come to an agreement. Jasper saved—by collective bargaining.

Now, after a sudden and unexpected reconciliation with Vanessa, who seemed to come out of nowhere, but who had actually been stalking him with method and alacrity, the same way she'd divested herself of him, Jasper felt somewhat pissed and doubly had, while at the same time, he'd never wanted to be parted from her. Instead, he'd been duped out of their connection, and now he was right back where he started, except all was different. He'd lost everything, been reduced to nothing. He'd lived briefly in a car wash, then a warehouse, then a dreadful efficiency, believing, as he always had in the back of his mind, that he would become the Invisible Man, and now he was back into a nice three-bedroom brick ranch Vanessa had put a down payment on during the years they were apart, as if she'd planned to have a husband and family. Whether, at the time she took on the mortgage, she thought or knew that Jasper would eventually become the man in the family picture frame, he couldn't say.

14

THE INVISIBLE MAN

Jasper was always trying to get Vanessa to read Ralph Ellison's novel *Invisible Man*, which he sometimes claimed to be the greatest novel ever written. Vanessa didn't even believe you could say there was a single greatest novel, or greatest movie, or song, or play. It was just one of those things people liked to say because it was grand and dramatic and gave them the power to confer, like God creating the earth in seven days. For him, *Invisible Man* was the ultimate universal existential statement. For her, it was a sad-ass black man, trying to get his shit together. And she'd already been through all that, more than once, with her daddy, a little bit with Jasper too, and didn't need to read about it. Jasper was more white than ethnic, in her judgement. He sure didn't look like his mama had rubbed loins with no non-white meat, and sometimes she'd suspected he'd given himself the name Delgado in court only to endow some more flavor on his cracker ass. Then she saw his birth certificate, and she did an internet search to corroborate, and yeah, his name really was Delgado, although she would have last-named him Brewster or O'Leary.

It used to drive her crazy that he'd printed out a quote from the novel on a white sheet of typing paper and put it on the wall behind his computer.

> *If only all the contradictory voices shouting inside my head would calm down and sing a song in unison ... I wouldn't care as long as they sang without dissonance ... But there was no relief*

She wanted to rip it down and shout, "Maybe you need to be on medication!"

Vanessa would much rather be a character in a novel like Henry James's *The Golden Bowl,* where it's all interior psychology, but in a cool way, like you're suffering and all, but enveloped in the narrating voice as if you were wearing a long mink coat to an upscale dinner party, at the Waldorf-Astoria, not that she even knew where that was, exactly, somewhere in New York City, it sounded romantic, that's all, like old money, and you wouldn't be eating Natchitoches meat pies or black beans with sausage and bread pudding, like she did her whole entire childhood, that's for sure.

If Jasper had a lick of sense, he should have sold that *Inca Armageddon* script to Amazon, with aliens and all in it, like she begged him to. That's half the reason she canned his ass. He secretly believed in aliens and zombies, for heaven's sake, so what was the problem with sticking a few thousand of them in a screenplay and letting them attack a Mesoamerican fortress? And she was raised on voodoo and zombies; her dad used to scare the shit out of them at night with tales of such. Even her mom told her once that the only reason their grandmother, with her black moods, didn't kill herself was because she was afraid that she'd come back as a zombie. Granmère claimed that back in the slave days, the masters had wanted to use puffer fish venom to turn all the slaves on the plantation into zombies, died and resurrected without souls, so they wouldn't have to eat, wouldn't get sick, and they could work around the clock without sleeping, only do whatever the master ordered. That's why Vanessa's mother never wanted her children to swim in the ocean or any brackish water, in case the grandmother turned out to be right. This is what it meant to be a Catholic in Orleans Parish.

Being raised among such, even after her degrees in microbiology and public health, her sitz bath of enlightenment, Vanessa didn't find the eccentric Jasper to be particularly strange. She wasn't going to disallow any of the phantasmagoria or extraterrestrials, even though her particular parish priest would have found that heresy, although he probably knelt to his private effigy of Bondye in his bedroom. For her, Jesus was in a way an extraterrestrial; he came to Earth to save us.

If Jasper had sold that script at the given time, when she was loaded with student debt, he could have helped her pay it off, and they could have formed a plan together to marry and buy a house with a hearth and a playroom and have a baby they could watch rock back and forth together after they wound up its mechanical swing. And they'd take a trip to the beach, where she'd push into the ocean, not worrying about the puffer fish lurking behind reefs. She'd taken lessons at the Y and swam laps there, but she couldn't go out into those brackish waves on her own. She needed Jasper alongside, the Jasper who, improbably, had been the captain of his swim team in high school and a life-guard the summer after! He was full of surprises like that. She was trying to imagine the nubile blondes smeared with sunblock falling all over him. The very thought of it made her smile.

Vanessa had gone ahead and bought the house on her own, as if making ready, even though the string of guys she dated ranged from arrogant to creepy to selfish, and she had sex with some of them anyway, her eyes open over their shoulder as they labored away, her eyeballs bugging out as if she'd opened them underwater to see what manner of ghoulish mystery floated there.

When she disrobed Jasper the other day, taking charge, being bossy in a way almost any man would reject, and he was so sweet and compliant, and she gazed on that scrawny body that used to be all good, lean muscle, and he didn't even seem to be aware he looked about like a boiled crawfish, taking her tenderly and reticently in his arms, gently laying atop her, the way that long-ago teenage life-guard had probably lain, gingerly, atop his first conquest, she was so filled with a weird mix of maternal love and raw woman desire for him, wanting to fix him yet suddenly he was fixing her by pushing into her in his determined way, as if saying, "I'm fucked up but I never gave up," that he gave Vanessa the most powerful orgasm she'd ever had, her hollering like her aunts did at church service on Sundays when that single, young, purple-dark minister used to get them riled up, shouting from the Book of Ruth, "Where you go I will go, and where you lodge I will lodge; your people shall be my people." Those aunts always thought they'd catch him for a husband, or if not, some other fine-looking churchgoing man, but they ended up finding their men at the pool hall and the racetrack, men given to cock-fighting and playing bouré with the Cajuns and spending half their paychecks before they got home of a Friday.

Vanessa couldn't explain why she loved Jasper so much, nor why she'd let him go so easily and foolishly, on an impulse, having to bear up under her mistake for three whole years, until Geeta threw him out, she didn't really know exactly why, because she and Geeta didn't talk after the handoff, except once or twice, but there was a strain, as if they'd all literally been in a threesome together and immediately regretted it. Right before Jasper, she was dating a pediatrician, who was awfully nice to her, a man from Lithuania with a cute accent, but it was all too perfect and too successful and too dull. He was sweeter than fresh-cut sugar cane, but he didn't have that devilishly active brain that was like candy to her, that refreshed her spirit, like when Isaiah says, *For I will pour water upon him that is thirsty, and floods upon the dry ground: I will pour my spirit upon thy seed, and my blessing upon thine offspring.*

During her and Jasper's three-year separation, Vanessa did read *Invisible Man* all the way through, after all, and one thing Ellison wrote stuck with her: *"Man's hope can paint a purple picture, can transform a soaring vulture into a noble eagle or moaning dove."* That's what she wanted Jasper to do, and be, that noble eagle and that moaning dove rolled into one. And she knew he could. He just had to put on a little weight first, otherwise he was gonna disappear.

15
THE LETTER

Dear Mr. Jasper Delgado,

Greetings to you, sir! I am a notary public in the city of Cusco, Peru and I normally werk outside the courthouse on Avenidda Sol on an old Corona that once billonged to my oldd Uncle Sixtu, a goat farmer who had little use for it, so he gabe it to me. The keys stikk freqqently, in addition to me having arthritis in my fingerzs. I use carbn paper and white out, so I Guess I am not exactly up to Xerox times. Odly, this tmpermental machine has helped me get something of a reputation as an auvant-garde Poet and everybody in the literary werldd is crazy about my ""alternative"" spillings. I can reed Shakespppeare in Egnlish ony I don't understand a lot of it, but neither did my teachers and they raid it in Spanish. I guessed you could say I'm an idiot-savant which is why I mmakke my living *typyiying on this old Corona for ignorant peasantz and others who need the servies of a notary. I guess you could say I am "notarious."*

I write this on behalf of a youngg ladie who claims to bee your sister. Her name is Inés. She sayz that she has beene tryng to trackkk you down. Your daddd dieddd last yr. In his Will he left you haff of his proprieties and possessions; a considerable sum at least by our national reckkkoningg. This includes a hacienda house and surrounddding lands. It was being used as a cooperative but would need an infuzsion of dollars to make it go. I have apppended the adddresss to thiz dokcument. She asks for confrimiation and reqqqests that you hie to the city of Cusco on a near date of your choozsing to divide the spoils of yr father's death.

With no ottther patricuiliar of the moment, I remained your attenuated servant,

Otomilo Gáspar Núñez Villareal Atayupanqui, Esq.

"Honey, this is a scam."

"I don't believe it is."

"You said you found it in your junk folder."

"That's where the algorithm put it."

"I'm not persuaded."

"The Divine Hand of God?"

"I don't think he works that specifically."

"What about all the preposterous misspellings and weird locutions?"

"It's not done in the way a scammer would. Scammers have a shaky grasp on the language. This scribe is a madman. But sincere. He's like a Melville character."

"And the requested cash infusion?"

"I don't have any cash to infuse. They'd be barking up the wrong tree. I'm not going there with a cashier's check or stacks of hundreds."

"Like the ones you were taking to buy your car?"

"I want to see what it's about, that's all."

"After we just got back together? And you're heading out?"

"I haven't decided. That's why I'm talking to you."

"But—who would leave you a hacienda?"

"Yeah, I wanted to talk to you about that. My dad—is—was—Peruvian."

"Jasper. You said Skokie."

"That's where I ended up with my mom. After."

"After what? Did you grow up there?"

"I'm not ready to talk about that. Just yet. This has awakened some things. And I haven't talked to anybody."

"No shit. You're closed-mouthed about your past. Even for a man, it's too much. I spent so much time imagining you had illegitimate children, or had been in prison, or were once a drug addict."

"No. Sorry to disappoint you. It's the usual family stuff, I guess."

"You're saying that you're going there to face your past, and you'll want to open up completely and come to terms with whatever knocked you off your struts, and then you can be sensitive, but not too sensitive, because that's a buzz-kill, but a partner who I could relate to and confide in, within the context of a healthy long-term relationship?"

"I never said any of that."

"Because in that case, I'm going with you."

"A minute ago, you said it was a scam and I shouldn't go."

"Not alone. I don't care about that hacienda or whatever it is. But I am going to be standing right there, beside you, when the revelations occur. No, sir. Not gonna be left out of that primal scene."

"I'm not aware of having a sister. She said her name is Inés."

"Well, when you meet this lady, if that bitch is not your sister, I'm going to grab her by the hair extensions or whatever they wear down there, and wrestle her to the ground."

"The women don't wear hair extensions down there. They all have naturally thick, glossy hair that they wear down their back in braids. It's so profuse it would choke a brush."

"Don't make me jealous. This woman is probably looking for an American husband."

"Are we going, then?"

"Let's look at some dates and tickets online. "

"I have to talk to Butch. This is a brand new job, and I don't want to lose it."

"Is he going too?"

"I can't imagine Butch would have the slightest interest in tagging along on this sudden adventure."

16

A LINEN SUIT AND A BOATER

"Count me in!" cried Butch.

"Do you speak Spanish?"

"Kinda sorta. I get my message across. A hacienda, you say, in need of improvement? Well, I am Mister Deep Pockets. To be perfectly honest, I've got significant amounts of cash I need to cool down and a foreign investment would be just the thing."

"Illegal funds?"

"I wouldn't go that far. It would stand up in a court of law. Never you worry. Papa's not going to get you in trouble. Papa's going to get you out of trouble."

"It makes me nervous when you refer to yourself in the third person."

"Look at it this way. You can go strictly on your own initiative, in which case you will likely get fired, because well, you're refusing to show up for work. Or I go with you to look at the investment, and we are performing a work activity together, by assessing a new business opportunity. If you're with the boss, you're on the clock, and you're earning a salary."

"This feels manipulative."

"It is."

"Yet it solves all my immediate problems."

"It does."

"I'm not sure, though, whether you should be thinking about investing money in something we haven't seen."

"You leave that to me. I'm the master of appraising dubious prospects. I'm not going to get burned. My gut tells me this one is a winner."

"All right. We were about to pick dates and make plane reservations."

"We?"

"Vanessa, my once and future girlfriend, and I are back together."

"Congratulations. Why didn't you say so? Can't wait to meet her. But listen, hoss. Butch, Sundance, and Emma would never fly in a plane. That wasn't even an option for them."

"I believe I said her name was Vanessa."

"Whatever. The three of them had to escape Joe Lefors. They got on a steamship and sailed to Bolivia to start afresh. I'm going to book us a cruise ship."

"That's slow and expensive."

"You leave the expenses to me. And what's the hurry? The old man's dead. The will can wait. Didn't you say it was sitting in your spam folder for a few weeks before you noticed it?"

"True."

"Hell, we'll find out what's what when we get there. Here's four hundred dollars. Go buy yourself a linen suit and a boater."

17
THE CRUISE SHIP

Diesel generator sets, boilers, compressors, steering gear, oily water separators, purifiers, evaporators, pumps and heat exchangers. Wastewater treatment and garbage handling plants. Three watchkeeping teams, each headed by a senior watchkeeper and comprising of junior watchkeepers (3rd or 4th Engineers) and a motorman. Lifeboats and davits, sprinkler system, hydraulic side-shell doors, watertight doors, vacuum toilets, freshwater distribution lines. Coffeemakers, ice-cream vending machines. Chlorination and maintenance of all the swimming pools on board and potable water, handled exclusively by the water technician. Heating, ventilation and air-conditioning, helmed by the Chief AC Engineer, assisted by Assistant AC Engineers, AC Technicians, fitters and wipers. AC chillers, air handling units, ventilation fans, refrigeration machinery, cold rooms, chilled & heated water system and related heat exchangers, high voltage installations, mostly 6.6 kV or 11 kV.

Tourists prematurely festive in loud yellow and pink shorts, Teva sandals or ill-advised heels and ersatz

Hawaiian shirts and t-shirts with corny puns about drinking too much, crowded the gangplanks, ready to stretch their elastic waistbands to the limit with the endless buffets of roast beef, mashed potatoes, shrimp, cobbler, watermelon, salt-water taffy, candy apples, squid eyeballs, beef jerky, buffalo steaks, platypus tendons, giant stacks of Pringles, chutney, bread pudding, foie gras, churros, endless sheets of peanut brittle, donut holes, shrimp arrayed around an ice sculpture of Cabeza de Vaca, head cheese, barrels of olives and peanuts, cheese curds, Frappuccino, thick slices of Spam with pineapple and gravy on top, blood sausage, bouche de noel, pasta in the shape of all the republics of Latin America, a 12-foot candy cane pole you could climb and lick as you slid down, frozen margaritas shot straight into your throat, vats of whipped cream into which you could jump with a brownie in hand, a lake of fire into which you could toss a raw, thin cut of flank steak and a chef dressed in a fireproof suit would dash in and fetch it for you, exactly as you ordered, whether medium rare or well done. In short, Butch had spared no expense in booking.

In the music hall, scores of college students on summer internships tap-danced fervidly to songs of their great-great grandparents, like "Winchester Cathedral," wearing bowler hats and twirling canes so fast over their heads they looked like propellors that would lift the dancers from the ground. A Katy Perry look-alike either sang or lip-synched her songs, it didn't matter which. A comic with eyes bugging out kinetically explained the differences between men and women and discreet canned laughter from the sound system encouraged the audience to agree his was a true account of the battle of the sexes. A man who looked suspiciously like Walt Whitman stood up from the audi-

ence and recited verses from Hart Crane's "The Bridge"
before he was hustled out.

> Out of some subway scuttle, cell or loft
> A bedlamite speeds to thy parapets,
> Tilting there momently, shrill shirt ballooning,
> A jest falls from the speechless caravan.

Jasper was trying to put on a few pounds, so he ate
hearty the first couple of days, after which he couldn't
sustain the pace anymore. Instead, he got drunk on rye
whisky, not having been smashed in years, after which he
made his way to the prow and shouted into the fused fury
of the unchained waters, "Condense eternity!" and
promptly threw up into said waters. Emma/Vanessa gently
led him to the stateroom to lie down, while Butch, who
stood outside because it was so cramped in there, gently
strummed "My Sweet Lord" on a brittle guitar he'd
purchased at the gift shop and was just learning to play,
skipping the chords he hadn't figured out yet.

Jasper hadn't expected Vanessa to accompany him to
Peru. However, upon meeting her, Butch Cassidy Kowalski
Fischer had immediately seen her as a viable third, less
based on anything he knew or felt about her, more on the
fact that in the movie *Butch Cassidy and the Sundance Kid*,
Emma had accompanied Butch and Sundance on a
steamship out of New York City at the outset of their ill-
fated trip to Bolivia. Butch had kept calling her Emma by
accident and couldn't get over the fateful fact that, in the
movie, she was attached to Sundance! Meaning Jasper. This
was a sign from above that her presence would be a
blessing on a trip—the one in which, in the movie, she ends
up coming back alone, while they both die bloody, ignoble,

bullet-ridden deaths outside a market stall, surrounded by local police and hundreds of federal soldiers, who gleefully keep shooting volleys of rounds long after the two hapless cowboy thieves lie cold and stiff on the crimson-soaked dirt.

Vanessa was relaxed because, as she remarked, all my bills are on autopay and I have several weeks of paid leave because I never get sick and I never take a vacation. Meanwhile, they had a free half-day docked in Cabo San Lucas to buy shot glasses bearing that name. Jasper didn't even want to think about liquor; he had a hangover, but he bought a shot glass anyway, because he might regret not doing so later, and where are you going to find a Cabo San Lucas shot glass at home? Unless you go on eBay, where dozens of them are on sale, including a Sammy Hagar Cabo Wabo 4-inch leather-wrapped one for $25 and $5 shipping.

Butch wanted to go parasailing. Jasper didn't think his stomach was up to it, so he blessed the other two to partake, saying he preferred to watch from the beach while nursing a smart water, not wanting to admit to himself, or to them, that he was discovering that he suffered from seasickness when in any boat smaller than the Titanic. Now he wasn't going to get to show off his funk dance moves, right when disco night was coming up. Emma and Butch went up towed by side-by-side boats, as if they were members of an aerial-water ballet, practicing for some massive show that would involve dozens of the cruise ship passengers, corpulent though they might be, who would disport themselves with unsuspected flair in synchronized parasailing, possibly spelling out CABO SAN LUCAS from the air with their bodies.

But no, Jasper was left only to watch his two travel companions, gracefully drifting and swooping, as if dancing a tango together, albeit many yards apart. Lazily, he wished for a crossbow in his arms, with a flaming arrow in it, to set each parasail on fire, though not in a way to hurt anyone. He only wanted them to drift down, as the embers and ashes of the sail were sucked harmlessly out to the deeper water by trade winds, whereupon Vanessa and Kowalski would be fished out, unhurt, by their lifejackets.

Instead, he acquired a sunburn by the time they got back, in spite of his ultra-high SPF sunblock. Their skin, in contrast, seemed to have acquired a special glow, peppered by sea salt (oh, oxymoron!) in a manner that made them seem to have gotten gorgeously encrusted by means of a dip into crushed diamonds. They were smiling like the king and queen of the cruise ship mock-prom.

"Did you see us?"

"I caught a glimpse."

"I'm famished! I know somebody was driving the boat and all I had to do was float around and take in the spectac-ular, azure view dappled with adorable sailboats, but it about wore me out!"

"Me too!" Butch enthused.

"Let's go scarf down calamari and huge, fat shrimp in a cocktail, and wash it all down with a pitcher of beer. After which, key lime pie! We could have a pie-eating contest!"

"That sounds fantastic."

"Are you up for it, honeypot?"

"I'll tag along. Could you hand me my shirt? I'm afraid my skin is going to break off in pieces if I sit up."

"Oh no! Poor little baby. I was going to say let's rent dune buggies and go tear up some dunes after lunch, the three of us. This is the most fun I've had in forever. But I'll take you back to the room afterward and put some cold cream on your skin to soothe it."

"It's okay. I'm going back onboard now. You kids have fun."

As she and Butch literally ran down the boardwalk toward the restaurant, Vanessa's afro wig, which she'd advance purchased for disco night, bounced like a lone tumbleweed blowing across the empty plain of a desolate, forgotten Mexican town.

18

GUANO

The gentleman in the bowler hat and three-piece suit, trying not to sweat in the hard sun, stared at the pile of shit in his hand. Offshore, a tethered boat pitched perilously close to the rocky shore, moving like a Mississippi colt that has unexpectedly been penned in when it wants to run free. Danton squinted to inspect the poop's consistency.

"I came here to buy guano, not reconstituted pig poop."

"Señor, I assure you this is the finest on offer. In the guano world, it is the equivalent of French Beaujolais."

"It is the equivalent of diarrhea. I'm seeing in here, just with the naked eye, traces of umber, powder stones, and half-rotted sawdust."

"Only there is inside it what the sea birds eat."

"Then they must be overflying garbage scows."

Danton knew he had to close this deal for the U.S. of A., more specifically, for Purity Imports, Inc. Even in the noon sun, his mind drifted back to where he'd lain with his mistress in an upstairs room at the Tremé-Lafitte. Her raven curls fell down her firm, naked shoulders like ivy spilling over a brick wall. Her body could stand up to being ridden. "Whenever I lie with you," he spoke softly into her listening, glistening ear, "I already lie beneath the earth. O you precious grave, your lips are passing bells, your voice their knell, your breasts my burial mound and your heart my coffin."

"Pass me the chewing gum," she replied.

"This is white gold, sir," insisted Pedro, his interlocutor.

"President Millard Filmore has declared that the global price of guano should be set at $76 per pound. That's more than fair. Last year, prices were two-thirds that."

"The market, señor. I hardly control it. These are monumental forces. Neither you nor I ultimately control them. We are slaves of the global economy. If only this island belonged to me, I might find a little room to negotiate."

The swirl of gulls above them looked like a cyclone forming. Danton knew it had taken hundreds of years for this quantity of avian excrement to build up on the Peruvian islands and that it was, in an immediate sense, a nonrenewable commodity. But why couldn't the birds just shit faster? Terns and gulls, maddeningly black and white, swooped and ascended, as if teasing Danton about his conundrum. He had a mind to draw the pistol he brought along for safety out of its sheath and peg one, just as an object lesson to the rest.

Danton sighed, and his mind returned again to the soft mattress in New Orleans, where he'd much rather be than on this fetid island where a halo of ammonia hovered over everything. Several Chinese nearby were using shovels to load the guano into sacks that were then loaded into carts to be transferred to the ship of one of his competitors. In Room 206 of the Tremé-Lafitte, the sole window lay open, and a playful breeze brought in the scent of honeysuckle, as ducks below on the lawn could be heard softly laughing to one another. Julia, the woman he loved but could only rent, reached for his trousers. Was she going for his pocket, or something else? Either way, it was always in the end about money.

"Macabi Islands. What sort of name is that? Did you know those were Jewish rebel warriors? The pious Jews rose up against the Seleucid king."

"Sadly, the Chinese and Negroes who labor here were only recently freed from slavery. But yes, San Martín did lead us to rebellion also. In any case, the genealogy of these islands' name is *Macaví,* a word from the Paracas culture."

"What are you, a professor? What are you doing stuck out on these islands?"

"It's a job. I happen to be Jewish myself, Sephardic. My real name is Abdelmalek, not Pedro. I was born in Morocco, but the Amazonian rubber boom drew many of us here. Then, I couldn't take the mosquitos."

"So, you traded them for flies."

"I follow the work. Bird shit and all, I get to live by the sea. I grew up on the Moroccan coast and haven't yet exhausted its mystery."

"Look, Abdelmalek. I'm missing out on the attentions of a perfectly good whore I happen to be in love with, just to come down here and close an exclusive deal with the Macabi or Nacavi Corporation or whoever the hell you are, so I can get recumbent on that floral divan upstairs where I get my heart broken and my loins massaged every Tuesday at 2 p.m., right after a lunch of striped bass and scalloped potatoes, followed by cherry cobbler and a digestif. Could we settle at $78 per pound?"

"I can sell at $82 with no exclusive right to purchase. That is $2 off what I am expected to charge."

A fly stung Danton, who began to slap his clothing insanely, as if an entire swarm of bees had attacked him out of nowhere. Maddeningly, Abdelmalek stood calmly fanning himself with a sheaf of papers, smiling patiently. The very seagulls that had threatened to form a cyclone had now mostly settled on barren ground in placid bunches around them, a few feet away, unafraid, not doing anything, simply looking stupidly at the ground, like a postwar army waiting for further instructions.

"You don't seem to understand. I hate this wretched place, even on short acquaintance. This woman, the one with whom I share a monetary-based concupiscence—she has bedeviled me. I've degraded myself beyond belief. Five or six times I've stood on the point of proposing her marriage, except that I'm afraid she'll laugh in my face. If I could only close this big international deal, that would be something to brag about, to persuade her I'm an entity in world business."

Abdelmalek had acquired a look of sagacity on his face, like that of a Talmudic scholar. His mouth could almost, though not quite, be interpreted either as a smirk or a quizzical moue. Another fly stung Danton, then another, but not his interlocutor. Why? "Señor, are you saying that getting me to go down $2 more per pound on bird shit, and agreeing to sell our shit only to you is going to allow you to win the wifely favor of a whore?"

Perhaps Abdelmalek was merely offering a gentle gibe, a friendly, empathetic teasing, because his unexpectedly sensitive mind understood with compassion the irony of the situation. Possibly, his jesting remark represented a ladder for forming a new understanding between them, after which he was going to offer Danton an exclusive deal at an acceptable price, giving Danton what he wanted, in fact, like a best man, facilitating Danton's questionable desire for a permanent and more honorable link with his weekly mistress. But the answer to that mystery will never be known.

Danton drew his pistol from inside his waistcoat and trained it on Abdelmalek. "You're going to sign an exclusive deal with Purity Imports, Inc., ten years, at $76 per pound. And we're going to hold you to it, no matter the fluctuations of the world market. Next time, I'm showing up with enforcers. So don't even think about fucking me over."

Danton felt an iron blow to his skull and collapsed face down into the pile of guano directly in front of him. Before losing consciousness, he barely had time to turn his head and see one of the Chinese ex-slaves brandishing a shovel over his lean, muscular shoulders, ready to strike a second blow if necessary.

After that, the story was Abdelmalek's to tell, in whatever manner he wished.

19
FLACO AND KINKY

Butch had been a bedwetter until the age of twelve. He was big and raw-boned from an early age, made all the sports teams, but this, his secret sorrow, made him turn down all invitations to sleepovers with teammates and earned him a reputation as an oddball. He developed a slight stutter and the first kid who made fun of it, half his size, got knocked out cold. Butch got suspended from school, threatened with juvi, but his dad, a literally fast-talking cattle auctioneer from San Antonio, persuaded the principal to let the matter go.

The father didn't send him back to school right away. Instead, he gave his son a turntable and the dad's LPs of Flaco Jiménez, as well as a bag of weed, saying, "Don't smoke it all at once," and left him alone in his room to sort things out on his own. That was the kindest and wisest of all his paternal acts.

Ya no quiero que me beses ni besarte
Ni mirarte, ni siquiera oír tu voz
Porque supe que tenías otro amante

Y en Laredo ya tenías otros dos.

I don't want you to kiss me, or me to kiss you
Or look at you, or even hear your voice
Because I found out you have another lover
And in Laredo you have two more.

Before he ever acquired an actual girlfriend, Butch learned, in Spanish he only half-understood, about two-timing women and heartbreak, about the melancholy that lies in the pulse of a bright accordion's squeeze, and how you got to dance it off, drink it off, laugh it off, because there will always be another señorita, just as beautiful and just as wicked as the previous.

The hiatus prepared him for the vicious and passionate going-steady social scene of middle school in Nuevo Laredo. That sea of fresh estrogen was one into which he jumped headlong to swim. He stopped wetting the bed almost overnight, never understanding what the cause of it had been. Yet he was left with a slightly brooding affect, totally unconscious, which, combined with his suddenly tall and muscular body, alongside his sensitive nature and a slight crudity that reminded girls of their own rough-hewn daddies, made him a popular boyfriend.

Butch lost his virginity at 14 to a bossy cheerleader with a nasty disposition who, for him, mewed like a kitten, and when she changed schools, other girls followed quick and fast after Butch on her heels. Nobody of the masculine persuasion bothered him or challenged him anymore, yet although he served as a high-school linebacker and a forward on the basketball team, also lettered in wrestling, and began to hang out with the other boys at bonfires, he managed to remain essentially a loner, who if it weren't for girls doing much of his homework and teachers turning a blind eye to his botched exams, Butch would surely have failed each grade.

The high school as a whole worked to throw a blanket over Butch's genuine intelligence, fulfilling the unspoken American compact that such as him ought to be given a berth, strictly based on the fact that if he'd been a bighorn sheep, he would have successfully butted away his male competitors. It was expected he'd get recruited by colleges after a standout junior season on the gridiron, messing up people toward whom he had no actual bad feelings, thereby justifying the corporate bad faith of the school in passing him along, and then they could keep his picture up inside the trophy case in the lobby next to the principal's office.

Only Butch was busy trying to learn to play the accordion, for which he had no talent whatsoever, smoking too much weed and reselling stereo equipment that arrived at his hands through questionable sources. His father found the hot equipment in the garage, questioned Butch, kicked him out, whereupon he found a cheap apartment, expanded his business, found a young woman out of his league from a "good" family from the sister city, Nuevo Laredo, Mexico, who got him off the weed, made him cut his hair and took him to church with her at Parroquia San José Obrero, where he only somewhat understood the Spanish mass, except that it weirdly reminded him of Flaco Jiménez's songs, only the impossible love was for Jesus instead of a female.

Aparición, his girlfriend, got him to sign up for Spanish lessons, enroll in the community college, and moonlight as a stereo technician, while she prepared for the border-crossing debutante ball of the Society for Martha Washington, at which she would debut a colonial gown, weighing

100 pounds and costing $30,000, made by the dressmaker Linda Leyendecker Gutierrez, the oil heiress who designed her dresses with "heavenly inspiration from God."

While Butch broke a sweat, putting in sixteen-hour days to be worthy of Aparición, in addition to finding the time and extra stamina to have sex with her on the sly when she required it, he somehow got the idea that he would be her consort at this social event, as a sort of audition for meeting her parents and possibly marrying into her society family, and began to worry about what he would wear, or whether he would have to learn dance steps of minuets, allemandes and hornpipes. She'd kept making excuses why she couldn't introduce him to her family, and why he kept having to meet her at the Motel Valle Verde for two hours at a time, spending money on hookups that he could ill-afford.

The ball came and went, without her ever inviting him. She was a success and broke off with Butch by text cryptically the next day. He found everything out retroactively when the banns for her wedding to the son of the prominent Garza Barrios family were announced in the newspaper. Butch briefly considered going and shooting them both, but he had renounced violence in middle school. Instead, he put on Flaco.

> She said if you're from Texas, so
> Where's your boots and where's your gun
> Well, I got guns that no one can see
> Well, after that we both agreed
> Spanish is a loving tongue
> But she never spoke Spanish to me
> Well, she never spoke Spanish to me.

His father made ribs that night, with a special secret spicy sauce and put on a new-old record for Butch. "This is our people," said his dad. It was Kinky Friedman and the Texas Jew Boys, singing "Are You Sure Hank Done It This Way?"

As pop and son ate the delicious ribs with their fingers, letting sauce smear over their facial hair, his father turned to Butch and said, "In the words of Kinky himself son, 'Find what you love and let it kill you and devour your remains. For all things will kill you, both slowly and fastly, but it's much better to be killed by a lover.'"

Then Butch cried for his momma like he never had let himself since she was hit by a truck when he was just a toddler, crossing the street to mail a letter to a convict, because she was always trying as a good Christian woman to improve convicts via the Postal Service. Butch plumb cried himself to sleep. It was one of the best nights of his young life.

20

LANDING THE MARLIN

Vanessa had a blue marlin on an eighty-weight line in a charter boat off the waters of Costa Rica. The guide had put out a good spread of fish patés as bait, he knew his stuff. He'd wanted to strap her into a fighting chair because she was so petite, but she insisted a harness was plenty. She'd done a bit of deep sea fishing with her dad in the Gulf, it was one of the things she liked best about him, those excursions, where he could get out all his aggression in the water and even seemed kind and solicitous and proud of her when she landed a big one. He'd always beam and shout out, as she held up the fish for the photo, "It's almost as big as you!" That tickled him to no end. In the Gulf was where she learned that you were a counterweight to the sport fish, not by your size, but by your movement and timing. It was no different than judo, really, or fencing. You weren't fighting muscle for muscle. Skill was power.

That's how she got into microbiology and succeeded in laboratories studying addiction. She was a tiny black woman, and men, especially white men, but all of them really, were all too ready to dismiss her, referring to her as cute, lightly touching her butt and pushing on it as if it were a plush pillow that they'd just won at the carnival by knocking down bottles. But she had conducted her study of men and their ways since early on in life. There was no remedy for most of them; you could only control the symptoms. But they were a lot like this marlin, sleek and scared and angry and full of piss and pulse. You had to give them plenty of line, let them run themselves hard, allow them do what they had to do, to an extent, so that they wore themselves down, hook already well set, blind fury at fever pitch, while you did a counter-dance inside the boat, sometimes almost getting pulled in, but you stayed light on your feet, nimble, moves and countermoves, enjoying that feeling of force against your forearms, the same way it felt when a man held your body fast during coitus and practically squeezed the life out of you, because he was that excited.

A crowd had gathered around Vanessa as the marlin leapt above the water line, still parallel to the boat, and crashed back into the waves several times. They were calling out encouragement to her, like a pack of Little League coaches, offering tips and advice, instructions and warnings, all of which she ignored. When she briefly stumbled, the guide, at her elbow, gently offered to take the rod, but she waved him off. Then, the marlin began to tire, and she was able to crank it in a few more feet for the next phase of the dance.

When she glanced out of the side of her eye, Butch stood agog, admiring her finesse. He was the only one who didn't say a word. Rather, he was under her spell. Yes, she knew he wanted her real bad. He didn't even know that, but she knew it as sure as she knew that each of her feet had five toes. He was a hunk of a man, super sweet, yet who could easily be head of the local motorcycle gang or else the local baker who gives you free samples. He had a shock of dark hair, appealingly half-combed, that you could have shaved off and made a decent lap-blanket out of. His body was made for tight clothes, but he wasn't vain that way, he liked them slack and comfortable, and even so, lots of ladies on the cruise, figuring out he might be single, or just not caring either way, had been hitting on him, dropping their purses after they walked by so he'd pick them up and they could strike up a conversation, or else stopping to ask him for directions. On a boat! Or just brazenly coming up and twirling his mustache. Yet he resisted all their entreaties. Like Jasper, he was a true romantic, the only kind of man worth having. And he was fascinated by Vanessa, but never beyond the bounds of tact. A woman had hurt him real bad along the way, possibly several had, and a melancholy underlay his affectionate bluster and Texas twang.

When they rode the dune buggies in Mexico, almost overturning them a couple times but managing to stay upright, she'd felt a thrill. She had literally gotten wet between the legs, and it wasn't the subtropical heat either! Vanessa wanted Butch, the way she'd wanted a man when she used to go clubbing and the man was a good dancer, like her, and could move her body around, suggesting how he would conduct himself in bed, because couples dancing is almost always a sex simulation, sort of a warm-up and audition, and she'd simply pluck him off the dance floor and have a toss with him, in his apartment, in the bed of his truck, and a couple of times even in the men's room with the wingman watching the door outside, because those were her wild days, ones she miraculously escaped unscathed. Butch called out, primevally to her loins.

Only those days were over. Long over. She'd had a

number of years of serial monogamy, going to her job at the lab, saving for a house, doing all those things that make you a citizen and possibly a wife and mother. She had girl-friends who were still keeping multiple guys on the line, being unfaithful and having promiscuous sex, her age, good jobs, and it wasn't a good look. They were living lessons of what she didn't want to devolve into, though if she'd given free rein to her instincts, that's exactly what she'd turn into. She had no illusions about her inherent virtue.

That's what church was for! That is why she went to Mass; apart from that, she loved candles and incense and singing and the soaring ceiling of the cathedral and even the grumpy old priest, who scolded more than preached, as if he knew that 90% of his congregants were going to end up in Hell despite all his best efforts. Every night, on her knees at the bedside, same as when she was a little girl, Vanessa ended her vespers prayer by saying out loud, "God, I'm not that good of a person. Please make me a better one."

Jasper was intelligent, so she couldn't fool him that she was not having some stirring of feeling, she couldn't hide it entirely, and he'd pick up on it, and she could have simply ignored Butch, been a bitch to him, but what was the point in that? They were here to have fun. She hadn't sinned, not yet, and she wasn't going to. As the marlin began to tire and she could tell it was going to be hers at last, she glanced over to Jasper, who wore ridiculously huge aviator shades, like a Hollywood celebrity on vacation trying not to be recognized. He looked damn sexy, even with that sunburn. Maybe that was just the eyes of love. She couldn't figure out why he attracted her, why he was the one she had to return to, she who could get any man on the hook, but he was her fucking destiny, praise Jesus. He sat impas-sive, taking in the spectacle of her, or possibly his mind was elsewhere and that was half the appeal, that busy brain.

Also, he was constantly turning out to be capable of unexpected things. Walking around, he was a klutz, but he could ski moguls. He had a good hand with a saw, a level, a drill, a hammer. He made her several beautiful birdhouses one summer, exquisitely turned and he hand-painted them her favorite primary colors. When she took him fishing on a lake, explaining how to bait a hook, turns out that he already knew how to fish, only didn't want to interrupt her and afterward, he filleted them expertly at the campsite while she drank beer. Jasper changed his own oil, grew his own herbs, and for a while, even roasted his own coffee and made his own beer, which turned out decent. He could read the constellations in the sky and identify bird and plant species almost anywhere in a way she hadn't ever bothered to master, and she was the scientist!

Jasper should have been a rich, famous world-beater, except he wasn't, and there was nothing to be done about that. By rights, they never should have been on this cruise with a man who fenced merchandise and was going to Peru half-cocked. But here they were, and she was going to ride it out, be the Emma, rather than sit at home sidelined while these two wild cards dreamed big and then messed it all up.

With a final few cranks, Vanessa brought the marlin to the boat and nodded to the guide to help her bring it over the side. The other charter passengers applauded her first strike, and she looked around with a faint smile and shrugged as if to say, "Shucks, this was nothing. I've landed a bunch of them."

21

HUMMINGBIRD

She had the same heartbeat as a blue-throated hummingbird, 1260 beats per minute, she was sure of it, except when she fell into a torpor on a cold night, when she hibernated, at which point it fell to 50 beats per minute. She could walk on hot coals dumped from a grill when her friends cooked out by the riverside, in violation of the law, because it was fire season, and she walked across the coals precisely to put them out with her feet like ice. She could regulate her body temperature that way. She could do cocaine in a crowd, lights twinkling on the riverboat, and it had no effect whatsoever on her bloodstream. She watched the others twitch-dance, while she moved lithely among them, touching this back and that, bestowing her blessing without getting involved with anyone. She was an android, not a real one but the equivalent, a simulacrum of a simulacrum. She was linear. Everything in her universe made sense.

She could attempt suicide by rope, pills, gunshot, jumping from a bridge, running out into traffic, electrocuting herself, swallowing acid and nothing would happen, not even a stomachache or a headache. She put one foot in front of the other, the way a verb follows a noun or a duckling follows its mother. She was all-powerful but too shy and modest to mention it. She would have made a good heroine in a gothic novel, surrounded by cosmic forces arrayed against her—necromancers, ruined anti-heroes, wolves or werewolves, thrown onto an ice floe to perish as she watched the mainland retreat, because she was the sacrificial victim of the tribe, or buried alive by an insane and vengeful lover, ants crawling over her, a goddess who metamorphosed right when she was about to get obliterated by the head god for disobedience, a female executive in a corrupt male world of depraved bank executives, not part of the club, they secretly wanted to pass her around like a commodity but couldn't figure out how to get away with it so they shunned her, planning to make her the fall guy for their financial scheme to dupe the American people.

She adopted too many pets, but they spoke to her in a secret language, literally spoke. She could decipher their mews and growls and squawks and hisses as if she were a linguist at an Ivy League school who had cracked the code of universal animal speech, decried by her colleagues as a charlatan but she would outlast all their pious heresies. She ate men like air, ate women like popcorn at a tear-jerker matinee, ate herself and regurgitated and out of her own vomit fashioned a new being, more beautiful than her current self, and her soul slipped as easily into that totem as if she were passing a dollar bill from an old wallet to a new wallet. She was a junkie whore, living in an abandoned house with rough men who were too strung out to actually rape her, so instead, they pawed her until she metamorphosed them into little glittering fish in an aquarium and watched them cruise through the water trying to remember what they used to be.

She was unemployed, but things were going to get better. Her car had stopped running and she didn't have money to fix it, but she'd figure out a way. She'd only just gotten over the flu and lay in her walk-up trying to recover, too weak to do anything except microwave the diminishing stock of frozen dinners. Her cat had run off, but maybe it would come back, once she could get to the store to buy another bag of cat food. She'd been turning t-shirts inside out, so the dried sweat wouldn't be as pungent, but pretty soon she'd wash all the dirty clothes, once she'd figured out why the washer wouldn't spin, and how to fix it. Her man had moved in with their upstairs female neighbor to be friends with benefits, but screw them, rather, let them screw each other. She was suffering from incontinence, at her age, possibly due to a bladder infection, yet soon she'd find that old bottle of antibiotics that she hadn't finished taking and possibly it would fix her condition. She had night terrors, dreaming that she was drowning in the bathtub only to wake up in her own bed soaking wet. Her workplace had called and called about her not showing up for work, first scolding, then offering to let her work remotely, then threatening to fire her, then asking her to at least come in and train her replacement, then silence. She had probably been fired at this point, not that she cared.

What was the motive for getting better? Who would she seek out even if she got on her feet? What kind of relationship could a woman hope for who couldn't keep her job and was so unappealing that even her cat and boyfriend ran away? How had she gotten into this position? She tried to force her mind to trace the trajectory backwards, establishing a strict chain of causality so that at least the demise would seem inevitable. If she could manage to reconstruct her recent past as an irrefutable logical proof, that would also suggest a logical final outcome. If the steps of her degradation pointed to her death, at a minimum she could accept that, calmly make preparations to kill herself and get the job done with dispatch, without lollygagging.

Yet she couldn't reason out the situation to satisfaction. No matter which way her exhausted mind turned over the events, she could do no better than see them as an arbitrary succession of non-related missteps, not even a matter of self-blame. Rather, her consistent bad luck figured as the random hate of the cosmos. Her life was comical in that it was accidental, therefore, not to be taken seriously. This being the case, she burst out laughing at her conundrum, cast off self-pity for such a ridiculous, pathetic figure as herself, and realized that she was nothing more than hapless in the hands of an uncaring fate.

She got out of bed. Inspecting the washer, she realized it was just a sock that had hung up the tub from spinning properly. The familiar noise of the machine summoned her cat, who must have been lingering nearby. Its yowls for food made her shower, put on newly fresh clothes and go to the store for cat food, and while she was at it, do a full shopping for herself. On the way down the stairwell to the street, she happened past her ex-boyfriend and his new squeeze and surprised them by giving them a polite wave and going right on by. This made her laugh again and put her in the mood for an espresso at the corner coffee shop. The caffeine buzz made her flirt, and soon, she had a date for Thursday with a guy who worked in a nearby office. Returning home, she put away the groceries, cleaned her house top to bottom until it smelled of perfumed disinfectant. She made a sizzling stir fry in the wok, laced with lots of hot chili, cracked one of the frosty wheat beers she'd purchased for this moment, and settled in with her cat on her lap to binge-watch her favorite series, about three female roommates taking turns leading tormented romantic and work lives. She enjoyed their suffering immensely.

The next morning, she showed up for work as if nothing. The boss looked surprised to see her. He looked like he was about to launch into a big lecture, but instead gave her a set of instructions that brought her up to date and waved her to her desk. In it sat a temp, whom she in turn asked to please vacate. The temp cried and left, literally running out the front door while sobbing.

It was a good day to be alive.

22

JASPER'S ORIGIN STORY

He'd spent several years of his early life on the Peruvian altiplano, on Lake Titicaca. In his admittedly fallible memory, everyone wore knee-breeches and either rubber sandals made of recycled tires or went barefoot. Balsas skated across the lake, and huts were made of straw, adobe or cinderblock. Everybody had windburned cheeks, which at first looked rosy, then by mid-adulthood, like skin damage. Lightning ripped the sky constantly, and once from his yard, Jasper watched a cow get electrocuted by a bolt. He remembered people casually mentioning this and that person getting hit by lightning coming back from a bean field or simply out walking. Neighbors would also speak of "not awakening the hail," so that it wouldn't destroy their crops. People lived casually, stoically, in the midst of not only poverty, but daily tragedy. They went to and fro with immense bundles of fresh-cut barley on their backs. He remembered them squatting as they salted fish, and he remembered the pungent taste when it was offered to his child's lips and his father enjoined him to partake.

Jasper didn't understand fully, until later, that his father was an anthropologist born in the city, a mestizo, not indigenous like them, and he was doing a long-term study on the relation between myth and ecological sustainability. What he could recall vividly were the arguments between his parents, how his mother asked why they had to live in this godforsaken, freezing, windswept place full of ignorant people who couldn't even speak proper Spanish, much less English.

She'd grown up on a farm in Iowa, her "origin story," as she sarcastically called it, but this rustication was too much. She'd disappear for weeks to the apartment they kept in La Paz, which his mother referred to as "a perfectly good shithole," and where she occasionally took Jasper along, where he'd mainly watch her lie in bed while he played with his toys or rummaged for dry cereal in the cabinet, though mostly she left him with his father among the Aymara and Quechua-speaking indigenous dwellers of the highest part of the Andes, so high that you could reach out and pull the stars over you like a blanket when the temperature fell below freezing and your teeth chattered despite the alpaca skin you were wrapped in.

During the mother's long absences, a woman would come and stay with him and his father in the hut, sharing the latter's bed made on the floor. This young Quechua woman disrobed in the kerosene lamplight, discovering her beautiful body, which Jasper dimly knew, in spite of his youth, was exciting. She had the large breasts and hips and sturdy build of women made for hard work and child-bearing. Her name was Antuka. In the utter dark, after the lamp was extinguished, Jasper heard the soft grunts of lovemaking. His father never tried to hide the fact of this woman from his son, nor did he ask Jasper not to say anything to his mother. Yet Jasper never mentioned the fact of her to anyone. Surely everyone in the village knew this open secret, and most likely his mother did too, for after a time, they separated.

It would have made sense for Jasper to stay with his father, who had taught him how to fish, make adobe bricks, repair the thatch on a dwelling, who carved for him little figurines out of eucalyptus, kissed and embraced his son often, told him myths, such as Manco Inca and Mama Oqllo walking together out of Lake Titicaca, their lake, to found the city of Cusco and by extension the Inca Empire. "We live in the imperial cradle," he said. "You're standing on the most prestigious ground in the universe." Jasper found that hard to believe, with the hens and the dog shit and women squatting and peeing around him in broad daylight, but his father said the words with such conviction that Jasper, for a time, believed them.

That's why, when the separation came, and given the pattern of the past, he fully expected to remain on the altiplano when his mother announced she was relocating to the United States. But she took him with her, and her father let him go without protest. Jasper felt as if he'd been hurled from the heavens to a distant sea by a powerful arm. The next time he heard from his father was five years later, when a package arrived wrapped in brown paper ripped at the corners and tied with skinny rope, covered with many colorful stamps, and addressed to Jasper Delgado.

Inside lay a brand-new, unblemished tome. On its pale green hardback cover were embossed the words: "ALTI-PLANO ATTITUDES: THUNDER, RAIN, LIGHTNING and the Creation of an Ecological Cosmovision." Jasper never opened the book to look inside. Rather, it lived on his bookshelf, then under his bed, then his closet, then it migrated with him in a cardboard box as he moved from place to place, until finally, discovering the book one day during preparations for another move, Jasper sold it on eBay, listing the book as "in mint condition."

23
THE NAKED STEPMOTHER

Daybreak. White and tan guanacos meander on the puna, yanking out stubbles of grass with their teeth. Volcano flamingos swoop low over the vast water. They land to fish for minnows in the shallows, plodding ankle-deep, stepping as if they wore wet socks. The Uros Islands float, unmoored. The barren plains roll up in the distance into hills of burnt orange and fire red and beyond them lies a succession of snow peaks. Frigid wind blows endlessly, chasing vizcachas down into the broken rocks.

José awakens first and goes to feed dry, shelled corn cobs and scraps of kindling into the stove to heat up the adobe hut before either of the other two awakens. Soon, there comes a welcome crackle and smoke begins to pour through the aperture in the roof. He places coca leaves into two clay cups, coffee essence into a third and listens for the initial hiss of the water that will precede the more heartening pings against the tin kettle as it begins to boil. Meantime, he unwraps the moist cloth from the fresh, salty cheese, slices it and lays the pieces on a plate. From a blue plastic bag, he extracts yesterday's bread, hard and cold but still half-fresh. Hanging from the ceiling is jerky, and he hacks off a few slices to complete the picture. José considers setting broad beans and corn to boil, but he'll let her do that after this simple breakfast and they can eat it for lunch.

Antuka stirs from sleep, in a patchwork blanket stitched from other exhausted blankets. He's offered to get her a new one, but it's sentimental, something about her girl-hood, one she slept under, one that kept her lap warm when she herded alpacas in the most remote stretches and spent endless hours alone and unattended. She claims that the blanket kept the condenados and the nina karru from taking her away to the underworld. He doesn't contradict her. For all he knows, she's right. It's been a long time since he tossed away the term "cultural beliefs," and just said, "a reality."

He's horny. They didn't fuck last night because they could hear his son's dry cough and it made her uptight. He tells her it's better that Jasper should go ahead and learn that this is what the world is made of. But women, it seems, are at bottom all Catholics. When Jasper's official mother takes her son back to La Paz for a few days, and José can give way to the full fury of his manhood, he and Antuka will do everything that can be thought of. They will rut. From childhood, she has watched animals couple, so she knows. Yet even alone, afterward, she tells him, "God was watching us that whole time." And he replies, "Well, I hope he enjoyed it."

Although José now speaks fluent Quechua and decent Aymara, he has been requiring of Antuka that she address his son in Spanish and that they try to also converse with one another in Spanish, so that Jasper will feel included. The pressure of this demand makes her cross. Her Spanish is almost incomprehensible even to him, the heavy, earth-bound accent. And given she's not an intellectual, she's a shepherdess and cook. He can't speak to her about cultural standards when she quite reasonably asserts that this is her land, her birthplace, and that José and his son are the inter-lopers. If the father learned the indigenous language and ways, why can't the son? It's her belief he already under-stands most of what they say in Quechua; he's just not going to show it or admit it. She knows things are bad between José and his wife. She's thrilled about it, childishly so.

At the same time, she's mature enough, or just practi-cal-minded, that she tells him, "You know she's going to leave for good. Prepare him now. If you don't, you'll lose him. Make him one of us, if you want to keep him. A beast. Otherwise, you'll have to let him go."

Antuka is only nineteen years of age, or thereabouts, by her calculations, yet she bears that kind of straightforward wisdom about what matters. She can't be entirely sure she's nineteen, it could be less, even sixteen or seventeen. It's never come up because she didn't even go to grade school and doesn't know how to read even if there were a birth certificate to be had. Her sense of time doesn't revolve around birthdays. Now that José is curious, or nervous, about her age, there's no one to consult about her birth particulars. All her mother ever told her is that it was a hard labor. Her mother was killed by a lightning strike while washing laundry in the creek, and her father, who knows. He doesn't pay attention. Half the reason Antuka made a play for José that day he came around with his digital recorder asking them questions about their use of manure, is because her father had been rubbing and patting her in the wrong way. He was soon going to drag her to bed because he'd already done so to her little sister the very night of her mother's death, and Antuka knew she was next on the list. After the first time she and José copulated in a field, she declared outright, "I knew I was going to fuck somebody this week, so I decided it might as well be you."

He finds her frankness strangely appealing. She does what she has to do to get along, and she gives him the best effort in bed partly from hormones, partly from passion, and partly because he's her best chance at going beyond the basics of existence. Not that she needs much. Salty cheese, jerky, bread, coca tea—that's fine by her. That's what she's used to. She asks for no more. And if it doesn't work out between her and José, she'll probably calmly kill her father with a rock and figure out some other way to get along. She's certainly not afraid of hard work. Antuka cooks and washes the clothes while José is busy interviewing, reading and writing. She gathers wood and watches after the animals she owns. She goes into Puno sometimes to get supplies, when he receives his check from the Foundation, or she stays at the house and watches over Jasper in silence, except that she sings him nursery songs in Quechua, the ones she was raised on.

> *Surphuy t'ika pallaspaiki*
> *Hakay maq'ta haku niwan*
>
> *Kayna wata tusuqmasiy*
> *Maytaq kunan kaypinachu?*
>
> *T'ika pallana pampapiqa*
> *Iru Ichullas winayusian*

Jasper seems to like her. At the least, he doesn't dislike

her. Unlike his mother, she's calm. Her silences aren't tense or pregnant. She likes to muss Jasper's hair, tells him he's *guapo* and has figured out he likes her quinoa chicken soup and she makes it for him whenever she hears that dry cough coming. All the same, in José's mind, his wife is like Medea, and he believes she would kill her own son, cook him in an Iowa meatloaf, and serve it to José before she'd let him slip into the caring hands of another woman, especially one who didn't suffer from depression like her, didn't even understand what depression was and would consider it a disease white people suffered from.

If Pamela ever confronted Antuka, she'd conclude, in her usual sarcastic manner, that the girl simply didn't have very many moving parts. How he'd ever dragged Pamela to this part of the world, he couldn't adequately explain. He genuinely thought she'd adapt. He hadn't understood that at that moment, Pamela's sheer terror of being left alone in Milwaukee was far greater than the unimagined scenario of going to the native country of the young professor she'd met at a cocktail party and whose charming foreign accent alone was enough by itself to get her into the sack with him, overriding her certain knowledge that she had no deeper interest in foreign cultures, foreign languages, foreign foods even, and that unconsciously, she assumed that a highly-educated, nay, brilliant wunderkind like him, who looked almost white and who spoke flawless polysyllabic English with a hint of a sexy Latino lilt, could certainly be expected to assimilate 100% to her midwestern culture, her mashed potato palate, her middlebrow taste in music and movies, her unexamined jingoism.

Hadn't he already? He was a tenure-track professor at UW Milwaukee, for heaven's sake, he'd quickly won a long-term grant from the Ford Foundation and without them discussing the matter, because they never discussed anything important such as finances, career expectations, gender roles, desire for children, she just got knocked up because she kind of wanted to and kind of didn't, basically, sex made her feel good for a couple of hours when she got a hard case of the blues, which was often, so she was mostly game. Except that she did forget to take her birth control pills when she was depressed and it was as much his job as hers to at least ask, that's what feminism was for, and if he insisted on just pouncing on her, attacking her, whenever he got an urge, what did he expect the result to be?

Jasper stirred and sat up. His alpaca skin slid down and exposed his naked chest. "I thought you slept with a shirt on," his father said.

"I did. But I got hot and took it off in the night."

"It's okay. Come here." The father rubbed Vicks on the son's chest and slipped a fresh shirt over him. Antuka had awakened and was looking from Jasper to José and back with sleepy eyes of love.

"I'm going to finish up a few things this morning, then you and I are going to take a bus to La Paz to see a doctor. You may need antibiotics. That cough has been going on too long."

"Are you going to leave me in the city with Mom?"

"No, we'll have a good meal in a restaurant and come back tonight."

"You can take a break from me, Dad. It's okay. I know you get sick of me. I don't want to bother you."

José pulled his son close. "Never say that. I never want to hear those words from your mouth again. I always want you close by."

"If you say so, Dad."

"And I'm not the only one in this house who cares for you."

"You mean Mom?"

"Well—her too. But I was referring to someone else."

Antuka got up, and slid her peculiar personal blanket off. Wearing only her clingy nightshirt, she began to lay the foodstuffs José had prepared on the table.

Without speaking, Jasper watched Antuka with great concentration, and it was at that moment José realized his son was memorizing in precise detail the young woman's naked body, when she got out of bed at midnight to close the shutters, and how entrancing it looked in the low lamplight.

24
VANISHING POINT

T he cruise was ending. Butch, making a team out of various women who were trying to pick him up, won the Thursday night trivia contest Muscle Cars in Movies, after having coached each of them in their staterooms with his encyclopedic knowledge on the topic. Having concluded that he and *Emma* were never going to betray the Sundance Kid, that the two hombres had a higher destiny than that, and knowing he was not willing to pay for such an indiscretion with even a metaphorical bullet in the heart, he instead bedded each of the aspirants in succession, but with the promise they would bone up, I mean, drill, I mean, sorry, study hard the sheet he made up for each on auto-cinematic marvels such as the 1968 Mustang GT, the 1977 Pontiac Trans Am (a model he'd actually owned, 400 cubic inches, 200 horsepower, 325 foot-pounds of torque, masterful compression), the 1955 Chevrolet 150, the 1974 Ford Falcon, the 1972 Ford Gran Torino Sport, and the king of them all, the 1970 Dodge Challenger R/T. With his All-American mindset, he came close to losing the match, erroneously (though in his mind, rightly) equating the world "muscle car" with American motor engineering. Jasper came close to beating him with his knowledge of foreign cinematic automobiles given to high-speed chases, such as the Lamborghini Miura, the Porsche 911 Turbo, the Audi S8, and the Ferrari 550. Secretly, it pleased Butch to have Sundance as his chief competitor, mano a mano right to the last round, as the gods decreed. They embraced in front of an applauding crowd, most of them were pretty shit-faced and only knew about SUVS. The men's renewed brotherhood was a relief, especially to Emma.

On deck that night, smoking cigars Butch had bought with his share of the prize money, having said goodbye to his weepy, tactical one-night stands, the boys stood on deck off the coast of Ecuador, hair gently tossed by Poseidon, only a few hours from the Port of Callao, where they would disembark. They philosophized about the difference between a vanishing point and a horizon. Both words portended a disappearance from view, but in different ways. The vanishing point, Butch ruminated, was possibly more existentialist, being the place where two parallel lines met. "*Appear* to meet," Jasper corrected, letting go a puff of smoke. "If lines are parallel, by definition, they cannot truly converge."

There was a thoughtful silence, after which Butch added, "Unless they're crooked lines." Jasper then allowed how the horizon was more optimistic, because it's where the earth's surface and sky meet, the terrestrial and the cosmic fused into one. "*Appear* to meet," Butch corrected. "Land and sky don't touch, so far as I know." Seeing his friend's melancholy look and recalling that he'd lost the trivia contest a mere hour before, Butch noted that if you really think about it, when you hike up on a mountain, which is part of the earth, clouds come down and brush the ground and wipe dew all over every last rock and bush. "Hell, even on the farms in Tennessee, fog comes and lies in the bottomlands of a morning, it gets so damn low it's right enough below the very grass, so how much more can the sky and earth meet than that, hoss? When you're right, you're right."

The two men finished a good smoke, tossed back the dregs of their bourbon and gave praise as the cruise ship's foghorn gave out three long blasts to signal that they had entered Peruvian waters.

That night, Butch fell asleep and had a wet dream that he was driving at top speed a Challenger with a high-performance 440 cci Magnum with four-barrel carbs and a four-speed manual transmission with a pistol-drip shifter.

25
THE SPANISH FLOTILLA

Crepuscular skies scented with falling zephyrs that smelled of burning cedars covered Sacsayhuaman, as if casting a blanket of divine protection over the warriors stationed there. Crooked queñuales ferns hovered beside the stone walls, like men too old for battle now, who could only give ineffectual advice to the young, warning them out of harm's way, when everyone knew that there was no way to avoid danger if you were a soldier. You could only watch over your shoulder for an attack, to find out that the war yell you thought you heard was only the cry of the cock-of-the-rock, mocking you, and the masked trogon answering with a trill.

Chaskar stood and laughed at his own momentary fright. So unlike him to get spooked, even for a moment. He wasn't the premonition type. He'd killed enemies up and down the Andes, including the headmen of villages they'd conquered, the ones who were too dumb to understand the good deal that Huascar had offered them in his succession of conquests. Take the women, some of our most beautiful. Let us enlighten you with new forms of engineering and

production, systems of running water, crop terracing, flawless distribution and exchange, for the small price of fealty.
That and turning over your property to the Incas and practicing obedience to their laws. Chaskar himself had been
born one of those ignorant savages, in a forgotten byway
without laid stone roads, without arm cuffs of gold,
without medallions of the same, without feasts of roast
meat and endless fermented corn beer to celebrate victo-
ries, without luscious young women falling into your
victor's arms, one after another, without priests who
designed buildings in precise fashion, situating a window
so that exactly on the winter solstice, the light of the stars
fell directly into a bowl of water situated in the middle of a
holy room. Those stars could be charted and the future read
in them.

Chaskar believed in this scientific spirit, the price of
which was the domination of the strong over the weak, or
else, ideally, those weak would be made strong, and even as
slaves, they would have the stamina to work long days,
whether or not they were located to a new region for
maximum labor efficiency throughout the realm, yet
somehow the new conquests would prosper, the men
muscular, and the new women they met, despite differences in language and customs, would be fertile as never
before, well fed, bearing many children, increasing the
empire. They could put aside their old superstitions to
embrace the light.

Conical cleft calyx flowers sprouted in full bloom. Their
abundance seemed to Chaskar an emblem of the endless
growth of this civilization, how it was meant to rule over all
of these fledgling, so-called societies, becoming the apoth-
eosis of all that had been, all that would be. His favorite
moment was to see thousands of dancers congregated, in

crimson, yellow, teal, and orange fabrics dyed from plants, finely woven on countless looms, riddled with glyphs and figures, whimsical seeming, but really, emblems of the State, as the Inca was carried in a litter past all these worshippers. This embroidery, worn on all their persons, spoke a language that was secret, yet their meanings were known to all.

Chaskar had risen high enough in military rank to understand the tension between the two ruling brothers, Huascar and Atahualpa, for both of whom he'd worked, as Atahualpa repulsed Huascar's attempt to take over his smaller portion of the kingdom. Chaskar had acted as a double agent, giving each information on the other, waiting for divine justice or sheer military muscle and tactics to sort the matter out, while he kept getting promoted for his competence.

But today on Sacsayhuaman, there existed a greater possible threat. His men had been reporting for some time about seeing ships of the air, which at first Chaskar had assumed were part of the recent arrival of this strange, sallow, bearded man Pizarro, who dressed in burnished metal, less beautiful than gold, but as if made to reject arrows and sword and spear blows. Chaskar was sure the Inca's massive, numberless forces could defeat this small band of fewer than two hundred men, most of them hard-bitten and sickly-looking, if mean and desperate. But ships of the air would be another matter. Perhaps they weren't Spaniards at all. Perhaps the gods to whom they constantly prayed en masse had finally decided to show themselves in a visible form other than the Inca. He'd kind of been waiting for that, because to him the Inca, either one of them, wasn't necessarily divine.

Chaskar wasn't really religious; he more believed in the

political part of things, but you never could say for sure. Even in matters of gods and men, you had to play both sides until you knew what was what. He'd had a tendency to put off ultimate decisions until the last possible moment, then to change his mind later. He wished his brother Kilali were here, rather than holed up with Atahualpa's men. He and Chaskar had a parting of the ways after their little sister was chosen for ritual sacrifice. Kilali was the religious one, so he should have been thrilled at his sister getting picked for the ultimate honor. But he was overly attached to Pasya, lovely, fair, with long lashes, delicate lips, and barely out of childhood into maidenhood. At first, it looked like she was just going to become one of the Inca's concubines, which would have been the best-case scenario. That would solidify Chaskar's access to Huascar, who had recently become shaky, moody, and overly superstitious. Instead, his sister was drugged and placed in a volcano. It was a bad way to die, for sure, no matter how much prestige got attached. The only comfort was that she probably had no idea what was happening to her, so possibly it wasn't terrifying. When Chaskar didn't seem utterly outraged and didn't resign his position in protest, that was the ultimate rift between the two brothers.

As the sun rose over Sacsayhuaman, a floating fortress, several times the size of their largest temple, pierced a cloud and hovered almost straight above Chaskar. Peaceable alpacas fled, knocking down their enclosure. It sounded like ten thousand torrent ducks passing over, or the hoofbeats of the men in his charge galloping into a blind stone alley and whirling to retreat. As crimson fire began to shoot from it toward the ground, burning his men alive, another airship came over the mountain's horizon, then another, then another, then another, until the air was filled with one great otherworldly force. Chaskar raised his bow to the heavens, as if to ward them all off with that single gesture. He was unafraid. If he survived, he would adapt to whatever new reality came, as he had his entire life, which had begun in total anonymity. But if this was indeed a flotilla of Spanish ships of another kind, he understood that neither Atahualpa nor Huascar would ultimately be victorious.

26

SIN CASHED

L anding in Cusco on a plane, you thread the needle into a narrow valley flanked by hills. Ausangate Mountain, where the godhead dwells, stands snow-peaked when the cloud cover blows off. Ears still popping, you can feel the *soroche* setting up in your thin bloodstream, even though you grew up in the highlands, and you hope that a cup of warm coca tea awaits you nearby, before the *condenados* and the *ñak'aq* with their horrible fangs and powerful claws seize you while you sleep to drag you into a dry furrow in a field and suck the fat out of your body, so the priests, their secret masters, can use it to grease the bells of the cathedral, and they will ring with sweet clarity up and down the valley, awakening the faithful to oaths and obedient acts and tithes, world without end, as pious mestizos and trembling old indigenous women who outlived their usefulness but have just enough strength to hold onto their fate, kneel in pews, making the sign of the cross next to the flickering candle lighting the portrait of the Last Supper, the one with a guinea pig painted in the platter at the long table's center by some long-dead anonymous artisan, the creature's little claws half-curled, its teeth tiny but vampirish, and the Christ who looks exactly like an Inca smiles knowingly, as you, the interloper, are sacrificed in that dry, distant furrow, because you had to return to the homeland, you had to know, you had to crawl into the haunted house wind tunnel of your past, barley chaff and dry corn husks flying at your face, crawl to the end against a hurricane force gale to see whether the celestial light of self-knowledge would usher you into the fulness of existence, no longer an orphan whose mother went in and out of psychiatric hospitals while you bounced among the houses of reluctant aunts and family friends, until your mother was hollow as the shell of a fire-toasted grasshopper.

"Those snacks were tasty, no doubt."

"It's like a bunch of birdseed smashed together with honey. But surprisingly delicious. Did you eat yours, Jasper?"

"No, I saved it for the hummingbirds."

"Oh, I want to see those. They're adorable!"

You haven't yet told your new-old girlfriend, now or ever, your origins, and that you have watched many a hummingbird dance around a k'antu flower before nipping at its innards. You'd lie in stubbly grass beneath a bush looking up, quiescent, as several of them hovered, and you'd imagine they were tiny archangels. Some days, they were an annunciation of dawn; others, harbingers of a miniature apocalypse.

The clustered taxi-jockeys bounce, like soccer players in the red zone readying to do a header on the ball and score a goal. They're calling out, pointing out you, specifically. They've been waiting years for this opportunity, hoping, planning, conspiring. They are competing to be the one to whisk you to an undisclosed location, where the semi-literate relatives of the notary public who sent you that letter will tie you with electrical cords and duct tape, beat you with the same sticks they use on their donkeys, then cut letters from magazines, old school, coming up with the semi-cryptic message WEV KITNACKED YUR MEN. SIN CASHED, and send it to the hotel where Vanessa and Butch will be sleeping off a night of pisco sours and lovemaking, to demand ransom, because there is no hacienda, there is no sister, there's only you, a knit cap over your head, one of those with the doggie ear flaps hanging to either side, lying prone in a dry bathtub, and soon, if they don't pay, you'll be made an Inca mummy, stashed down there in the cata-combs, where tour guides will come past explaining the preservation techniques used, because the people who built Machu Picchu were geniuses, scientists, experimenters, agronomists, astronomers, givers of life and prophets of doom. If you'd never been forced to leave, you wouldn't be an outcast, a white-man equivalent. Instead, you'd have been issued an old Corona with worn keys on which you could slowly write more first chapters to throw into the garbage, which would be better, because then you couldn't write them so quickly and you wouldn't have so many to throw away.

"Jasper, ow! You're squeezing my hand, honey. That hurts. Are you nervous about meeting your sister Inés?"

"No, I think it's just a little air sickness. I'll be fine." He waved down a van and negotiated a price in Spanish, drawing impressed nods from his fellow passengers, and soon the luggage was loaded and they were on their way to a hotel in the historic downtown.

27
BENTLEY BENTAYGA

Interior walls had fallen or been wrecked. Plaster, cement, stucco and adobe were smashed into piles of rubble. It looked as though a fierce battle had been fought on this terrain, and indeed there were multiple bullet holes in one of the walls. The chandelier of the dining room lay on top of a long trestle table. Other rooms had ancient sewing machines set on the floor, and dismantled looms lay propped against the walls. A bag of gray wool leaned into an open doorway. Through a dirty skylight fell dim rays that only succeeded in casting garish shadows and lighting up the tangles of spider webs that had taken over every corner.

The room had the dusty agricultural smell of the grain storehouses Jasper knew from youth. He could hear the distant buzz of a transformer, perhaps connected to an aboveground telephone wire. Jasper had the feeling he was about to be assassinated. "Inés," now via text message from a possible burner phone, had asked to meet him alone, so he'd taken a taxi out to this location, one that had been difficult to find except the driver was an old man who looked like he'd been everywhere and seen everything.

The old man, rosary beads swinging from his rearview mirror while from his radio sang Cardi B, *Big bag bussin' out the Bentley Bentayga,* kept complaining that he wanted to move to the United States, to Los Angeles, and Jasper kept telling him that it was a bad idea; things were no better there, if no worse. The political atmosphere had become poisonous, the populace become racist, the inflation out of control, the wildfires omnipresent, the snowpack disappearing, and the best case scenario was that the man would be there what he was here, an old taxi driver working twelve hours a day to make ends meet, as well as an illegal alien, who would possibly get deported and be right back where he started, if not stuck in Mexico with the Haitians, the Guatemalans, the Venezuelans, and everybody else.

"Still," replied the man in a calm, reasonable voice, one he'd no doubt practiced on many gringo passengers, "I just want to see Universal Studios once before I die. I just want to do the *Jurassic Park* ride."

Into the dusty silence walked a petite but sturdy woman, maybe a decade younger than Jasper. She was dressed in jeans, high-laced boots and a quasi-military jacket that was stylish yet could also have been a hand-me-down from a member of the Shining Path. "Brother," she said in accented English. As Jasper began to make up in his mind many possible objections to her use of this word, the half-playful, half-mistrustful smile that crept over her, and the way her eyes looked into his, as if she were recognizing a distinct physical similarity between them, conspicuously in the face, the set of the jaw, the long, almost unruly eyelashes, the round eyes that forever seemed slightly surprised but could suddenly narrow with skepticism and the fact She, an obvious Andean mestiza with strong hips and thick legs and hair dark as a rain sky at 3 a.m., also had hazel eyes, exactly like his.

"Inés," he replied, giving possible credence to that being her real name, but not being able to utter the word "sister."

She didn't rush to hug him. She sat on one of the long tables, drawing no closer, used her finger to remove a dust mote—one of many floating in the half-light—from her right eye, and lit a cigarette, throwing the pack to the other end of the table, where he stood, and then the match book. Jasper didn't smoke, but in the interest of proper semiotics, he lit one up and puffed right back at her.

"You're good-looking, brother," she said, those hazel eyes still appraising, "in a half-breed kind of way. I wish you were more Indian, but you're not. If I passed you on the street, I'd say you're just another gringo, about to ask directions to the Temple of the Sun."

"How do you know I'm your brother?"

"Half-brother, actually. We have the same dad. My mom is Antuka."

"You have a cell phone. You speak English. But you sent me that half-literate note off a barely functioning typewriter. Using a notary public. Or did you write it yourself?"

"No, that's a real guy. I pass him on Avenida Sol all the time and we talk. I found an email address for you from a college you used to teach at, I guess, and I just gave him a general idea of what I wanted to say, about this place and let him do the rest. Then I digitized it and sent it from an account I created only for that one mail. My personal account for you. I wanted to see whether you had a sense of humor. I guess you do."

"Why did you wait so long to contact me?"

"It took years to figure out who you were, and where

you were. Mom didn't want to tell me anything. And Dad, I guess you didn't keep up with him, and I barely remember him, because when I wasn't even two years old, he got pulled off on some research project in Ecuador and he never came back. But when he died, I got my hands on some of his papers. They got sent back by missionaries in a big, sloppy bundle. Mom didn't even want to look at them, so they became my property. In there, it said I was his daughter and had various addresses and emails for you, a couple of returned letters. I had enough information to cyber-stalk you. I even got one of your novels off Amazon for five dollars. You're a pretty good writer."

"Thank you."

"Well, here we are. Did you think I was from the Shining Path and that I was going to kill you or take you hostage? Or just that I was going to scam you for your life savings?"

"What? Don't be crazy. None of that."

"Not even the money part?"

"I did wonder, but unfortunately for you, I ran through my life savings last year, playing the stock market."

"Too bad. If you were flush, we could really fix up this shithole."

"Who knows? Maybe we can anyway. How did you learn to speak English so well?"

"Lovers." Jasper remained speechless and she laughed. "Too much?"

"Not at all. Vanessa's going to love you."

"That your woman?"

"She is."

"Is she a good one?"

"She is."

"I'm glad. I want my brother to have a good woman."

"It's our second time around, but maybe we'll figure it out this time."

Inés threw her cigarette butt to the floor and stubbed it out with her military boot. "I've been longing to see you, brother. I went through a lot to make that happen." She walked toward him with the decided step of an assassin and threw her arms around Jasper, pulling him to her with those mighty arms and squeezing him tight. Jasper cried his heart out while she patted his back until he was quiet.

28

THE CANDY BAR

J oseph agreed to hike Iron Mountain with his new
best friend, Darien, a lanky silver fox whom he'd met
several months ago at a four-handed dinner party for
Darien's girlfriend of the moment. As the two women
talked, Joseph kept Darien company in the kitchen, where
the host expertly tended to the tri-tip he was re-basting out
of the oven, wearing gloves that looked like they came from
Williams-Sonoma. The girlfriend, Adriana, had married her
psychiatrist while in treatment, but it hadn't worked out.
Darien had wolfish teeth, bleached white to show them off,
and smiled a lot. He explained that he loaned money to
high-risk clients out of a personal fund he'd accumulated
over time by investing in real estate. Darien seemed to
know a lot about money, its origin, nature and movement.
He was a fan of the Cato Institute and Daniel Klein. He
dressed "casually" as if about to go to a job interview as the
manager of an expensive overseas resort. He kept house
better than most women. At first blush, he was a bit like
someone out of a New Yorker short story or one of those
Woody Allen movies.

Joseph had come to the party with Christy, a Korean-American psychologist he was dating, a friend of Adriana. As Darien mixed up a pitcher of old fashioneds, being careful to spill nothing on the gleaming white tile floor, while the last rays of twilight caught the pitcher and lit it up momentarily like an aquarium, he suddenly turned to Joseph, with a conspiratorial wink, and said "It's easy dating women within a few years of my age bracket. They just need someone to drill the pussy." Then he removed his apron, again revealing his starched pinstripe shirt and pressed flannel slacks.

Darien had perfect hair, artfully moussed and mussed ever so slightly, as if he were Anderson Cooper's musician brother, and he stayed ultra-trim by marathon running and hiking. He only ate once each day, usually the same meal of tri-tip, roasted potatoes and asparagus. Darien had strong opinions about everything and sometimes sent editorials to newspapers. He was a Libertarian who believed people should have to pay to drive on all roads. He had no sympathy for the homeless, no sense of responsibility. Everything was a transaction, and your only real responsibility was to yourself. He was renting out his own home and living in a lesser rental because he made more money that way. "It's just good sense," he explained, in four irrefutable words.

Joseph wasn't entirely sure why he hung out with Darien, whom he occasionally excoriated verbally in a half-joking manner and whose even more extreme friends offended his sensibilities with their rants about privatizing America and their hero-worship of the current president of the country. Darien never professed an opinion about the U.S. President, perhaps because he fancied himself a truly independent thinker rather than a closet herd follower. Rather, he sat at the head of the table nursing a cabernet while he let the friends do the dirty work of making politically salacious statements designed to stir outrage in the listeners.

Joseph, sensing little by little the extremity of Darien's views, and his person, had kept his own politics close to the vest, pretending to be an independent rather than the flaming liberal that he actually was. Their friendship had quickly evolved into a chess game, each man veiling his moves and using distraction techniques. Yet Joseph couldn't help but notice the sardonic smirk on Darien's face as his Libertarian friends heaped one extreme assertion on top of another, getting drunker and reaching a quasi-fascist register of rhetoric, Darien knowing that his friend was getting upset and waiting for him to out himself, by means of his own rhetorical outburst, upbraiding these morons who, like half the country, had abandoned all rational thought in favor of demon-worship disguised as good economic sense.

But Joseph held it together, finally excusing himself to go out and smoke a cigar on his new friend's terrazzo patio. The smeared Los Angeles sky, with its excess of ambient light even in quiet neighborhoods like this one, half-eclipsed the stars, bringing the ceiling lower, but at least Joseph could breathe as he lay back in a chaise lounge to recover his senses. Even the bark of neighboring dogs struck his ears as pleasant.

As he listened to a nightbird whose call he couldn't immediately recognize, the patio door slid open, and Darien handed him a glass of fresh, top-shelf bourbon with a cluster of ice chilling it. Joseph thanked him. Darien had figured out his favorite brand and kept it in stock and close at hand. He couldn't understand how his friend could be so personally kind, forever solicitous of Joseph, frequently inviting him over, always insisting on being the one to cook, looking over his taxes as a favor, buying his books, reading them, and praising his friend with utter largesse as an author in the company of his more urbane assembled friends at the semi-frequent parties he threw. It was best just to try not to think about the matter. Troubling as they were, Joseph's responsibility was not to police Darien's politics. He wasn't going to change.

By now, Darien had broken up with Adriana, and was on to another "drilling" project—he'd run quickly through several—which he wittily compared to Alaska, saying he was trying to secure rights to her wilderness area. His borderline misogynistic jokes and playful-pornographic drinkware didn't seem to bother these women—attractive, even conservative professional women who could have had their pick of men, it seemed, but were content to put up with his asides and his insistence that they pay for fifty per cent of everything on dates. Darien was utterly strict on that point. He even boasted about it, but at least in public, the women didn't complain, and they seemed saucy and flirtatious with him, trying to snag him before he moved on to the next prospect. Is that what it took, a trim body, being taller than six feet, having money—even if you didn't really share it—and displaying stupendous self-confidence? Were people still that primal when it came to him and her? On the surface, Darien looked like a cybernetically produced metrosexual who represented an amalgam of what women said they wanted and what they actually wanted. A smooth operator with a hard edge.

The new girlfriend, half-drunk, plopped down on the leather sofa next to Joseph and said, a little glumly, "I actually think that you're Darien's real girlfriend. The one he wants deep down. He can't stop talking about you. He was going on and on about your latest book of poetry while we were in bed, forcing me to listen while he read pages of it out loud. And we'd just had sex! I finally shouted, 'Why don't you just marry Joseph?' That shut him up."

"I'm sorry," answered Joseph, though he didn't know what he was apologizing for.

The girlfriend rubbed his arm and looked at him earnestly, sorrowfully. "Does he make you pay for your cocktails, like he does us?"

"No," he answered, with a surge of inexplicable guilt.

Without really meaning to, during their evening sessions on the back patio smoking cigars and having a cocktail, Joseph began to reciprocate some of Darien's anecdotes about his sexual escapades. As with politics, he didn't want to give too much away, even though Darien wasn't reticent. But he found himself telling how Christy used to encourage him to say to her out loud a fantasy she had about Joseph being a hacienda owner who called up humble women from the village, the first day of each month, to audition to work in his employ for negligible wages. For some reason, this audition required the women to strip and walk around him in a circle, suggestively, until he would imperiously call one, then another, to a spare wooden chair placed in front of his chair, a few inches away. The woman would then be instructed harshly to use her fingers to open her sex and let him inspect it.

This was the only way that Christy could have an orgasm. The telling of this same story to her continued each night, him like a one-note Scheherazade, until finally he said to her, impatiently, "This is starting to feel like a job." Whereupon she broke up with him. Now he was the singlet, and Darien the one with feminine company. The new one was a petite, sparky former actress and dancer, bubbly and openly affectionate, smart, quick, a graphic designer. She'd just gotten over cervical cancer and seemed glad to be alive. Joseph sat Darien down and said, "This is the one. I strongly advise you to get off the dating apps, because I've seen you trolling them on your phone. Have you ever been strictly monogamous? Take her seriously. The other day, she poured her heart out to me and said, 'Why doesn't he treat me nicer? What does he want? Please talk to him.' And so that's what I'm doing. You're almost sixty. What are you waiting for?"

"For her to give me a blow job. I know she's got cervical issues, but at least that. Besides, when did the two of you get so cozy?" As if he wanted to deflect, by being crude and by missing the point of the conversation on purpose. Joseph wanted to hit him for his crass remark. Instead, he said, "I wish I had your luck," got his keys, and left without a word. The two men didn't speak for a few days. Until Darien called and, making no reference to their previous conversation, invited Joseph for the two of them to hold a cocktail party, where each would mix up his best three libations and whoever at the party was sober at the end could vote on which was the winner. He looked up recipes and made old-school cocktails: Singapore Sling, Mint Julep, and Dirty Martini.

Some people started dancing to the host's carefully curated mix tape, probably created based on market research and a demographic profile of the guests. For Darien, everything had a matrix. In the midst of the increasingly noisy happy vibe, Catherine, the graphic designer, slid onto the love seat between Darien and Joseph and laying her head on the latter's shoulder, complained half-aloud with a drunken sigh, "I don't know what to do. You know, Joseph, my girlfriends have been telling me all night I should be with you instead of him." Darien was within earshot, but never showed any sign of having heard a remark meant to make him jealous. But after a few minutes, he got up and danced with the wife of one of his Libertarian friends.

Later, Joseph saw them through the blinds of the door to the patio, arguing. After the guests had gone and the hosts had cleaned up, the two friends embraced, congratulating themselves on a successful party. When Joseph walked the half-block to his car, he saw Catherine standing by the passenger side, purse slung over her shoulder.

"Take me home," she said.

"Where's your car?"

"I came with my girlfriends, the ones I mentioned."

"Okay. That's weird they left you. But I can drop you. Where do you live?"

"I don't want to go to my house. I want to go to your house."

That night, Catherine gave Joseph everything she'd been holding back, all the Alaskan wilderness she'd denied to Darien on the pretext of her cancer. She didn't ask Joseph to tell her any stories about haciendas, or stories of any kind. Instead, she made up for lost time.

A few days went by, the friends seeing one another once to watch a game, during which Darien let drop casually, as if saying he'd changed brands of milk, that he was seeing somebody new, and that Catherine was up for grabs. "I think you should go out with her. She's always been more attracted to you than me; let's be honest."

Joseph hadn't seen her since their satisfying one-night stand, nor, out of respect for his friend, was he going to. It was nothing more than a slip-up among two inebriated people who shouldn't even have been driving in a car alone, much less huddled in bed together. "Darien, you didn't listen to me last time. I'm telling you again, open yourself up to her and take her seriously. Call her right now and take her back."

Darien slammed his glass on the coffee table, sloshing liquor onto the teak, and stood up, looming over Joseph. "Don't tell me how to conduct my affairs. I said if you want her, she's yours. I'm done with her. Otherwise, drop the subject."

Joseph said no more. But in a few days, he sent Darien a text, saying that he had taken advice and was dating Catherine. "I'm happy for you, bro," texted back Darien, adding several varieties of happy face and silly face emojis —something he'd never done before. When they saw one another again, at a downtown speakeasy, Darien suggested, "Let's go hike Iron Mountain to celebrate."

"Iron Mountain? That's a beast. A little out of my league. Besides, you hike too fast."

"My true companion: as we've discovered, nothing is out of your league. I'll be your guide. I know you're ready for it, after our last few tough hikes. Noon Friday at my house. Bring plenty of water."

The air was already hot when Joseph pulled up at Darien's curb. Darien, of course, had to drive and had everything arranged in his compact hybrid, leaving exactly enough space in the hatch for Joseph's day pack and camel-back. He didn't like putting anything in the pristine back seat, even though it was empty. On the drive, Joseph, for the first time, appreciated the extent of the wildfire burns in the San Bernardino Mountains. The wilderness was huge and ran deep to the north, and if split with barren canyons, it was still populated with plenty of trees, bears and bobcats. The fire hazard was high everywhere after months, years of prolonged drought. Joseph hadn't bothered to bring bear spray or a whistle, nothing much except plenty of water, as instructed, and energy bars, bulk nuts and dried fruit. For all he knew, Darien had tri-tip stashed in a Ziploc, but he certainly would have brought, as usual, a compass, whistle, spray, and he subscribed to the All Trails GPS feature on his phone, which gave a much more accurate location reading. This didn't even seem necessary, given that Darien had already done Iron Mountain three times, in addition to Mount Whitney and many other peaks he boasted of, always making a point of citing the exact time it had taken him to summit.

Joseph had to admit he was a bit lazy. He was in good condition, but he didn't like to hike fast, and he always brought the minimum.

"Walking stick?"

"I forgot it."

"Forgot to buy one, you mean. I keep telling you to get one. Someday you're going to need it."

They alighted in the parking lot by one p.m. Two hawks soared in circles above them before disappearing up the mountain to get lost in the sycamores. Wordless, Darien fell onto the trailhead and set a stiff pace. It was going to be one of those. Joseph resolved to say nothing, just try to keep up. He could hear water sloshing in his camelback. He was already thirsty but would have to ration until he took the measure of the climb. On they went this way for an hour, seeing only the occasional sparrow and squirrel. Besides, he was too busy looking at his feet on this crumbly trail, eroded by too many urban hikers. This hike was the toughest in the area, so fewer people attempted it. Iron Mountain's reputation was "unfriendly scree."

An hour in, they stopped to briefly rest and drink. It would be six hours round trip if they made good time.

"It's weird you started midday. Didn't we want to beat the heat?"

"Normally, yes. But I had things to do. You didn't have to come."

"Hey, don't get pissy on me."

Darien slapped him on the back. "You're right. I'm having problems with some of the people I lent to. No sense taking it out on you. One just declared bankruptcy."

"Sucks for them."

"For me, you mean. I'm the one out $80,000 if they default."

"For you, then."

"Ah, it's okay. It's only money." They hiked for another hour, Joseph really having to haul himself up. He was winded but was trying not to breathe hard. "Okay back there?"

"You set a pace."

"I can slow down if you need me to. I only want to be back before it gets dark. We brought no camping gear. In these chasms, it's always surprising how quickly the sun goes. I don't really want to be some creature's night snack."

"It's okay. Push on. I'll let you know when I'm knackered."

Joseph began to pay attention to each turn in the path, trying to memorize landmarks. They hadn't seen anyone all this time. The sun, arid as it was, seemed like hot liquid being poured over him.

"Let's leave our bottles here," said Darien. "There's no sense hauling them up and back. It's just dead weight. I'll hide them behind these rocks—not that we're going to see anybody here to rob them—and we'll recover them on our way down. It will be like finding a present on your birthday."

As they neared the top, Joseph chuffing and getting a little asthmatic, and Darien quick-stepping in his modified ramrod posture, looking like a park ranger in his neat outfit, broad-brimmed hat and lack of perspiration, the panorama opened up, displaying the enormity of the wilderness. It was close to Los Angeles, yet a world away. At last, they reached the peak. Everything looked the same to Joseph. He didn't know whether he was facing east or west, north or south, except for the sun's position. He hoped Darien wouldn't quiz him, as he sometimes did. He'd already half-forgotten the landmarks on the way up and was glad he was the follower, not the leader.

They sat on separate rocks, close together. Joseph, who had only eaten toast for breakfast, had already consumed his nuts, dried fruit, and energy bars. He was on the last mouthful of his camelback water until they got back to the bottles. Uncharacteristically, the germ-phobic Darien handed Joseph his canteen to drink from and nodded for him to keep chugging until his thirst was slaked. After, he broke a candy bar in half and shared his food—something he never did.

Joseph had relaxed enough, now that he was rested, to feel the endorphin buzz.

"That's the fastest I've ever summited this," said

Darien. "You should feel proud. We cut a full fifteen minutes off my personal best."

"Oh, wow. I thought it was just me. Makes sense that my legs are cramping."

"So, she sucked your cock?"

"Excuse me?"

"I mean, I never got that far. She must have been really pent up by the time you got to her. I assume her cunt is all healed up."

"Don't talk like that. I don't know why you want to be crude all of a sudden."

"Don't get me wrong, bra. She never really was my girl-friend if you get what I mean. I was being a gentleman all that time, really patient, until she felt like it. But there was nothing wrong with her mouth that I could tell. Finally, I said, 'Can't you just get on your knees and show a little gratitude?' But I guess that remark sealed my doom."

"I told you to take her seriously. You treat them all like transactions."

"Do I? Then a white knight like you rides in, treats them right, gets treated to the leftovers."

"You're pissed. I'll break up with her."

"Now you're making it worse. Don't you love her? You're just going to ditch her? The one that I really wanted? I'm insulted."

"Okay, I'll keep dating her."

"Listen to yourself. Yes. No. Yes. No. Asking my permis-sion after the fact. You're the one who doesn't know what you want. Did you fuck her the night of the party?"

"I'm not answering that question. You've got a weird look on your face. Like you want to knife me."

"I did bring a knife, but I'm too tired to get it out. You don't have to answer. She sent me a selfie sprawled on your bed, wearing panties and one of your t-shirts. Jonny Lang. I recognized it."

"I can't believe it."

"Oh, believe it. That will teach you not to hook up with vindictive bitches when they're in that wounded animal stage. She used you to get back at me. Are you that stupid? Did you really think it was your urbane charm? Of which you have none."

"Okay. You're right. I did. I'm sorry."

Darien grabbed his friend's hand, gave it a big squeeze and didn't let go. "Forgiven. Let's not let a spoiled little dame come between us. It's exactly what she wants; to break up our friendship. Now, let's go conquer the downward slope."

As they descended among groves of tall juniper and the wind dropped away, the hills enclosed them more quickly than he'd anticipated. He never remembered how soon the sun set in these kinds of places. It wasn't yet four, but it felt like twilight. Joseph had stashed his half of the chocolate bar in his backpack, knowing he'd need it at some later point. Darien was setting a merciless pace. Although Joseph's calves and quads were starting to cramp more severely, he tried to endure the pain, not wanting to disturb the fragile peace that had miraculously followed his confession. Darien occasionally glanced back with the characteristic impatience Joseph had grown used to. He could never explain why he subjected himself to the borderline abuse of Darien's quasi-militaristic approach to what he considered a mere leisure activity. Joseph knew he had "real" hiking friends, the competitive, gung-ho types who would spout off the times and difficulty grades of their recent ascents, who would do "forty peaks in a year," and other such macho challenges. Why did he want Joseph to be part of this aspect of his life? Just to impress him? To build him up? To grind him down? Wasn't it enough to be cocktail buddies?

The distance between them increased as shadows fell. They must be getting close to the stashed water. Joseph's mouth felt full of sand. Had Darien hiked past the water bottles on purpose? Was this some sort of lesson in endurance? Joseph fully believed that Darien, like a fakir, could probably go days without water, that possibly he was a lizard metamorphosed into human form. At a sharp bend in the path, Joseph thought he recognized the hiding place and got down on his hands and knees, tearing away path-side weeds, scrounging among the rocks littered there in search of the precious bottles. He was faint. His legs hurt so much he could barely stand. Why hadn't he insisted on a slower ascent? A long rest at the top? Because stupidly, he wanted to impress Darien, show he was up to the level.

He found no water bottles. Now Darien was gone. Joseph ran forward, hobbled, limping, hoping to catch sight of his guide. But there was only another bend; no one in sight. He called out two or three times but received no answer. All at once, the forest, which had felt shrunk, seemed vast, endless, flowing in all directions, as the light turned silver. Joseph loped, like some half-human creature. He doubled back and took another path. The descent was nothing but a slag heap, scree upon scree, and as he sat on his butt and tried to scootch down, his pants tore, while loose stones rained down from his feet to the next pitch. When he got to the bottom and ran frantically from one trailhead to another, both of them unfamiliar, identical, Joseph realized he'd made a bad decision. Now he'd have to climb the slag heap, laden with rubble, all while his strength diminished. That way, he wouldn't lose the trail he'd been on in order to enter a labyrinth.

Slowly, painfully, he ascended on hands and knees, in the half-dark, like a man groveling for his life. Every couple of minutes, he screamed for help, only to hear his echo return, its ugly, self-incriminating sound. There was no answer. He'd grown weak, thirsty, hungry. When he reached a small, relatively flat spot in the ascent, he knew this was where he'd spend the night, exposed, with no tent, no sleeping bag, not even a decent jacket. In this remote area, on a Saturday after dark, there was unlikely to be anyone passing, certainly not before Monday, if then.

He lay on his back and looked without pleasure at a patch of stars that had opened up in the flat clouds. No moon lay in sight. He cried silently, without tears. All he wanted now was to sleep—better said, to lose consciousness. But now the wind blew against him, bringing the scent of the forest to his nostrils. His throat felt like it was growing shut from lack of water. And he was getting hungrier by the minute. He remembered he had half of a chocolate bar still in his pack, the one Darien had shared with him, only that, and rooted for it, finding it gooey and half-melted. As he dug it out, Joseph heard a rustling in the bushes just below him. "Darien!" he cried out. His friend had second thoughts and came back. Or maybe he'd planned this mental cruelty all along. Maybe he'd been stalking Joseph from a few yards away, enjoying his deterioration into unmanned panic. Or was it possible he'd had a pang of conscience, of regret, realizing that everybody makes mistakes and that's no reason for them to die alone in the wilderness?

The scent-carrying wind kept rising and falling. In one of the dead silences, Joseph heard grunts and a definite growl. A bear was coming. It had smelled the chocolate. Joseph tried to hurl the glob as far from himself as he could, but most of it was stuck to his fingers or smeared across his palm. He tried to lick it off with his dry tongue, immediately realizing that all he was doing was putting the scent on his breath, which was coming faster with each second. The distinct sound of heavy paws crashing upward toward him resounded like meteors crashing to earth. Joseph closed his eyes to await the apocalypse.

29
AT THE MONASTERY HOTEL BAR

The four of them sat in the bar of the Monastery Hotel, surrounded by a sleek, tasteful decorative version of the penury and self-abnegation that the monks must have undergone. Stucco in the building resembled chrome on a muscle car, lending it an instant glamour. Pictures of winged heralds of Christ in bright blue and red attire discreetly hung from the walls, while the visitors sat in wingback chairs sipping cocktails beneath a wheel chandelier adorned with little bell lights. Sconces held unlit candles, and stone arches ran exposed from the mid-wall to the ceiling. Beneath the foursome's feet, the vivid reds and blues of the patterned carpet picked up the note of the angel attire.

Vanessa found Inés charmingly keyed up but was happy when three drinks managed to settle her down to a normal level of social discourse. She'd been quasi-hitting on both Vanessa and Butch with an air of desperation, but Vanessa quickly realized that she was only trying to fit in, which was odd, because this was her place—not the bar; maybe she wouldn't have chosen such a destination to drink, not with those army boots. Psychologically, she did want to put Inés a little bit off balance, to make sure that the situation was real, because she saw that Jasper's heart was vulnerable, he was liable to do anything the girl asked and that was one of the reasons, the main reason, Vanessa had come along, to protect him from his sentimental impulses. She didn't want him to flame out right when Vanessa's and his romance was getting rekindled. This could be his finest hour, or his worst, but he needed a chaperone; that was the truth. Butch was not fit to supervise anything or anybody. He apparently had a lot of cash; it was burning a hole in his pocket, and he looked prone to throwing it away on that questionable hacienda, not even having inspected the title or gone into the legalities of co-owning property in a foreign country.

Butch, a straight whiskey man, had betrayed himself by following Inés's lead and ordering a "Cusco mule," one he left mostly untouched because after one sip he obviously couldn't stand the taste. Inés had pulled her chair a little closer to Butch's. Butch was clueless about women, or better said, overly susceptible to their attentions, and his macho exterior hid, barely, a soft-hearted man of the kind it would be easy to take advantage of. Vanessa liked Inés. But Inés also represented an existential threat to everyone else in the room.

"When you look at the city lights from up here, it's like when the Inca priests looked into their sacred bowl of water when the stars shone through the window of the temple. If we took sleeping bags out to the old hacienda house, you'd see more stars bunched together than you've witnessed in your whole life."

"I'm up for it," said Butch, "as long you can score us some good weed."

"I can do better than that," said Inés. "A shaman is a close friend of mine. Ever done ayahuasca?"

"I'd love to," said Jasper, sitting up straight in his wing-back chair, almost spilling his scotch.

"Count me in," echoed Butch. Calculating for weight, I'll probably need a double dose. I once tried LSD, and nothing."

"You are the last person in this room who needs ayahuasca, Jasper," said Vanessa. "Your mind already exists in a state that most people take drugs to try to achieve."

"Well, that's no fun. I want to deviate from my set point. Don't be a spoilsport."

"I'm not trying to spoil anybody's fun. I know I'm a designated driver type. I only don't want you to have a psychotic break with reality, honey."

"Big brother can handle it."

Vanessa didn't want to get on Inés's bad side, right when the girl had the advantage of novelty and supposed blood kin. Therefore, she changed the subject. "Well, who knows? But anyway, what would be the cost of turning that hacienda into a feasible living space and a cooperative workspace?"

"I think half a million would do it. A million at most."

"Dollars or Peruvian currency?"

"Dollars."

"That could happen," said Butch. "If the conditions are right. I'd have to see who exactly we'd be working with on construction. And have it all in writing."

Inés didn't hesitate. "Hell yeah. All on the up and up. Jasper and I are the sole co-owners of the property. But if we had the right investor, that person could be an owner too."

Vanessa realized that left her out, but she didn't really

want to be in anyway. She only didn't want her man to get burned. "Are you expecting people to move down here?"

"What people do you mean?"

"Your new brother, for instance."

"He's not my new brother. He's been my brother all along. Only he didn't know it and I didn't know it."

"I'm happy for both of you."

"What I think is that before we take any practical steps, we all need to get some sleeping bags, take ayahuasca together, and get to know each other better."

"Fuck yeah."

"Oh, mama."

Vanessa said nothing. Refusing to take ayahuasca would make her the outlier. Could she just pretend? She didn't know how that worked. She might be able to fake it somehow. She'd have to agree to get in a position to gauge the situation. One wrong word now and all advantage would be lost. "Let's do it, then."

30
JASPER AND GASPAR

His dad had been a light-skinned mestizo and when you get right down to it, 99% of the racial argument comes down to phenotype, in this case favoring the invading Spaniards (original sin), and his mom was some mash-up of Scottish, Irish, English, German, Swiss, Italian, Dutch, Anglo-Saxon with a dash of Mediterranean mostly in the eyelashes and butt, so kind of promiscuous European mongrel stock, like underwear that's 60% cotton, followed by rayon, spandex, nylon, polyester, acrylic (this latter obtained from wood pulp), in decreasing percentages, so that you can make any extravagant claim when you're half-drunk at a cocktail party and suddenly blurt out "I'm _% Arapaho!" and the number changes depending on how drunk you are and who else is in the room, ranging anywhere from 1% to 25% and who is going to challenge you, really unless there happens to be a full-blooded Arapaho on the premises, who dominates you by a stable, universally accepted criterion such as beating you at arm wrestling.

But growing up on the altiplano, above all, hearing the

sound of Quechua spoken and sung, had affected Jasper more than almost anything in how he thought about himself. It's what had made him a writer. Even in the hottest summer, there would come a moment when the cold, distant wind blowing off Titicaca would shiver through his bones, having cut through the sweat on his skin and his warm muscles. That disruption kept him from belonging anywhere. He would have given anything, sometimes, to have that firm attachment, more than ideological, more than religious, rather, downright spiritual, that some writers he met seemed to possess. "By God, I'm a Mississippi man and that's that!" Didn't matter whether they believed in the Civil War, or whether those monuments should be thrown down, or even whether catfish was a superior meal. They just felt it, that's all. A sense of place to which they continued to belong, that went beyond what you did in the voting booth. They finished one novel and went right on to the next. Whether they wrote three or thirty, they were complete, for the most part, and they got published, reviewed well or poorly, sold good or bad, made money or not, and their oeuvre was put in a resting place that was at worst a mausoleum and at best remained a part of living history for decades, even centuries. Jasper had written his entire life, with short bursts of passion and talent, to no visible effect, almost as if he'd never existed.

Jasper had been deprived of a sense of local security. Yanked off that miserable lakefront high in the Andes, right when he was getting comfortable. With all his innocent, semi-incestuous feelings for Antuka, to whom no other woman compared until Vanessa came along. If nothing else, he should have been the next Faulkner, sublimating his feeling into an indelible book-length verbal portrait of that naked woman in the half-dark sighing, memorialized, etched in fire, full of passionate wrongness, and people reading its pages, after throwing that apocryphal novel down and unresistingly picking it up again, would read to the end and murmur something about "the human heart in conflict with itself," no longer able to judge right and wrong so easily.

Instead, Jasper saw himself as a man taking one picture of himself after another in a photo booth, on different days, in different clothes, with different hairdos, slowly aging, but always recognizable as himself, pasting solipsistic Polaroid selfies into an old-fashioned album with static plastic pages, and the images would yellow over time and eventually crack, their only story being an invisible one of tracing Jasper's life by looking from one image to the next, implying a timeline, causality, an underlying philosophy, and an invisible story that added up to a meaningful existence.

When he was a boy, Antuka had put him in charge of one of her goats. She kept a small flock that she would tend herself, running them up the hillside to graze. This one goat, Gaspar, was lame. On top of that, the goat had been rejected by its mother because it was mean by nature from birth and would bite her when she was trying to nurse it and with other goats trying to get to her teat, she didn't have patience or time for this ill-tempered creature. She ran it off to a corner of the pen, where it sulked and grew skinny. Jasper took it upon himself to nurse Gaspar, who became his first pet. The goat did bite him three or four times, but Jasper, who was amused he and the goat had essentially the same name, especially the way Antuka pronounced it, over time calmed the creature down to the point it would limp-walk by his side without even a rope. When Antuka saw them together, she would give Jasper a tender gaze, but not without remarking, frequently, "If it weren't for you, we would have roasted that damned goat and eaten it."

Jasper told the goat his hopes and dreams in a way he never confided later in life to his girlfriends. He was good at doing handsprings and told Gaspar he wanted to be an acrobat. He sang Quechua huaynos to the hills, love songs far above what was right for his age, lamenting the loss of a girl when he'd never even had one. He admitted to his lame pet that he knew how the rickety little goat felt, because he himself often became low in spirits and like he wanted to die, but you just had to walk on and let that slow fire burn inside you, hoping that someday something good would come along and put it out, quench it for good and ever.

> *Polleraypa watun kuti kutishan*
> *warma munasqaycha engañawashan*
>
> *puka chalinaysi kuti kutishan*
> *warma wayllusqaycha engañawashan*
>
> *The edge of her skirt is spinning, spinning*
> *The woman I love has been unfaithful*
>
> *Her red scarf is twirling, twirling*
> *The woman I want has betrayed me.*

One warm afternoon, a straw hat keeping the sun off his cheeks, Jasper fell asleep against a rock as Gaspar nibbled a patch of grass nearby. He woke with a shudder, and looking around, he saw that the goat was gone. All that afternoon, he spent roaming over the hills, braying the goat's name, until the sun dropped and shadows lengthened over the valley. Either someone had stolen his precious hobbling goat, or else it had other plans and limped its way to a precarious freedom.

When he ran home spent and bawling to utter his tragedy to Antuka, she cleaned his weepy face with a dish towel and simply replied, bringing him to her skirt for an embrace, "They do that sometimes." He refused to accept her wise stoicism, and though he didn't openly oppose what she said, he spent the next few days sulking, refusing to eat the food she set out, sleeping little, sometimes jumping up in the middle of the night because he thought he heard the goat's plaintive bray. He even imagined that it had died and its ghost had come back seeking his companionship.

Two weeks later, as he walked aimlessly along the lakefront, he heard the goat's voice again, this time in broad daylight. At first, he didn't turn around, refusing to be tricked once more by his senses. But at last, he gave a volteface and there stood Gaspar, perilously skinny, tottering on its legs like a newborn, eyes half-closed. Jasper ran and seized the creature, giving it a hard squeeze that made it yelp. He felt a surge of love greater than anything he'd felt even for Antuka. She prepared a bottle of pureed oatmeal, water and canned milk, stuck on it a modified nipple, and he offered it to Gaspar to suck, as if he had literally been reborn. With the patience of a mother, he tended his still-limping goat back to health, scolding him for not having at least eaten grass during his odyssey. There was no reason for him not to graze as he normally would. But then it occurred to Jasper that Gaspar, like him, had turned lonely and lost his appetite in the absence of his beloved master, and understanding that, Jasper ceased to criticize.

31
AYAHUASCA

J asper watched the others throw up into buckets inside the ruined hacienda house. Ironically, he who had developed crippling nausea on the high seas, here turned out to have an iron stomach. The shaman had laid out woven tapestries, old ones with holes in them that had runes woven into their black and crimson background, as well as part of the alphabet. Coca leaves had been scattered across their surface, as well as cracked sepia photos of people Jasper didn't know, possibly dead ones, who could at this very moment be exerting power of life and death over him. Those people had candy bars and cigarettes placed near their images, coins and barrettes, little dolls made of sticks and thread, stinky cheese, a pair of baby shoes weathered possibly by being left out in the rain or just age, who knows, the shoes might be one hundred years old, older even than the shaman, whose deeply lined and pocked face didn't seem to bother him in the slightest, he had a full head of hair, not even very gray and he stared penetratingly like a handsome man does, one who knows he's always going to have groupies no matter what, because his head is packed with wisdom, his loins with the fire of the stars, his heart with the soul of Tupac Amaru and the cool beatitude of Jesus Christ, like somebody who speaks multiple languages without effort, code-switching with ease while everybody else catches up to the situation.

How much of life is conducted on sheer confidence, in all senses of the word, self-security but also the ability to take others in, whether for good purposes or bad, maybe they were right this instant in the hands of a confident man who was going to get them all doped up and tie them up for ransom, or murder them, but in truth, his eyes seemed kind, there was a tender gleam inside the gaze of the predatory hawk, admittedly Jasper could be overreading the situation because he was super high. Now the shaman had picked up one of the consecrated cigarettes and was having a smoke; maybe it was a ritual smoke, part of the ceremony, or maybe he was just craving nicotine and pilfered one of the cigs off the altar because nobody was going to smoke them anyway.

You probably got bored watching foreigners trip their brains out while you had to be more like the hall monitor to make sure everybody was okay. Did consecrated cigarettes taste better than regular tobacco? Did they get you high, bring you closer to God? Or were they just like communion wine, which you didn't get drunk on, it was more the idea of the blood of Christ that you got off on emotionally, paradoxically making church less weird so that you could enjoy your fellow parishioners, rather than feeling competitive about who would get first to the promised land.

Surprisingly, the trip was a lot like the Peter Max posters that Jasper collected, saturated pastels with repeating figures and shapes, cones and rays and flowers and waterfalls, half-abstract, cascading over one another, based on actual objects in the room, so not true hallucinations, more like fanciful adaptations of existing reality. This wasn't scary to Jasper because his brain waves had always been weird, and the room now appeared as a literalization of the kind of thought-images that occurred to him on a daily basis, just with a more vivid color scheme. He was fairly calm, because he'd thought an apocalyptic scenario would set up fairly soon, a bad acid trip of sorts, complete with paranoia and possibly even a schizoid break with reality, as Vanessa had feared for him, whereas this had the leisure of sitting back eating peanuts at the Folies Bergères, lots of movement and energy and high-kicking legs and colorful, bustling fabric and leering overly-painted faces, but without any scent of evil.

Jasper went over to Vanessa, who had just hurled mightily into a bucket. If anything, he was worried about her, but she waved him off as she wiped slime from her mouth with a sleeve, sitting on the ground and rocking, muttering, "I'm okay. I just needed to get that earth-ball out of my stomach." The shaman went over and put one hand over each of her ears, which seemed to settle her, and her eyes went dreamy, so Jasper left her alone.

The thought that dogged him, the revelation, was that he was a technician. Maybe that's what limited him as a writer and doomed him to so many single chapters. But where was his soul within those truncated verbal transactions? Was he merely drawing on a repertoire of style, stolen from others? Or conversely, was he the opposite of a technician, so trapped within his immediate experience that he could only write versions of himself, the ultimate solipsist? Shouldn't his ayahuasca trip be placing him within a hall of mirrors, infinitely reflecting his image to the exclusion of any other, magnifying his innate narcissism?

But that wasn't the case. He was fully present, fully aware of everyone else in the room. More than ever before, he felt down into his bones the utter insignificance of himself. He might as well have been that bit of light in the corner, real or imagined, refracting off an old, dirty, cracked mirror leaning against the wall.

He wanted to go over to that mirror, to look at his head broken into pieces in the glass, like the victim of a heinous traffic accident, extracted from mangled metal with the jaws of life, but all he had to do was experience that thought and there it was, his shattered head, he was both looking at it and inside it, simultaneously, without contradiction. There was no separation of the self into internal and external. What should have been a terrifying moment, on the contrary, made him feel liberated from himself, as if he were one of those children's kaleidoscopes, he used to have one, where you held it in your hand and turned it slightly, and the colored fragments of glass shifted to a different place every time, giving you a refreshed perspective. He used to spend hours looking at the kaleidoscope from a window seat in the upstairs of his mother's house. All his novels should be like that, so simple yet so complex.

It occurred to him for the first time—a thought he couldn't corroborate at the moment—that if he put all the chapters together, maybe they made a whole novel in themselves. Maybe they had a secret order, like the Kabbalah, one not evident to the outside observer, but that could be discerned by the cognoscenti.

32
COUP DE FOUDRE

Butch felt nothing but love for everybody in the universe. Especially for Jasper and Vanessa, and Inés, she was pretty cute too and he sure would like to love her. It could have just been the ayahuasca, but he didn't think so. Hell, he'd done reefer aplenty, cocaine, speed, meth only once, heroin only twice, because he wasn't really an addictive personality, amphetamines like a million times, though not really psychedelics. So, he could be susceptible, yes, still all he had was a great big old feeling. If you wanted to know the truth, he'd been turned into a giant heart. He'd beaten the shit out of a bunch of guys over the years, first as an angry teenager, later on sometimes as a bouncer, though he tried to avoid altercations, later as an enforcer for a drug dealer, and even now, as a businessman, he dealt with some rough customers, people who would try to run out on you without payment, or even show up with associates to try to shake you down and then you had to kick some asses pointedly in order to establish that you were not going to be fucked with.

He wasn't violent by nature. It was really the circumstances. And he'd seen such ugly things in his life, including death and rotted corpses he dug up and buried once for somebody he was trying to ingratiate himself to, so hallucinating, what did you really have to be afraid of? Life itself was trippier than any drug he'd consumed. And ayahuasca, hell, it was some kind of pissant Indian substance, about as powerful as a box of Juicy Juice. Yeah, he did vomit, as advertised, but god damn it, he'd hurled a lot more than that when he got hold of some hamburger that hadn't been defrosted properly. He didn't cook it all the way through, and spent the next twelve hours with diarrhea, shitting his britches several times until he finally took his pants off and sat butt-naked on the toilet for hours, getting a ring around his ass, only getting up to drink from the spout of the bathroom sink so he wouldn't dehydrate entirely. He'd puked out his share of liquor too, used to binge drink, no sense lying, but that was a long time ago.

The point being that he wasn't susceptible to hippie native visions. All that was going on was that he was a giant heart, floating about shoulder-high to a mare off the ground, transparent, it was his heart, he reckoned, but there was nothing else, he had *become* the heart, as it floated around, bouncing off the wrecked furniture, but apparently it was puncture resistant, it sort of bumbled on, rising and falling, it felt kind of good not to weigh two hundred and forty pounds, mostly muscle but a little bit of gut too, let's be honest, by his figuring he couldn't weigh more than 0.3 ounces, and though he didn't seem permeable, when he got to Inés, who was sitting calmly cross-legged, who knows maybe she did ayahuasca every night, maybe it was like a vitamin for her, and as the heart touched her it enveloped her body and she passed inside, so now the heart was lifting toward the ceiling, carrying at least 100 pounds of cargo, pretty impressive that 0.3 ounces of metaphysical mylar could support that and not burst and not crash to the ground. Was his soul like helium? Or his consciousness, mind, whatever the fuck. The philosophers, despite all their blather, never did quite get that shit figured out. His breath, maybe, was keeping her afloat.

All he knew was that he was falling in love with Inés. Call him changeable, but that thing for Vanessa was only cruise ship horniness, easily assuaged when he fucked those three young ladies on board; the truth is, he could have remedied the feeling with his left hand and a squirt of lotion. But Inés, love at first sight. Coup de foudre. There was something sturdy and solid about her and she looked like she didn't take a lot of shit, but she didn't have a bitch face either. Maybe one of those women who makes you a better man. Kind of like what Vanessa was for Jasper. Truth, that dude would be fucked without her in his life. He would still be at the car wash. He loved Jasper like a brother and wanted him to be happy and would spend all his accumulated wealth to buy this hacienda outright if he had to, though a loan was preferable, but he would do it if that's what it took for him and his possible future wife Inés and possible future sister-in-sister-in-law Vanessa to experience collective joy. That was in his power. Only he really hoped Inés wouldn't fuck them all over or kill them, that would be such a letdown, especially because she was just so damn cute with those strong high Indian cheekbones and those expressive eyebrows but soft little doll lips, her mouth had a perfect shape that anybody who glanced at her, man, woman, child, dog, or shaman, would immediately want to kiss them, you simply couldn't help yourself.

And now he was carrying her around like one of those virgin queens in a Catholic parade, one who would bless everybody by blowing kisses from inside the heart-shaped bubble, untouchable yet everybody in the crowd lining the street felt a close personal connection to her, they were kneeling and strewing petals over the heart-shaped bubble, shouting "We love you, Inés," they were flat out worshipping her but Butch didn't mind at all, he was quite willing to share her with the entire world, for the moment anyway, because right now his heart—which was the entirety of him!—had grown almost to the size of the room, and even then—even then!—it was overflowing with love. For the first time in his existence, he understood with the entirety of his 0.3 ounce body that love was not a commodity; rather it was infinite, there was enough for everybody, god damn it! And he just hoped he could remember that when all this ayahuasca shit was over so that he wouldn't be a jackass. He was sick and tired of fencing stolen goods and dealing with petty, mercenary people, because that shit rubbed off on you, even if you were more or less a good guy, little by little you started getting sharp at the corners, not a balloon shape at all, and doing quid pro quo and figuring out right away what was in it for you.

He hadn't meant to befriend Jasper, it was just an odd impulse he'd acted on because he'd been an asshole to him, but never in his wildest dreams did he figure he'd be in a broken-down hacienda house doing ayahuasca and would turn into a giant heart.

Letting himself drift to the ground, he let the virgin queen disembark. Butch fell on his back, closed his eyes, and laughed his ass off.

33
THE SAINTS COME MARCHING IN

Somehow Vanessa knew she, the most fastidious of all, would be the one to vomit most copiously. It was one of those situations where you're hurling your entire life out through your esophagus. She'd hoped that she'd be carried off into a rapture of stereoscopic, Technicolor, old-school rapture, with a soundtrack by Curtis Mayfield, her wearing hip-hugger bell bottoms and a crop top, braids sponging out into a mega-Afro, maybe a pistol stuck into the behind of her waistband just in case, huge hoop earrings and either crimson or white lipstick, she couldn't decide which.

But no. She was so maddeningly self-controlled that she couldn't get high, only sick. Part of the reason she couldn't let go is that the shaman seemed especially interested in her, not so much hitting on her—of course, a man is always going to be a man—but rather trying to get her to channel her African ancestor deities: the *loa*, Papa Legba at the crossroads, with his erect phallus, walking with a cane; Maman Brigitte, with her black death rooster nestled in her lap; Baron Samedi, lewd and outrageous, top hat and tails, dark glasses; Erzulie, the most womanly of women, the cosmic womb, all sexed up; Ogun, the manliest of men, machete hanging by his side and an eye for the ladies; Damballah, the giant serpent, whose coils shaped heaven and earth; Oshun, the river of pleasure, her hair orange and gold and her dress green and coral.

That's where Vanessa wanted to be, in the river of pleasure, clothed in green and coral. Her life had been one of achievement, meeting deadlines, striving, being the first one to leave the party, unless she stayed to help the hostess clean up afterward. She didn't have unprotected sex unless in a long-term relationship, and both parties had gotten an STD test. No exceptions and she never had sex while drunk. This ayahuasca was literally the first recreational drug she'd ever done. Not even marijuana. No, she couldn't even call it "weed." Weed was what grew in your yard, only not in hers, because she had a lawn guy. And no, she didn't flirt with him. She saved her money, paid off her credit card, didn't make impulse purchases except the occasional cash register candy bar. She had a monthly budget and stuck to it. Never had she driven without insurance, and she had never submitted an insurance claim because she didn't drive while high or like a maniac. She observed the posted speed limit—okay, within five miles, because sometimes you're on a desolate stretch of highway at night, and it says 65, and somehow the gauge creeps up to 70. Other people could do what they wanted. Her friends and boyfriends could call her a tight-ass, but she wasn't going to be pulled down. She kept hearing about lifting up her people and she wasn't so sure about that, but she paid her own way through college, working night and weekends, graduated without debt and that had to count for something, only she wasn't going to spend her time encouraging crack heads and lazy asses, no sirree, everybody had to haul their bucket of water. She tithed to the church and gave to special missions when asked.

So, what in the hell was she doing with Jasper in Peru on her hands and knees puking up an earth ball? Vanessa was a fastidious woman and she normally was not gonna vomit unless she had to. Even then, it would have been because of some freak fever, because she didn't overeat. She would make sure she got as quickly as possible into her own tidy home, with Febreze air freshener right at hand and a cake of ammonia in the toilet bowl, tissues on the counter, Listerine, and she would change her toothbrush after that, she had three fresh ones in a package.

Nonetheless, here come Papa Legba showing his dick, using his cane like a baton. Erzulie right behind, showing her behind. Ogun and Samedie strutting in matching tuxedos, sticking their tongues out, leering at Brigitte and Oshun, who were doing the funky butt. Damballah's thick coils wound and unwound as it slithered among them, brushing the cuffs of the men's pants and winding around the ladies' well-turned ankles. Confetti was falling from the ceiling, thick, endless, covering the floor and all the surfaces and Jasper, Butch, and Inés. "Walk on Gilded Splinters" was playing from nowhere. Everybody hooted and hollered, pulling out little cornets to toot and accompany, as if it were New Year's Eve or the Rapture. Where was Jesus when you really, really needed him? He had just sat this one out. Left Vanessa to her own devices in this godforsaken hacienda house. She had half a mind to just run around and copulate with all the men, including the shaman, and Inés too—why not?

Only she had the acid taste in her mouth, the nastiness of her own saliva and stomach juices, so no, she wasn't going to be kissing nobody anytime soon. Best to just lie against the wall. Her eye fell on Jasper. He looked anxious. That boy fretted too much. If he would calm down inside, he would be alright. There was goodness in him, a lot of it. Whatever happened between him and Geeta, he had never treated Vanessa bad. She only hoped that the ayahuasca could miraculously heal those wounds, whatever they were.

Vanessa decided she wasn't going to be jealous of Inés, rather encourage this new connection. She knew in her heart that girl didn't mean harm and really was his sister. What had it taken for her to summon him back and him being a piece of work. Inés didn't know the half of it. Maybe it would take the both of them, Inés and Vanessa, to wrangle him into respectable shape. Vanessa knew she was an improver by nature; she wasn't going to accept everybody as they were. No, that was a bunch of New Age bullshit, because people had all kinds of quirks and kinks that had to be ironed out, so Jasper, she was going to go easy, but he needed a sustained, strong, Christian black woman's hand so that he could straighten up and fly right. Sorry, but that was the bargain, and in return, he would get love and compassion from the one person who understood him for exactly who he was.

34
SWITCH HITTER

Inés had gotten him here. She hadn't taken the ayahuasca along with the rest. Okay, that was a little white lie; she had drunk Gatorade from a cup by prior agreement with the shaman. She'd tried ayahuasca before, to no great effect; it just didn't seem to combine with her body's chemistry. But she needed to be clear to observe Jasper and these other two. She knew they didn't necessarily trust her. Jasper wanted to, she felt that, and Butch who was the money man had warmed to her, but in his eyes, she immediately read that he'd been burned many times. Vanessa was the wild card, the one who held the key to Jasper, the one she couldn't afford to alienate. The two of them weren't natural allies, the one a bit prim underneath and the second, her, rough around the edges, and both of them were wary by nature. But maybe that's exactly where they met, on the field of skepticism.

Her father had gone to Ayacucho to do field work, embedding himself in a little village, lived there for several months to study the economy of river fishing and had disappeared. Maybe he'd gotten too free with his liberal ideas, going native, as he tended to do, and he ended up sleeping with the wrong local woman. Somebody claimed he slipped and fell during a mountain trek during the rainy season, but nobody had found a body. Inés knew better. Her father was more sure-footed than those goats you saw grazing way up the steepest hillside. An earthquake couldn't have made him trip. But she didn't have the heart to talk to Jasper about that; not yet.

Because she came off a bit masculine by the standards of the locale, people had been known to call Inés a dyke. She liked women, but she liked men, too, and she thought at least her busty figure, even if she didn't have the usual earth-shaking hips of the women around here, would buy her some credence. She liked Butch all right. As his ayahuasca trip progressed, he was getting giddy and horny, you could see that, and he came and hovered over Inés, talking about how he had a big heart, or was a big heart, when what he probably meant was that he had a big hard-on. And she wouldn't have minded one bit dragging him into the next vacant room over, or him dragging her, either way was fine, and she had a presentiment that he and she would understand each other immediately, without having to resort to a bunch of categories du jour, gender-fluid, lesbian, switch-hitter or whatever. Who cared? Some of the ancient gods had both sets of genitals, so really, what was the big deal?

God, she hoped they would stay. She was afraid they would try to convince her to go with them back to the U.S., but though her English was decent, and she didn't suffer from even slight xenophobia and could certainly adapt, this was her place. She might as well be a *huaca,* an earth being, one of those sacred rock formations that grew out of the ground and whom her mother and many others of her ilk treated with reverence, prayed to, and relied on for their well-being, making them into some combination of priest, therapist, and best friend. Inés sometimes went to talk to one of the *huacas* to see whether that would spark for her, because she just couldn't do Saint Sebastian and Saint Cecilia and all that. The Jesus side creeped her out, in addition, there was all that colonial dominance behind it. But she knew she was just faking it with the earth-beings, same as faking a friendship or an orgasm, you knew you felt nothing inside, even if nobody else figured that out.

Inés did want to believe in something, have fervency, lose her mind a little bit, the way she did when she splurged on going to one of the local clubs when they did the 80s British synth-pop bands and customers started to crowd surf. It felt cool to be lifted up by all those hands. But you couldn't exactly make a religion out of Duran Duran and The Clash, could you? Inés had taken a big leap of faith by contacting Jasper. Her mother Antuka had talked about him in such a tearful, agonized way at first that Inés thought he'd died. It was only after several years of witnessing her weeping fits that it came out Jasper had been taken off to the U.S. by his actual birth mother—Antuka wasn't even his blood mom!—and he and Inés were only half-siblings.

For a while, this truth made you angry, because how was her mother going to get that torn up over the offspring of somebody she'd basically just been sleeping with, and valuing him more, in a sense, the son of some crazy gringa bitch and the ex-lover who she had a love child with, her, Inés, whose father then went off to Ayacucho and left both of them on the altiplano, deadbeat dad, yet she held this so-called son in higher esteem than her own flesh and blood daughter, right there with her toughing it out, tending her god damned annoying goats and often cooking the meal while her mother sat in the corner moping over the missing men.

Thank God at least she'd moved to Cusco, where you could get tattoos and body piercings and there was rock and jazz as well as the good, catchy native guitar, and you could do a little coke from time to time, only enough to take the edge off, and lead recreational trips, five-day hikes with Americans and Europeans who tipped well, kayaking, mountain biking, you were good at sports, it kept your physique in good shape, you became fluent in English as a result and you understood French, German, and Italian pretty well. If you'd ever gone to university, God only knows what you could have become. But your life was all right. You just needed a mate, if possible, and a half-brother if the fates allowed. You'd had a few "foreign affairs," but those people always went away, of course, and travelers of both genders, however spiritual, had broken your heart.

Now, her dad had left this hacienda. How he came by it, through what stratagems and deals, she had no idea. It had been in probate for several years, despite its wrecked condition, maybe because of the land value, but it suddenly was cleared, and it could be something beautiful if her non-believer's prayer turned out to be answered, once everybody was done tripping and came to their senses.

35
FRANKIE AND JOHNNY

The ayahuasca had done its job. Social strain relaxed. Inés took them river rafting through the tour company they worked for. They went to Sacsayhuaman, the Sacred Valley, Machu Picchu, ate roast guinea pig, bought baby alpaca sweaters, and Vanessa loaded up on silver jewelry. Butch kept buying intricately engraved gourds with scenes of native life and Peruvian indigenous history on them from pretty native female sellers who accurately identified him as a soft touch and let their smiles do most of the work. He even bought a mandolin and flute, though he knew how to play neither, yet he swore he would learn, in spite of not being able to carry a tune, as had been established during their car rides. He had an unreasonable attachment to the song "Frankie and Johnny" and its many verses. Those purchases were followed by tapestries and stuffed llamas. Soon, he had to buy woven baskets to carry them in, then luggage. He'd either have to ship them back or pay exorbitant excess baggage fees when they returned.

"*If* I return," he quipped, noting the displeasure on

Vanessa's face, said, "I'm just cracking." But that comment stood as a gunshot through the arcade.

Discussions on the hacienda began. Legal titles were shown, an attorney was brought in to attest to their veracity. Inés and Butch and the lawyer went to a bank to discuss loans and collateral, how such a partnership would work, and Butch, who wasn't as flighty as he acted, had all the documentation to show his (legal) assets, in addition to mentioning he had a robust fund of disposable cash. This latter remark was met with no batted eyelashes, calmly and stone-faced, as if to say, "If you want to put an infusion of cash into our beleaguered economy, by whatever means, God bless you."

Builders and an architect went out to the property, measuring and kicking rotten plaster, digging out samples of wood, and in a few days returned to the group's hotel with a set of blueprints of the existing area and a new one of the proposed rebuild. Costs were discussed, and a provisional agreement was reached, though everybody involved said they wanted a few days to think it over and talk.

Vanessa, whose business this really wasn't, as she was not an investor nor the spouse of an investor, had to admit that Inés was conducting herself with great tact in the matter. She'd said nothing to Jasper about staying on, and Jasper wasn't making any extravagant statement either about wanting to relocate. He was just listening, not having been asked to invest either, as he had no money with which to do it anyway, just a half-title in the property. He seemed mature, calm and reflective, almost as if the ayahuasca had peeled off some damaged, bad skin he'd been trapped in. Only she awoke to find him crying in bed one night about his father's death, which seemed perfectly natural, a delayed reaction that was finally coming home, in a healthy

way, because he now had a sibling with whom to share that
grief. Vanessa was clear on the fact that she didn't own him
and wasn't going to debase herself by being possessive.
Only a part of her kept waiting for a smackdown to come
from some corner, but there seemed to be none. Maybe it
was merely her learning that she wasn't in control of this
experience, that she couldn't or shouldn't manage it. So,
she kept her mouth shut and ate her trout sushi with
toasted corn.

Vanessa had more than enough to think about
regarding her own situation. She should have been the
head of the laboratory by now. It was in her generous
nature to fill in for others' shifts, to let the higher-up
researchers "pick her brain" when they found out that her
insights on addiction were at the level one would expect of
a top graduate student. Several times, she was asked why
she hadn't applied to an advanced degree program, and she
was too embarrassed to say that she'd been accepted to a
so-so PhD but had let the opportunity pass, hoping she
could instead get on first as co-author of a research paper,
or if not, become head of a lab, then maybe not have to
worry about pursuing an advanced degree at all, even
though she experienced guilt about not doing it for "her
people."

But what had her people ever done for her, the ones she
grew up with, except try to hold her back and fit her into
the New Orleans party scene and get her matched up with a
man out of their crowd, a pretty stockbroker who would
have gotten her knocked up and pretty soon she'd be just
like her momma, depending on a man with a lot of quirks
that would come out over time and when she complained
about it, her momma would say "He makes two hundred
thousand dollars a year! Just learn how to suffer and be a

wife," whereas with Jasper she knew all the quirks ahead of time, she could read him like a menu at a catfish restaurant.

Did they not promote her at the lab because she was black? Because she was a woman? Because she wasn't actually good enough, despite what they said? If she was so good and was the most conscientious person in the lab, why wasn't she getting regular pay raises and going up the ladder? The project had money for that. It's like she was getting gaslighted, "You're really too good to be in a place like this, but in the meantime, don't forget to scrub out those vials like a kitchen maid." She'd grown up thinking there would be a direct reward for being good at what you do, punctual, kind, conscientious, having a strong work ethic, not gossiping about your peers, sticking to business, performing each task to satisfaction down the line, and her whole credo was based on that. Like a fool, she had believed in meritocracy.

But it turns out it was more important to be part of the club, to go out for drinks afterward with the crew after you just did a double shift and only wanted to get home to heat up a frozen Thai dinner, shower, getting into P.J.s at six p.m. and binge watch *Bridgerton,* which she'd already seen twice all the way through. And when you didn't go along with the dogma, acting like you were all part of a family, that failure to engage subtly pushed you to the outside. Truth was, one of her supervisors had hit on her a couple of times. He was witty and quick and knew just how to do borderline flirting where it was hard to go to HR with it; the man had obviously had a lot of practice. And that PhD she got into, the one everybody second-guessed, the professor who'd interviewed her couldn't stop looking at her tits with his shifty eyes, letting his gaze veer off to the bookshelf whenever she caught him doing it and he made it clear she would be his personal assistant. No, she didn't want five or six years of that cringey leer.

Vanessa had never complained about anyone during her undergraduate years. She sucked it all up, the slights, the micro-aggressions. She held some outdated fantasy that nobility of spirit and hard work, trying to be a good person and outdoing everybody else with her GPA meant something. But it only meant something to some people. Maybe she needed a mate like Jasper, who knew he was cracked. Beneath all her strait-laced apparent normalcy, maybe she was every bit as weird as him.

36
EDEMA

No one would ever tell, but Butch had almost died auditioning to be a Navy SEAL. During Hell Week, when 90% of the seamen washed out, he hung in almost to the bitter end. Basic Underwater Demolition had been brutal, dangerous, and reckless. There had been concussions and broken bones among the men. He knew previous aspiring SEALs had died before, fighting the frigid waves, slipping from the grasp of the human chain they were forced to form as they fought through the water. A lot of them were using performance-enhancing drugs to get an edge. It was ironic how many drugs he'd used later in life, but at that moment, he had a purity about him, a naiveté that if you worked hard enough, you'd get your dream. Seaman Kowalski, eighteen years old, simply gutted out the endless push-ups and pull-ups, the running with a 170-pound inflatable boat over one's head, not being given water for an entire day. He'd never been more fit in his young life, but he felt like a piece of paper blowing in the wind. The seamen dropping out of the competition immediately got labeled turds. The remaining men ran and crawled on hot sands without breaks.

He was sure heatstroke was what was finally going to put him down, because he knew he was running a high fever. But in the end, it was lung edema. In week three, he was spitting up bloody fluid and he couldn't breathe. He could barely get through the cold water swims on four hours of sleep per night. Medics were having to give him supplemental oxygen, the way you give it to high-altitude climbers trying to summit K-2. He filled a quart bottle with bloody sputum. It was the final couple of days and the medics had gone home for the day. Kowalski lay burning. One of the instructors came to his bed and yelled at him that he was worthless, and he needed to quit. He spit a gob of blood in the man's face and got slapped as a result.

In the middle of the night, as he felt shadows closing over him to end his life, at least with the dignity of not having quit, there were strobing lights outside. One of the men, against regulations, had called 911 and an ambulance had been dispatched. The instructors were furious at this breach of privacy. Kowalski, stupid as he was, back then would have been mad at the anonymous tipster too, who would no doubt be ferreted out and punished, banished from competition at the eleventh hour, but Butch was too weak to have any feelings as he was taken on a gurney to the ambulance and intubated. It was a struggle for weeks and he recalled in his hellish sleep-wake the doctors discussing his slim chances of surviving. But he pulled through.

He'd almost been a SEAL. He knew what the commanders were subjecting them to was wrong. He'd figured that out early on in the contest. But he wanted it anyway. Seldom did he reflect back on those days. Only his father knew the full extent of the torture he'd undergone, and then he had passed away, leaving only the memories of Seaman Kowalski and his erstwhile band of brothers, all sworn to a fucked-up code of silence that they would obey, partly out of unnecessary shame.

Butch had lasted another three years in the Navy, not doing anything particularly distinguished, but not being a particular rebel either. Finally, he just couldn't do it any longer. He went back to Texas and helped his father out, who had bought a little ranch that never amounted to much and finally had to be sold. But they had fun together roping and riding, getting up early to keep the livestock moving and healthy. He learned about sales and butchering. He kept that buff physique. Then he went to Española, New Mexico, for no particular reason other than he had passed through it on a trout fishing trip to the Four Corners.

That's where he tried crack and meth. Luckily, he didn't get addicted. Instead, he learned to drink hard. He helped some guys steal merchandise off a food truck. After that one experience, even though he didn't get caught, he realized that stealing on your own was too dangerous, so he turned the men down when they wanted to jack a car. They ended up getting busted and sent to prison for five years. Somehow that stroke of fortune convinced Butch that he should be at one remove from theft, as a middleman. He was making a modest living selling merchandise off eBay, enough to open a mechanic shop, working on hot rods and regular cars, and selling legit. There was no reason he needed to sell stolen goods on top of that. But guys he knew from before were coming to him, telling him his shop was the perfect front and that they would literally buy him a warehouse, put the title in his name, if he'd go in on commission. He wasn't expected to sell to customers directly. All they needed was a place to modify the cars as necessary while they created fake titles.

He said yes, though he couldn't explain exactly why. It was simply something bad in him that had to express itself. He saw himself in the mirror, still bulky and strong, but forty pounds fatter than that muscular youth who almost died from edema. He kept waiting to be discovered and punished with prison. But he kept getting more and more successful, and it was hard to get out of the many relationships he'd built within his business network.

Then he ran across Jasper in the car wash. There was something about him. Also, he represented to Butch what he himself might become. Now, he wanted to do something good to redeem his life, one that was lucrative but otherwise empty. Everybody around him called him jovial and fun, but he knew better. Here he was in Peru, with Vanessa, Jasper and Inés. He didn't care if he had to spend his whole bankroll if it would make these people happy. Some people gave donations to universities or for polio research. This was his charity, even if all they got for it was a pretty hacienda house, a restoration of something gone to shit.

37
NIGHTHAWKS

T wilight fell over the folds of the mountains and receded, giving Jasper a view of more stars than he ever remembered witnessing. They were so closely packed together that they seemed to touch one another. He'd seen star-laden skies in the Southwest when he camped, but these hovered closer, like an aerial armada of distant ships that would fill the air as they drew closer to land on a virgin planet.

He'd insisted on coming back to the hacienda house alone with a sleeping bag. Everybody else had advised against it, but he'd been stubborn about it. Finally, Inés had said she'd go with him, otherwise it was a no-go. Vanessa and Butch agree that they'd stay in Cusco. Everybody had rented cell phones, and they made sure they had each other's numbers. Vanessa gave Jasper a big hug. She seemed happy that he was going to have some alone time with his new half-sister.

Inés was able to borrow a car for the night from a friend. They bought roast chicken, bread, cheese and beer, and cigarettes for Inés, who said she liked to smoke when out in the countryside. As they'd driven there, she joked about *condenados,* haunted spirits, coming around at night. Or maybe she wasn't joking because she wasn't smiling when she said it. The chicken was greasy and lukewarm by the time they got there but it still tasted good. In the dark, the silhouettes of half-walls around the courtyard looked like genuine ruins, the kind you'd pay money to see. They washed their hands in a work bucket that some laborers had left, half-filled with water. They realized they hadn't brought drinking water, so beer was all they had. It had stayed cold in the cool night air. A scraping chirp came overhead, faded, as if with distance, and came closer and louder again, several times.

"Nighthawk," said Inés. "Looking for insects." She looked cool and pretty in the glow of the kerosene lamp, her features soft, a beat-up green cap on her head from some long-ago revolution, sipping from her bottle and smoking a cigarette in a simple and sincere manner, yet still a little theatrical.

"What was Dad like?"

"Absent a lot. But let's not get into that right now. I want to enjoy my achievement of getting you here with that stupid letter. You and your beautiful girlfriend and that hunky friend of yours."

"Is he?"

"Definitely. I like them stout and brawny. Would it bother you if I got with him?"

"Got with?"

"You know what I'm saying."

"You're two grownups. I'm not his chaperone. Besides, I barely know him."

"What?"

"I'm serious. I met him at a car wash a few weeks ago."

"I thought you two were like childhood friends. Why is he willing to invest in us?"

"Beats me. He's like my gigantic fairy godfather. He insisted we come and splurged us to a luxury cruise."

"Well, maybe you deserve that." Inés unrolled a towel and out onto the dirt spun two pistols.

"What the hell? Where did you get those?"

"Never you mind. These are Taurus G2cs. The budget pick, but they deliver. Twelve rounds. You ever shot?"

"It so happens that Butch has been taking me to the shooting range. Are you two in league?"

"No, big brother. But I dare say he and I think alike. She handed him one, and a box of shells. "I suggest you load it."

He got to work placing them into the cartridge with delicacy, like a teenage girl laying her keepsakes in a cherry-wood memory box. "The haunted spirits?"

"You get thieves out here sometimes. There's nothing to steal here, but they may have seen construction going on and think there's equipment to steal."

"Now that a gun has been brought out, we have to use it. So says Chekhov."

"Another friend of yours?"

"Never mind."

Inés pulled something else out of her backpack, a rolled joint. "Want to smoke some weed?"

"I don't know. After that ayahuasca, I'm feeling overly susceptible. And thieves? Shouldn't we be on our guard?"

"Come on. The *condenados* around here are slow. Like zombies."

"Is this herb treated with anything?"

"Honestly, a friend gave it to me for this trip, as a present for your arrival. I was saving it for this special occasion. Trust in the universe. It's brought us this far."

Jasper sighed. "I guess so. It's just that my brain chemistry—"

"Makes two of us. Must be genetic. But isn't everybody kind of crazy?"

"I guess so."

Inés took a hit and passed the joint to him, then exhaled. "I'm so glad you're in my life, Jasper. Whatever that ends up meaning."

He took a hit, held in the smoke, let it out. They passed it back and forth until it was gone and drank another beer. The stars had expanded outward, creating space between them, as if to prove that space really was curved. He leaned back against an adobe wall, feeling the warmth it still held from the day's sun and pulled the sleeping bag over his body. He felt good and was getting sleepy. He let his eyes shut as the nighthawk continued its occasional swoops past their refuge.

38
NOT A GRAVEYARD OF FIRST CHAPTERS

J asper sat against the headboard with the laptop balanced on his knees, reading and scrolling. Vanessa, one leg flung over the back, read the history of a maverick physician in the 1600s who transfused calf's blood into a madman. She had a feeling the madman wasn't going to make it, but she wished him the best. The strains of musicians playing in the streets wafted up to their room. When she'd gone down for a Coke, dancers still clotted the plaza and all the side roads, as they had for days. Their stamina at this high altitude was impressive to her, even though she'd grown up watching similar parades at Mardi Gras, where you can't necessarily tell a saint from a sinner; it's just one long conglomeration of sensory excess. Here in Cusco, flower blossoms were thrown and judges sitting at a dais on the nearby square through squawky sound systems were excitedly announcing each troupe of damsel devils with ice-blue eyes or leather-jacketed businessmen with priapic noses.

Out of the side of her eyes, she saw Jasper set down the laptop he'd been reading almost without a break for hours.

She also set down her book. Vanessa had wanted to break into his solitude earlier, but after the incident at the hacienda, he'd gone into a mental retreat. She was prepared for it to last for days, in which case she'd just go see the Sacred Valley on her own, until he emerged into conversation.

"I figured something out," he said.

"What's that?"

"I've been rereading the first chapters. I couldn't stand to look at them for months on end. Each one seemed dead on arrival, another evidence of my insufficiency. I could only picture them as a graveyard, one I was carrying around with me everywhere I go, making it even less likely that I'd ever write another novel. I haven't even tried writing for the past year. I decided to open them this morning. I literally copy-pasted them all into a single document, so I wouldn't have to keep going from one to another. And I've been reading."

"The verdict?"

"I haven't gotten that far in thinking about them. I've simply been trying to piece together what happened. Where I got stuck. You can't say much about something that's just in its initial stages. I know I should have been more forgiving of each one. They're mere words. And I've always been harsh on myself. Even my bestsellers, I wanted to claw them back. Any bad review I received, I perversely welcomed it, as if knowing in advance I deserved to be criticized."

"Why are you such a masochist? I enjoyed *Antarctic Knob*. You used to read it to me in bed and we'd laugh our heads off. We decided it was a comedy."

"I don't know. But even when I concoct tales out of nothing, based on no one, it still feels personal."

"Have you considered the fact that maybe it is personal?"

"Funny you should say that, because as I've been reading through these in succession, I've come to the realization that they're not a graveyard of first chapters."

"Now you've got my full attention. Which part of that statement is true?"

"Both parts. What makes them a graveyard is them being first chapters. Like a head without a body."

"Please don't get back onto zombies. That's not a good topic for you."

"I mean that taken together, they make up one single novel."

"Wow. That never occurred to me. You were always so trenchant about presenting them as funereal monuments to your eternal insufficiency, world without end."

"But it's only true if I add in my life—our lives. That's the unwritten part of the novel. It's what I still have to get down in words."

"Your life and mine?"

"Yes. But also, Butch and Inés's. Only when you take that and the chapters in its totality does it make sense."

"Have you been reading the Kabbalah again?"

"I'm serious Vanessa."

"When and where does it end? With you trying to kill Incas before they get onto their spaceships?"

"I wish I hadn't told you about that yesterday. Please let it go no further. No, it wouldn't end there. That was a great ending for *Inca Armageddon*. And maybe I'll rewrite the ñak'aq attack someday and pitch it to Hulu this time. But we haven't finished living the part that ends the story. You, Inés and Butch opened the path by you running into me on the street—"

"Hello, I was looking for you. Did you so soon misre-member that encounter as an accident? In a novel, you'd never accept that kind of coincidence."

"Okay, somebody gave you a tip and you were looking for me. That's even better. And thank you for doing that. But Butch, him finding me in the car wash, that was totally a coincidence."

"Let's call it fate. Sounds more literary."

"Agreed, fate."

"And Inés reaching out to us right at that same moment—"

"So unlikely, yet somehow necessary."

"Again, if you recall, you told me she had sent that email weeks ago. You had simply neglected to look in your spam folder."

"Alright. Nonetheless, I was motivated to read through my spam at the right time. Why? The hand of the Almighty. Then the three of us going on this trip in summons to her letter, on that improbable cruise."

"This is starting to sound like a novel."

"Bringing us here, where we face off against pottery thieves, putting our lives at risk."

"You're laying it on thick, but I don't object. When they make it into a movie, let's just have those skanky robbers be actual zombie Inca warriors, the four of us beating them back with semi-automatic weapons, the spaceships and all that, and let's not explain it away as a dream or hallucina-tion, or an act of imagination. That really happened."

"Agreed. It really happened. It certainly felt real to me."

"But it's not the climax of the tale? Because any high-salaried blockbuster director—"

"No. The four of us must travel through the highlands toward Puno, to Lake Titicaca."

"Where you used to live with your dad and your sexy stepmother."

"I told you about that?"

"You tried your best to be inscrutable and emotionally unavailable, so as to ruin our otherwise fairly decent relationship. But you did let a few things slip out, such as your profound yearning to regress to infancy so that you could suckle from her dark, ample bosom without anybody having to call Dr. Freud."

"That is so wrong to say."

"It's okay. You were a relative child. That was your first experience of sex and love all rolled into one. It's probably how you got to me."

"What do you mean?"

"I'm saying sometimes I got the feeling I was one shade of brown from me becoming a black woman fetish for you."

"Ouch."

"The Black Virgin. There's nothing wrong with it, per se. As they say down on this continent, *rico es rico*."

"I would never make that claim about you."

"Oh, I had a white-boy fetish about you. But I grew out of it and started seeing you as a person."

"Thank you for growing out of it."

"You're welcome. But about this trip."

"Yes, I hope she's living there. Inés ought to know. I want to see her. How things turned out for her."

"Never a good idea."

"Nonetheless. In addition to that, Lake Titicaca is where Tupac Yupanqui and his wife Mama Oqllo emerged from the water onto land."

"I don't know who those people are."

"Not people. Inca gods from the Tiahuanaco era."

"Oh, the Incas again. You're just going to put them into everything. So maybe it is Inca Armageddon after all."

"They were the mythic founders of the Inca empire."

"Your spiritual grandparents. Now that you mention it, I remember *Lonely Planet* had a thing about them."

"Can we go?"

"Suits me. We're waiting to see what the government is going to do about your all's property. And when we get back, let's do Machu Picchu. I will burn as much of my unpaid leave as possible."

"If I only have been writing this one novel, even if it's been taking a long time, I haven't failed. It's a work in progress. It wasn't yet ready to be finished."

"Nobody ever called you a failure, Jasper. That's your word."

"Geeta did."

"After you blew all that money. Okay, so you fucked up there. Send her a check if that property really does end up being worth what Inés says it is. But don't get carried away. Twenty thousand will soothe her feelings for a lifetime. I know the woman and how she thinks. I only ask that you and I have the relationship we always wanted, one so excellent that it makes her insanely jealous, and she tries to use that money to buy you back from me."

39
THE SHE-CALF

T birthed Inés, here on the altiplano, where the wind blows hoarse like the notes of a zampoña. They said I was José's mistress, but no, the white woman, the sickly one who always fled to the city, to her apartment, was the other woman. How could someone that skinny contain life? She couldn't cook a meal, couldn't feed her man, couldn't keep him happy in bed. She wasn't made for these bone-chilling nights. Why did she even come to our shores?

They called me *mula* because they didn't see me holding a baby, even though they perfectly well must have heard the cries of my child's birth through the open window. The midwife even swore that I had borne a daughter, but they demanded, "Well, where is she?" Inés grew and grew in my belly, kicked and kicked. I knew she was going to be big. I insisted on taking the cows to pasture to graze and make those steep hikes, even though I was large with her. Animals in the field just keep living when they're great with the burden of a litter, even our little guinea pigs scamper about the earth floor, always in motion. Living beings are meant to run and roam, and in a way, it's a shame that we have to pen up the animals for their safety and our profit.

Everybody said no, rest, you're going to abort if you do that. Maybe that's why later, everybody's official story was that I miscarried. Because the truth, the one we whisper and tell in our stories at bedtime, frightening the children before they go to sleep, is too strange to be believed when it comes down to the fact. "Oh, those are fairy tales," they say. But then they'll arrive at their houses late in the evening saying a ñak'aq followed them down the winding trail in the dark, eyes glowing, to suck out their fat with horrible fangs, and we're supposed to believe them. I guess it's only real if it happens to you.

When I kept growing, they said, the baby will be born wrong. I thought they meant breeched, like my neighbor woman who died from that condition, howling like a sudden widow, where we could all hear the agony. But no, they said, "She'll be born an animal, some kind or another." The town was always talking about blood moons and such nonsense. At least, that's how I thought then. I know I'm ignorant, unlettered, unschooled, whatever you want to call it. I know José had a doctorate, whatever exactly that is, a bundle of studies and hundreds of books read, the ones that were always lying around the hut, not a word of which I could read.

He would try to teach me sometimes and I'd fly into a fury, crying out, "Don't I have enough to do? Don't I care for the animals and you, cook all your meals, warm our bed with my body, mend your clothes?" And he would leave me alone, getting sad and withdrawing for a time. I know his intentions were good. But it was impossible for him to understand how terrified the thought made me, almost as if a curse lay inside all that knowledge. I forever wished that just once, he would have said, "You're smart, Antuka, in your own way. It doesn't matter whether or not you can read." If he'd stayed around more, I wouldn't have needed to read. He could have done that for both of us. I was so ignorant at first that one day, I held up a book to my ear to see whether it would speak to me. Maybe that's just called hope. If the radio talks, why not a book? Then recently, somebody said there's something called "audio books," and I knew I wasn't entirely wrong to think that possible.

Anyway, I never paid any attention to the neighbors' warnings about my running around so much. Besides, did any of them offer to help me, besides little Marianito? Ducks would fly across the lake, honking. They were scolding me too, telling me not to be a shepherdess to the cattle, not even touch them until after the baby came. I wasn't afraid. A wayfarer had tried to rape me up in the high fields once, in the shack where I slept near the cows to keep out of the biting wind. But I grabbed a stick and hit him so hard it busted his crown. He bled so much I thought at first he was going to die. After a while, he ran off, his poncho stained red with his own blood. Nobody ever found his body, so I guess he was okay.

I was worried, though. The baby went beyond forty weeks and I looked like a cow myself. I couldn't even get out of bed the last week, even though I didn't feel bad. Only I couldn't sleep because the baby moved constantly. Then it happened. The midwife came and as I quickened, and finally started to push, she got hold of a leg and said, "It's furry." Even then, I wasn't too concerned, because some of them have that lanugo and come out looking like little monkeys.

Except that when she got it halfway pulled out, she

expelled breath, as if bothered, and as the rest of the baby slid out, slick in its placenta, she said, calmly, "It's a calf."

I thought that was a manner of speaking, until she held it up to show me. It really was a calf, scrawny and wriggling and bloody. I said, "Bring it to my breast, I want to nurse it." She had been getting the creature wrapped up to take it away, maybe strangle and butcher it, so I had to act quickly. I repeated my request, louder, desperate. She looked down at it in her arms as if gazing at a monster. Then with a sigh, she cleaned the slime off it, ignoring my continuing pleas, but at last, knowing I wasn't going to give in, she brought the calf and laid it across my stomach. "It's a girl," she said. At that point, José had left me. He didn't even know I was pregnant. The she-calf suckled from my left breast, then my right, after which she sighed with contentment. "Her name is Inés," I said. Then I looked at the midwife slyly. "You were afraid she was going to look mixed-race, just because José is a mestizo from the city. But you got even more than you bargained for."

"You got more," she replied, cleaning up the mess rather than look me in the eye.

I kept Inés in a separate little corral right outside my room. I wouldn't let her mix with the other animals. I didn't want her to think of herself that way. Yet I could see her yearning, straining her neck over the fence toward the others, and she would ignore me. That hurt my feelings, but I never said anything about her sulking. I wished and even prayed to the *apu* that José would return and tell me what to do. I was sure he wouldn't bat an eyelash if I told him that our daughter was a calf. He might just make a dark joke like saying, "Who's the father?" and then he'd help me figure out how to handle the situation.

I thought about how if she stayed in this household,

eventually I'd begin to think of her as something to milk, or a source of meat. Or worse, just a pet, not good for anything. I'd never been sentimental about my goats, chickens, guinea pigs, or cows. They had been born to produce eggs, milk, and eventually, they would end up on our plates as cuts of meat. That was just the way of the world, and nobody questioned it.

That's when I decided to build her a pen up in the far reaches of the puna. I wasn't worried she'd be stolen. Other animals had been kept up there, by many of us, and we looked out for each other if we thought there might be rustlers. If a stranger came around, we'd know it at once, and the neighbors took turns sleeping up in the shacks at night, making the rounds as sentries. But it did mean she'd be alone for long days and nights. I felt bad about it, but I didn't trust myself to know how to handle her. She left me uneasy. Maybe that made me a bad mother.

Thinking back, I must have been crazy because Jasper had been taken away, and this was my only child, because I'd aborted twice before her and now, I was about to banish Inés from the house, afraid the neighbors would find out the truth, begin to believe what at first, they'd be skeptical about, and want to kill her, as the midwife had wanted to. They would consider her bad luck, an evil spirit, because some of them are just ignorant. So, up to the puna she went to live in her pen. I had an arrangement with a neighbor to set out food and water for her when doing his rounds if there wasn't enough grazing grass and if the rain hadn't been enough to keep her trough full. Often, I'd awaken at night, thinking of going up to check on how she was, but I couldn't make myself do it. I knew if I looked in her eyes once, I'd have to bring her back and one way or another, she'd end up slaughtered.

A boy named Marianito used to help me out. He could shepherd and do chores, keep the pens clean and I'd even taught him how to care for a sick animal. He had a gift. Marianito must have read my mind, because one day he said, "Inés is lonely. I went up to see her and she's low in spirits." Only he would use a phrase like that, at twelve years old. He was innocent. "I volunteer to go up and see her every day for a couple of hours, if that's okay with you."

I agreed. He began to visit her, and he'd come back, full of spirits, sprigs of grass in his hair, while I heated up milk for him and gave him hot bread I'd baked. The season of lightning began, and Marianito worried she was going to get shocked. I tried to argue with him that lightning strikes everywhere, she could as well get hit standing right here by the house. He grew moody.

"You know we talk," he said.

"In your imagination?"

"No." He had a stubborn look on his face. "She shares her dreams with me. And I sing her songs."

"What dreams?" I found myself asking, half in scorn, but half as if it could be true.

"She wants to marry someday."

"You, I suppose."

"She didn't say." I had embarrassed him, and he turned his face to the wall. Then he looked back at me, not pleading but as if stating a well-known fact about maternity. "You have to bring her back down to the house."

"I'll go see her," I said. "And if she speaks to me as well, I'll bring her down."

Marianito jumped up and grabbed me by both of my sleeves. "She might not talk to you. It took me weeks to get her to talk."

"We'll see."

"Okay. But be gentle. She's a shy creature. Do you want me to walk up with you?"

I found myself laughing. "To translate? No, I'll figure it out."

The next morning, I got up early, made myself a lunch and got on the path. Marianito said he would do all the chores himself, to leave my time free and so I wouldn't have to hurry. He'd arrived early to make sure I kept up my bargain. I wasn't sure I would know Inés by sight, but when I got to my pasture, I recognized the pen we'd built, one with slats that had gotten somewhat weathered and even a couple had fallen. Easily, she could have escaped. Either she was obedient, or dumb. As I got closer, I couldn't help but notice her beautiful, big brown eyes, set off by thick lashes. They were the shape of mine. The contours of her face were sleek, not broadly bovine, and even her body was trim, not emaciated, but rather something of the shape of a woman, with a slender waist and hips flaring at the back. Marianito must have been taking extra good care of her, perhaps taking her food and personally ensuring she had plenty of water. Her coat shone the way a horse's does, or the hair of a woman who shampoos with eggs and gives her locks one hundred brush strokes. Suddenly, I was mortified by my neglect and ashamed of myself as a mother. This was my only child.

My first instinct was to flee, but sensing that, she calmly said, "Come embrace me, Mother." I climbed into the pen, circled my arms around her neck, and leaning against her sturdy body, hugged her hard and stayed that way for a long time. Both of us cried, her lowing in a manner both touching and slightly comical, but I was in no mood to laugh right then.

"I'm bringing you back home," I said.

"That's all right." She didn't seem distressed or upset. Her tone was, rather, practical. "We can catch up later. I can tell you all about watching the clouds roll past the sky, the lightning hitting the mountains and causing small avalanches, and how and when the wildflowers blossom." At first, I thought she was being sarcastic or blameful for my absence, but I realized she was only speaking of what she knew. Probably her conversation would be more interesting than mine.

"Then, what? We descend together now?"

"No. There are certain things you have to do first. A carpenter must build a brand-new bed in which no one has slept. Also, a table and two chairs at which no one has ever sat. Kill your youngest chicken that's fattened. Get a bottle of precious wine; send to the city if you must, but it must never have been opened. Buy cheese, still wet, and from the baker, choose the first loaf of bread to come out of his oven that morning. Pick flowers the very day of my arrival to put in a vase. On the table, with everything else, set a fresh candle that has never been lit, and a box of matches. I'll come at the next full moon. Nobody but you and Marianito can be there. Dress him in brand-new pajamas that no one has ever put on and leave him alone in the bed. You will have to sleep in the smokehouse."

"All right," I answered, not even questioning any of these strange demands.

"I will come at midnight. Now go."

Once again, I wasn't offended, nor was her tone brusque. She was only stating her requirements. Of course, when I returned, I got on my assignment right away, using Marianito to run to the carpenter and so forth, without ever explaining what she had told me. He didn't seem to take it amiss, simply did what I asked as if it were the most normal set of requests in the world. But I knew that he would ensure that all was done exactly according to instructions.

I had to take a bus into the city three hours away to get the wine. I wasn't sure what would make it "precious." The price? Finally, I asked the store owner which was his favorite, and he handed me a bottle of red wine. The flowers, I didn't know whether she meant wildflowers that grew by the house, or something special, as if for a wedding. In the end, I went to the house of a friend I hadn't seen for a while, one who lived in a desolate place, but had many bushes of k'antu flowers, where the bees liked to congregate. I offered to buy a big bunch, but she said, "Don't be silly. I'll give you as many as you want. Why have you been such a stranger? They used to call me the recluse; now it's you. Stay and have coffee and biscuits." I promised to return soon to do that, except today I was in a hurry. She cut me an armful of bright red flowers, wrapped them in my shawl, helped me fasten it to my back, gave me a warm kiss on the cheek and said, "Don't forget me, Antuka. You still have a good friend here." I thanked her profusely and left.

The next morning, I woke at dawn and went to the baker's so I could be the first one there, to stand in the cold for an hour if necessary, while he warmed his clay oven and brought out the first batch of bread. To my bad luck, an old woman stood there, one of those gossips, already waiting, apparently having nothing better to do. She looked me over from top to toe and said, in that malicious-inquisitive, fake-friendly way that people assume when they want to get into your business, "How's your health?"

"I'm enduring," I said. She didn't know quite how to reply to that, me not having given her any real opening. Instead, we stood in uncomfortable silence. At last, the baker opened the door, as he was on the verge of bringing out the first batch, the aroma of which both the old woman and I had been smelling from outside the wooden door, both of us salivating. She had first pick, but I quickly said, "Would you mind if I pick the ñawi—the first loaf? I have a special guest coming today and I'm feeling a bit superstitious about it."

She was a stubborn sort, but she was more intrigued by having something to gossip about. "Who is your guest?"

"I'll tell you if you let me pick first. And I'll pay for you to have three loaves."

She was superstitious herself. But my offer was more tempting than her everyday fears. "Very well then." She stood aside and let me have the first loaf. I went ahead and bought two, just in case and paid the man for five. I put the loaves in my shawl and shouldered them. She did the same with her three. "So, who is your mysterious visitor?"

"Let's step outside first, to speak in confidence."

"Of course." Out we walked from the oven-warmed room into the frigid dawn. Luckily for me, the temperature would keep our conversation short. She was already shivering. "I tell you this in the strictest confidence. Not a soul may know."

"Yes, yes, whatever you require."

I knew perfectly well she'd be sprinting home afterward to spill my news to every neighbor within earshot. I knew what I was about to say would fuel her verbal fire, but in a way, it would serve me to throw her and everyone else off my real track when Inés came.

"I've taken a lover."

Her face lit up with malicious glee. "Who is he? That young bachelor by the square?"

"No, not at all. He comes from far away. No one has ever seen him around here."

"You poor thing. I know it's a sin and all and Our Lord Jesus would never approve. On the other hand, we all know that José has left you, a man you were already living in sin with. He has a girl in every town, that's common wisdom around here. Those biddies along the lake used to talk of nothing else when doing their laundry together. You might as well have a man of your own."

"I appreciate it that you're so understanding. Promise me again you won't breathe a word of this to a single soul."

"My lips are sealed. And blue, for that matter. I'd better hurry along before I turn to ice." And off she went at a gait she probably hadn't achieved in many days, to act as the town crier.

The full moon was due. I casually invited Marianito to stay the night, saying that I suddenly felt frightened, which was totally unlike me. Marianito was generally happy-go-lucky, and he liked me, so he went back and told his mother he was staying over. I sent along one of my chickens as a gift to make sure she'd say yes. Pretty soon, he had returned, smiling.

"Come here, little one," I said, though in truth he was almost as tall as me. "Take off your clothes." He stripped naked and I bathed him with a sponge and put on him the fresh cotton pajamas I'd bought in town. They fit him exactly. We sat on the bed together, me rubbing his head to make him sleepy, while he took my other hand in both of his and examined it, as if he were going to tell my fortune. Twilight had faded, leaving a profound dark and through the open shutters, which I had neglected to fasten, the stars seemed to have fled the sky. I could smell barley from a distant field, or possibly it was her scent. I didn't know whether to seat him at the table so that she and he could eat together. Her highly specific instructions hadn't included that detail. But my sense was that she wanted the house still and quiet. Even the guinea pigs who lived under the kerosene stove for warmth weren't making their usual weep-weep noise, as if in anticipation; rather, they lay quiet.

After a time, Marianito slid under the sheets, now half-asleep and asked me to sing him a song. I did.

Valicha, lisa p'asñaqa
Niñaschay deveras
Maypiraq kashanki

Sapanka achawasipis
Niñaschay deveras
Sarata kutasian

Cuartelpunku cuñapin
Niñaschay deveras
Maqt'ata suwasian

The lovely girl, Valicha
Really, girl
Where are you?

Over in the mill-house
Really, girl
You're grinding corn.

From the door of your room
Really, girl
You steal the hearts of young men.

He dozed off and I was about to close the shutters but decided to keep them open. Without changing into my nightgown, I went out to the smokehouse with a blanket and lay down beneath hanging racks of beef ribs. The wind came up but even beneath its gusts, I could hear her soft footfalls. I wanted badly to see her. I slid halfway out of the smokehouse, staying low to the ground, and there she came, half trotting, half floating, moving at a graceful speed, a nimbus of light around her. In she went through the door, which I'd left ajar. I knew I should stay right where I was, but my fears told me this might be my only chance to see her. I'd be careful and only peek for a moment. I had to know what these preparations were all about.

But would she smell me? Surely, the scent of the flowers, cheese and bread would keep her distracted. That and Marianito. Crouching, I ran to the window where I'd left the shutters open. She came in and sniffed the flowers on the table, the open bottle of fresh wine, and the cheese and bread I'd set out. She ate nothing, only imbibed the aroma of everything.

From there, Inés went to the bed where Marianito lay sleeping, and drew her ear close, seeming to enjoy the sound of his deep, regular breathing. She brought her lips close to his, and I thought she would kiss him, but no, she only wanted his scent in her nostrils.

Then it happened. With a sudden but prolonged shoooooof! her skin slid away from her body, revealing a beautiful young woman. Those deep brown eyes and lashes were now complemented by a human being with a sturdy, yet shapely and attractive figure. I couldn't help gasping, and her slender neck bent to turn her head toward the window just as I ducked down. After a long moment, I raised back up ever so slightly to where I could see. She was looking down at the boy with tenderness. Inés slid into bed beside Marianito. Pulling back the sheet and unbuttoning his pajama top with her newfound fingers as he lightly groaned, she inspected the pure skin of his chest. Also, she slid off the bottoms and drew her face close to his calves, knees, thighs, and his listless, small sex. I thought she was going to try to arouse him, but no, she simply slid his clothing back on while he remained in a profound slumber, and when he was dressed again, she snuggled up beside him, pulled the blanket over them both, and went to sleep.

I kept vigil as long as I could, entranced by the calfskin sloughed off on the bed beside them, as the candle burned down and guttered. However, I was startled awake on the ground in the white dawn, frost on my skin, shivering, the shutters above me now closed. I picked myself up and ran inside. Marianito was sitting up, rubbing his eyes. The calfskin was nowhere to be found. And Inés was gone.

40
GHAZAL OF THE BETRAYED WOMAN

Against the wall your laptop makes a crash,
    betrothed.
It's the last thing I have left to smash, betrothed.

I don't need any possessions, not now.
I should have sold them all for cash, beloved.

I picked splinters from my fingers—a dozen
And my own blood made my hands washed,
    betrothed.

Her messages, did they sound like poetry?
The ones you'd dragged into the trash, beloved?

All my unguents, perfume, the camisole
The oil in my hair, didn't make me lush,
    betrothed.

My small apocalypse means nothing—mere
    hysterics

When the world outside has crashed, beloved.

Wildfires raged up the coast, unchecked
Reducing our timber house to ash, betrothed.

I didn't torch it, though I fantasized enough.
Then it went up in a flash, beloved.

As if God almighty had been in on my plan
Her hands setting fire to each bush, betrothed.

A power in me has been unleashed—disturbed
I must be careful what I wish, beloved.

You'd loaded your clothes in the car, before.
As if knowing you might perish, betrothed.

We should have split right then, before you
      balked
But I didn't want to be selfish, beloved.

Instead, I hung your suits in our new closet
The ones my arms hugged and lips brushed,
      betrothed.

41
ZOMBIES

"Wake up!" Jasper was jerked to his feet by Inés's strong arm. "We've got to stop these bastards." She swooped up his pistol and pitched it to him. Out of coffin-size holes in the ground, harsh light flooding from the depths, burst hideous beings, flinging earth to all sides. Orbs of light swung from their wrists. Bloodshot eyes bulged from their skulls; lipless teeth leered. Their dark clothing was half-rotted, hanging off half-rotted flesh. Five, ten, fifteen, twenty, they advanced en masse. Fangs protruded from each side of their mouths, at least a foot long. Their tongues snaked out and retracted. Around them, eucalyptus trees swayed in a high wind, dead branches breaking off and flying up into the sky in the movement of small cyclones, as if the branches were corpses being claimed for the Rapture.

Jasper always knew something like this was going to happen. And it would occur just when things were starting to go well. Your girl wants you back, you have a new best friend, your half-sister is showing you love, you've actually got a posse, you half-own a hacienda that could turn into a business opportunity, and then some shit like this has to take place. "What do we do? Are these the ñak'aqs you told me about? The fat-suckers?"

"I've never actually seen one, but it looks like one to me. Shoot as many of their asses as you can."

"Are these magic bullets?"

"Standard issue. But we'll find out what they'll do."

Wind funneled in and out of open windows and spaces for missing roof tiles, setting up an eerie alarum, the groan of all the collective dead of centuries past, who had congregated here for the apocalypse. He knew he had brought them to this place. He never should have saved that laptop full of first chapters or referred to them as a graveyard. It was only tempting fate. He never should have written so much about death. Geeta had often told him he had a morbid streak and that he should stop obsessing about humans ceasing to exist at his comparatively young age. She read his story about the guy who takes his friend up to the mountains to die and simply shook her head, saying, "Who thinks up this stuff?" Vanessa at least understood him a little better, coming from that line of voodoo people, where the living and the dead are merely half a step apart, where the two existential states combine into a permanent liminal state, and that way, nothing takes you by surprise, this surfeit of underground dwellers, for instance.

Still more zombies burst out of the earth, to the point that he and Inés were surrounded by the hideous, reeking subhuman beings. He never should have written that cheeseball spec script for *Inca Armageddon*. His mom used to say, "Think something enough and it becomes real." No sooner had Jasper had that thought than Inca costumes, busy geometric fabric tunics, red capes, wide gold belts, spiffy sandals, feather headdresses, shields in hand, appeared on every single one of the living corpses. All of them! And the clothing was brand-new, as if out of a catalogue! No way. It wasn't fair for rotting flesh to be clothed in spanking new attire fit for a catwalk. But he had made it happen. Jasper always knew his mind was essentially powerful, except that he couldn't necessarily control its train of thought. Why, oh why, hadn't he left the laptop in the dumpster, where it belonged? Some things were meant to be buried and stay that way. You shouldn't exhume, especially, what was never truly alive, except in your own wishful fantasy.

Now the otherworldly Inca specters, gnashing their fangs, were closing in, but in classic fashion, half a step at a time, lurching, raising the possibility that maybe Inés and he could escape if they could just open a way in the dense circle of self-disinterring warriors.

"Hey! Any time, half-brother." The way she said *half,* which had sounded affectionate before, came off as disdainful. Okay, she was stressed out, obviously, don't take it personally, that was one of the four agreements.

"Can't you shoot first? You have more experience. I have a feeling you're a deadeye shot."

"My knowledge is theoretical. Give me a break. You're hanging around with a guy named Butch. You said he was taking you to a shooting range to practice."

"The targets were not zombies."

"A target is a target. It's not like they're moving that fast."

"Fast enough that if we keep talking, they're going to be on top of us in a couple of minutes. The problem, Inés, is that I'm afraid the first shot, while it might deter one of them, could provoke the other five hundred to rush us in a bunch and devour us."

"I'm willing to take that chance."

"So, shoot."

"Be a man, big brother. Your helpless little sister is asking you to take the lead."

"You don't look helpless. Anyway, this is a classic feminist moment where women show they don't need a man to resolve their situation."

"Feminism is overrated in certain situations."

"This is starting to sound like Cervantes's *Colloquy of the Dogs*."

"I love that story!"

"You've read it?"

"Like half a dozen times."

"That makes me happy, us having Cervantes in common. His short fiction is underrated."

"If you don't act soon, we'll have something else in common. We'll both be dead."

The collective groan of the long-defunct Inca warriors increased in volume, as if they were all praying to the evilest of their deities. "Okay, do you know that moment in *Butch Cassidy and the Sundance Kid,* where Joe Lefors has the two anti-heroes trapped on a mesa above the river, the posse is closing in, and Butch has to persuade Sundance to grab the other side of the gun belt he took off, and leap fifty feet to possible death, even though he doesn't know how to swim?"

"Yes, I'm a fan of that movie. But I think the better analogy is at the end when the entire Bolivian army has them surrounded and they run out together, guns blazing, and get riddled with bullets and die in a bloody blaze of glory."

"You're right. I was just trying to pick one in which they survived."

"Either scenario works for me."

Jasper had a sudden, unexpected pang of sadness, wishing that Butch Cassidy Kowalski Fischer could also have been at his side right then, to share this thematically powerful moment. In a sense, it's what they'd come for. But you don't always get to pick your 500 against 1 buddy. As soon as he had that thought, there was Butch, right next to him, cradling between his outstretched hands a Colt 1851 Navy Revolver. Jasper wasn't even sure how he even knew the name of that gun and could recognize it on sight, under extreme stress. Yet our minds are full of recondite facts that we read in passing and which meant nothing to us at the time, only trivia, only to resurface at their predestined moment. Predestined—that was the precise term for him and Vanessa. Not novelistic coincidence. And when his mind went to Vanessa, there she was too, in a cop crouch, holding steady a Smith & Wesson. Now the odds against the Inca warriors had doubled.

"Everybody ready?" There were grunts of approval. "Okay, on three. One. Two. Three!" He squeezed the trigger. The muzzles of the pistols flashed in the half-dark. Their reports echoed around the courtyard. Jasper got one warrior on the shoulder, another right below his headdress near the left temple. Inés and Butch were downing the interlopers like wooden ducks in a shooting gallery, with a ratio of one vanquished zombie per bullet. Vanessa, almost prim, took her sweet time to locate and aim, hitting each zombie only when it was up close and about to devour her. But she hit her mark, reloading calmly and squeezing off another one right in time. Jasper's shots were literally hit and miss, part of an insane, frenzied rhythm that he realized was highly theatrical, panicky, yet his very excess of movement and the wild yells and shouts he was giving off were proving a deterrent in themselves because all at once, the Incas, who numerically held the upper hand, had realized the bullets really were magic and their supposed superior strength had become useless.

But no, there was something more than that going on. A magnetic force seemed to draw them backward. Right when the zombies had opened a route of escape for the foursome, who were running low on bullets, a gigantic, vibrant whir commenced above them and the sky was flooded with blue-green radiance, as if the stars had collectively descended from heaven. Looking up, Jasper saw throbbing orbs, each thousands of times his size, descending over the hacienda's terrain. As they neared the ground, dozens of portals opened in each, round holes in a round orb, gauzy yet distinct. The Incas ran for them and as each approached, he was sucked inside, by ones, twos, threes, until not a single one of them remained, nor any spear or shield, only the oblong cavities from which they'd emerged from the ground. Yet those, too, like the portals, began to seal, until only a few dozen remained exposed, surrounded by patches of flung dirt, like scars that had been ripped open.

The giant orbs rose in concert, perfectly equidistant from one another, looking like turquoise suns and they ascended high, in an aligned, coordinated, almost balletic move, putting distance between themselves and the ground, until they vanished beyond the sky, no longer even pinpoints of light. Their electrical hum had subsided. Instead, Jasper heard a cock crowing to announce pale streaks of dawn and a light chill. He let his pistol drop to his side as darkness closed over him.

"Jasper!" He opened his eyes and looked up. Over his body, which leaned against an adobe wall, his sleeping bag tossed off to one side, stood Inés, Butch, and Vanessa, all with looks of concern on their faces.

"Hey. I must have drifted off. Did I dream all that shit? Please don't tell me I was only having a long and complicated nightmare."

"I don't know what you're talking about," said Inés. "You've only been out for about thirty seconds. You fainted."

"So, I was up and around?"

"That's an understatement," said Butch. "Your gun was blazing. You must have got off fifteen rounds. I was afraid you got hit."

"What about the rest of you? Were you hit?"

"No. You winged one and the rest ran straight off. Then I grabbed your gun."

"I hit several. Not as many as you all. But I don't know, maybe ten? Twelve?"

"What are you talking about?"

"Among the four of us, we must have fired a couple hundred rounds."

"We don't have arms," said Vanessa. "I don't even know how to hold one. I'd probably shoot myself by accident."

"I didn't bring one," added Butch. "Customs and all that. Wish I had one just now, because I would have popped off a few."

"Better you didn't," said Inés. "I don't want you in jail. If anybody asks, which I don't think they will, because there were no witnesses and no deaths, we're just going to say I'm the one who winged that guy. I'm a citizen here and most I'd get would be a suspended sentence. But probably not even that, because it was clearly property invasion with criminal intent."

"Damn right," said Jasper, getting to his feet. "There were hundreds of them."

"Uh, hoss," corrected Butch. "I think you must have bumped your head. There were only four of them, same as us. We might have plain old scared them off, but you rolled over and grabbed that pistol when you saw that one of them was carrying a gun and you played it smart, grazing him with a bullet to impair his shooting arm. Classic move. I'm impressed at your marksmanship. They dropped the stuff they were stealing and that was that."

"Where did you two come from?"

"We showed up in the middle of the night. We didn't want to be left out of the party, so we gave you all the time to hang out, and we joined you at about three a.m. You don't remember?"

"No. Inés, was that weed we smoked strong?"

"Definitely. I was tripping for a couple of hours. Statues wearing high heels, like John Fogerty once said."

"That explains it."

"Why? What did you hallucinate?"

"Never mind. Let's just say it was the climactic scene of a television series that never got made. But what were they stealing?"

"Inca pottery. I'd seen some guys lurking other times I was out here. They were surveying the property. Grave robbers, as it turns out. Funeral pottery, probably Inca. The pieces they had dug up before we caught them in the act are intact." She held up a gourd-shaped vessel with a handle on each side. "Happy hour pitcher."

"I knew it! My vision wasn't for nothing. It's like in a Steven Spielberg movie, where you build a suburban house on sacred ground, and all of a sudden thousands of malevolent spirits come rushing out of the ground in a vindictive mood."

"If you say so."

"That's what I left out of that script."

"Oh, yeah, *Poltergeist*!" said Vanessa. "I saw that as a kid. Only in that one, the developers moved the graves somewhere else. In New Orleans, the graves only get moved by a flood. Otherwise, you can't mess with that shit. Dangerous."

"What does this mean for our rebuild? I mean, the hacienda house is already here. We're only bringing it back up to code."

"Probably," said Inés, "the government is going to take this land off our hands at a hefty price. It's part of the national patrimony now. They've been trying to buy land from the owners up at Sacsayhuaman for years, but those farmers won't sell. They keep upping the price. They could declare eminent domain, maybe, but they don't work that way, because they don't want political backlash. It's a sensitive issue. But I recommend we entertain offers. What say you, brother? This hacienda isn't sentimental to me because I didn't know it existed until recently. I'd rather see them excavate the ruins properly. And we can always buy something new, if we still want that cooperative, and we wouldn't have to rebuild it."

"I'm fine with that. I'm just glad we survived the Inca Armageddon."

42

ANTUKA STARTS HER DAY

She drags the totora reed boat to the bank. Nobody is there but her. There used to be at least a dozen fishermen knee-deep, pushing off to fish. But no more. The shore is littered with dead frogs, discarded paint buckets and bags of soggy trash. In the water are toxic levels of lead and mercury. This she knows from the scientists who come around with questionnaires, the way José used to. He tried everything he could to get the government to listen. Most of his trips were to Lima to talk to politicians, or the designates of the NGOs, whom he would bring to Puno and Juliaca to tour the vicinity, to translate in and out of Quechua so that they could speak with regular people, people like her, about the problems of water pollution.

José wasn't off with other women. She knew that in her heart. If eventually he drifted away, it was because he couldn't stand to watch this world degrade. He found funds to go to the United States, Germany, Sweden, to give lectures to concerned progressive environmental groups and skeptical government committees. Once in a while, he would get excited, telling Antuka that they were talking about building a purification plant, but for one reason or another, it would always fall through and she would have to listen to his angry tirades, not directed at her, but to the system that underlay everything. She knew he wasn't mad at her; it was nothing personal, she was just the final set of ears. It was difficult for her to say to him that she didn't understand a lot of what he was talking about, especially since he himself wasn't always sure. He would blame the right, then the left, then the progressives, then moderates, then the state, then the people themselves.

Many times, she wanted to take him by the shoulders, make him stop talking, and say, *just take me away from here. Take me to Sweden. Take me to Germany or Los Angeles. Or Lima, even. I don't have the answers you want. I don't have some deep indigenous wisdom, some magic proverb that will unlock the mysteries of the gods and show you a path you haven't thought of. Probably I won't learn the language of whichever country you choose, not well anyway, and if you take this lake away from me, I'll simply be an ignorant migrant peasant woman, one of those who stays in her house and doesn't talk to anybody, who keeps the house clean and prepares the food, wondering when you'll get home so she'll have somebody to talk to, somebody who cares about her and at least has been to where she was born and has some common points of reference. But then in a way, I'm already that person, you made me that way, waiting around for you to come, neglecting my friends, no longer content to sit around and talk gossip, because a man from a bigger world singled me out, lifted me up, made me think I was better than them, so that I withdrew and got a reputation as standoffish, I was the object of gossip, the more so as you were a married man and on top of that, married to a white woman.*

I loved you, I really did. I took you back whenever you chose to show up, with whatever excuse, no matter that the neighbors had inflamed my heart with stories of your conquests, tales that I could neither prove nor disprove. But you made me into somebody small, illicit, not like these mestizas in Puno who take up a man and drop him and get another one, laughing the whole while, then they go to their jobs in the shops or the factory boasting about their conquests. They found a way to make themselves the heroine of the story, bragging about how much money they got from this or that one, and a good time in the sack too, and nobody seems to care whether those men are married or single, white or Indian. They're just marks and when the girls finally settled down with a regular, single, local man, there was a pact of silence among all their girlfriends and kin; as far as they're concerned, their niece is still a virgin, and they go on to have children and show up at church every Sunday, where the priest gives them a wink as they go in, and later at the altar serves them communion.

But me, I came too soon for that. I was the black sheep, the bad woman, the scapegrace. The natural and supernatural worlds came down on my head. Even my own daughter disparaged me.

Noqa pobreqa
Mana taytayoa
Mana mamayoq
Mana Piniyoq

I'm a poor soul
I have no father
I have no mother
I don't have anybody.

Untreated sewage water drains from two dozen nearby

cities and illegal gold mines high in the Andes dump up to
15 tons of mercury a year into a river leading to the lake.
Hypodermic needles, tires, old shoes and used diapers are
scattered among the potato fields that line the shores. She
sees them all the time when she goes for walks. Scientists
who came found mercury, cadmium, zinc and copper in the
fish and warped cells. The green totora reeds and camou-
flage-colored Titicaca water frogs she once spotted in abundance have thinned in numbers. When she washes a blouse
with the lake's water, it turns green, and if she heats the
water to make mate, it tastes salty and bitter. When there
isn't rain, she rows a boat ten kilometers out from the shore
and gathers water in barrels. That's where she's headed
now. The water deeper in Lake Titicaca is cleaner than what
she can collect from the banks and can be used to cook,
bathe and drink after being boiled. With one foot, she steps
into the squishy mud at the water's entry, and with the
other foot, pushes off, swinging her hip to settle herself in
the narrow reed boat as the barrels clank against one
another.

43
THE RED SAIL

Baron Marcel de Gitaine, Lyon aristocrat and heir to a Javanese rubber plantation, planned to windsurf 100 miles across the Taiwan Strait separating China and Taiwan to carry forbidden messages from rebels whose every communication was being tracked. He was no stranger to peril. He'd blasted across gelid whitecaps in the Bering Sea, landing in Siberia, official Soviets none the wiser. Night had been his friend in evading military ships trolling to catch him active in the South Pacific. All else he carried on his person was a canister of green tea, a drink that kept him alert and hydrated and gave him comfort. His Taiwanese wet nurse used to feed him green tea from her patient nipple as an infant to keep the sleepy baby awake longer, so she could contemplate his intense green eyes.

In a way, it was she who had made him into the hyper-aware athlete and adventurer he'd become. In his journey windsurfing from the Marquesas Islands to Tahiti, which was supposed to take less than a week, he'd fought off sharks, chapped his hands to blisters, and surface-burned his retinas. No matter.

But crossing the China Sea, he vanished. For ten days, American airmen searched from above, while ships did the same on the sea. The Chinese, too, helped in the search, lest there be any stain on their reputation. While they didn't approve of the Baron, they hadn't done anything to impede him. Taiwanese went from town to town, hoping to catch sight of him drinking green tea in a village café. An absence of storms gave them hope, though the wind gusting up to 41 miles per hour made others think he'd slipped from his board and been unable to grasp it again. Had he gone off course and drifted south, he'd have found himself in pirate-ridden seas.

His red sail should have been easy to spot in the dark-hued China Sea. But no one could find the Baron, a man who'd never strayed from the moral path in life and had always found his way back along a physical one of his making. His rectitude had been his flag. He'd never taken on a mistress; never inherited the rubber plantation, so he could not be accused of having exploited the workers. On the contrary, the Javanese plantation workers created an oral tradition in which they imagined the more just treatment they would have received at the hands of this unfindable son. To the extent they spoke, there came into being a movement to make the plantation a cooperative.

The workers set out to unionize. Gun thugs were brought in. Workers got shot. But that very violence against the self-named and extralegal Baron Marcel de Gitaine Syndicate forced the father to enfranchise the workers, raising their pay and living conditions and even introducing profit-sharing. In Taiwan, in oblique protest of China's imperiousness as a state, carved wooden statues of Gitaine, the Liberator, began to dot the Taiwanese coast, creating the strange spectacle of a man in search of himself.

It was said that a secret society was formed to venerate him, in the manner of a cargo cult. Native windsurfers insolently crossed the Taiwan Strait from both sides, though the activity was now banned, in order to strike up friendships with those men on the other. They discovered they weren't different at all in their hopes and dreams. A windsurfing contest was founded in the Baron's honor, as if the organizers half-hoped he had merely been keeping a low profile and might come back to participate in it. When he didn't show, they began to call him The Martyr.

The disappeared Baron's wife was troubled. She couldn't really grieve, since there was no corpse and since many people still believed him to be alive, if lost. The governments, all of them, refused to categorize him as dead. The Baroness at first tried to answer the increasingly voluminous mail she received, venerating her husband, or ex-husband, whichever he was, in prose verging on nominating him for sainthood. It wasn't that she had bad memories with which to refute their hyperbole. Always he'd treated her gently and kindly, if somewhat absently. He was so busy windsurfing, climbing mountains, and kayaking through deep and dangerous canyons, never considering that she might become a sudden widow, that there was no time for husband and wife to argue, unless it were for her to put her foot down and demand that he stay home.

After a while, the Baroness ceased to answer the letters. She couldn't sleep, no matter how much brandy and warm milk she drank. At last, one night, while the cuckoo clock chimed three a.m., Baron Marcel de Gitaine appeared, sitting on the hearth as if on a shelf of surfside rock. He looked diminished or perhaps merely dehydrated. He must have peeled off his wetsuit, for he sat pale and naked before his spouse. His body was beautiful, and she wished she'd been able to partake of it more freely and more often. Instead, she now had to share what remained of him, his distorted memory, with thousands of people. She realized the Baron wasn't recently lost to her. Rather, he'd never been hers. The situation of their marriage was no different than if he'd been lying, like the other Barons, in the beds of many mistresses, each of whom would take a piece of him from the Baroness.

Though he offered her an indulgent smile, as if to say, "I'm dead. Don't be angry," she waved him away with a dismissive gesture and he faded like a log that has burned to embers and finally dissolves into ash. She fell fast asleep, experiencing the first good night's rest since he'd disappeared.

When the clock struck four, a woman on the verge of old age awoke in another French town. Smiling, she suddenly thought of the Baron, whom she'd once nursed at her breast, until she'd put her nipple away and fed him green tea instead. Making the sign of the cross and glancing at the image of Saint Christopher on her nightstand, she accepted responsibility for his fascinating, short life, his inspirational impact on many, and his sudden, brutal death after he'd drifted far from help and slipped unconscious from his board to vanish into the sea.

44
AYAR MANCO AND MAMA OQLLO

In the lands near Lake Titicaca, men lived in a wild way, without laws to order their savage lives, naked in caves, feeding on raw meat and wild plants, without justice and without an established religion that would let them develop as a society.

The Sun God felt sorry for the life they were leading and sent his son, Ayar Manco, whom he charged to found the empire of the Incas, accompanied by his wife Mama Oqllo. He and she walked straight out of the pure waters of Lake Titicaca, the highest navigable lake in the world, whose name means "stone puma."

Ayar Manco received a golden rod from his father, the Sun God, with the mission of heading north and wherever they eventually stopped, he had to drive this golden rod into the ground. The place where it sank into the earth would become the site chosen to create the Inca empire. After they traveled several places, they reached a majestic valley surrounded by imposing mountains and climbing to Huanacauri Peak. There Manco sank the rod, naming that place as the center of the universe, Cusco, the navel of the world. The upper part was Hanan; the lower, Hurin.

Ayar Manco was rewarded with the name of Manco Capac, who was put in charge of teaching men useful tasks such as farming, fishing, science, religion, hunting, livestock and construction of stone-based dwellings. Mama Oqllo was in charge of teaching women weaving to provide clothing for the entire town, cooking so their people could stop eating raw meat, and caring for the home. In this way, they could live clean and unadulterated lives and luxuriate in the prosperity they had created all of which had its origins in the deep blue waters of that enchanted and crystalline lake.

Manco Capac, accompanied by Mama Oqllo, assumed the throne of the Inca Empire. From their powerful loins issued the world of today.

45
THE BLACK VIRGIN

Vanessa fell through the sky, her face the head of a comet. She could see the Andes Mountains from above, its impressive length and the many contours, its streams of water flowing from the peaks to irrigate plots of the sacred valleys, and a vast wooded reserve, where vicuñas took shelter. The marine stratocumulus clouds parted to give her a better view as she drew nearer Earth. The deeper waters of the Pacific had been pulled to the surface to cool the air above, prevailing winds pushing them inward, the water vapor then condensing into droplets and forming into clouds. The mountain ranges blocked these low-lying clouds, letting them form into dense banks.

The bus the foursome had taken, eschewing the luxury train because Butch wanted to "get down and dirty with the native scene," had a flat. It would seem a simple matter, but the tire had been repaired so many times that it had essentially become a tire made of other tires, resistant to a patch of any kind. You'd think there would have been a spare, but no, because that spare, as it turns out, was used to replace another dead tire made entirely of patches, and the bus company had never replaced it. They were stuck in a spot in the road where there was exactly one wayside restaurant and not much else. The bus had limped there, otherwise they would have been nowhere and would have had to sit in the bus for hours.

Supposedly somebody was going somewhere for a tire, but the driver seemed not to be in a particular hurry. Instead, he and the restaurant's owner were off in a corner doing a slow-quaff of a quart of beer, then another. Possibly if he kept on this way, he'd have to sleep it off and the passengers would spend the night there, though there would be nowhere to sleep except slightly reclined in the bus seats. Or else the co-pilot, who had been sent on the errand for the mystery tire, this was announced to inspire confidence, would perhaps take over the wheel if the regular driver was too tipsy.

The foursome had managed to snag one of the tables on the porch. It had its disadvantages, in that a heavy downpour had begun, monsoon-style, almost eclipsing the soft green mossy hills that rolled up into steep walls on either side of the valley, creating the sense of being in a self-contained world. Trinket sellers had congregated around the outside tables, trying to sell to the trapped tourists, but had eventually given up and now sat bored, except for a resourceful young indigenous man who went around practicing his English with everybody.

Several dogs had also taken shelter under the tables, inside and out, as if the occupants were their masters. One woman, who had obviously shampooed and blow-dried her llama, was trying to keep its beautiful coif out of the rain, with mixed success. Dressed in a traditional costume of vivid red and contrasting black, the hat on her head, sewn with little mirrors and yellow embroidery, worthy of a centerpiece, she was passive-aggressively trying to get people to take pictures with her and the compliant llama for an unspecified amount of money, before its hairdo wilted due to the radical change in humidity.

Vanessa was situated at the very corner of the veran-dah, right next to a noisy gutter pipe that sounded like a thirsty man just returned from the desert guzzling from a jug. Its flume plashed at the base, sending rainwater bouncing in all directions. The low but steady wind, punc-tuated by gusts, did its best to send draughts of light spray over Vanessa. Jasper offered several times to change places with her, to leave her less exposed, or to drag the entire table further in, at the risk of crowding neighbors, to keep her dry. But Vanessa had bought an alpaca poncho, the tight weave of which repelled the rain, leaving only her weave and face exposed. Granted, she had carefully applied makeup before the trip and refreshed her weave just so, to be worthy of her encounter with all passersby and fellow passengers.

Yet somehow, she had become the rain. Its spray on her face reminded her that humans are mostly made of water, and she wouldn't have been surprised if she had simply dissolved into a puddle and gone spilling out among the liquid gushing from the rain pipe, or ascended to the clouds, a surprising Black Virgin among the Quechuas. The female sellers of trinkets and the woman with the permed llama would pick up the rosaries hanging from their necks and begin to murmur beautiful words in their native language, could be the Ave Maria, the one she herself had said countless times at mass, in fact she had a rosary on beneath her poncho, one she often wore as a good luck charm and also for express prayers, the ones you need to get off in a hurry, whether it's praying that your old-new boyfriend would have a successful encounter with his not-mother childhood fetish, or that the co-pilot would successfully get back with an actual tire made of solid galvanized rubber.

Perhaps she would ascend, voodoo goddess queen among the Inca-Catholics. They would understand her, living daily among that strange admixture of Catholicism and their own ancient religion, as she existed in that liminal space between the African gods and the Christian ones. They would adore her, briefly, as she rose, the firm contours of her body beginning to loosen, expand, turning first to water, then to mist, a holy cloud, spreading wider and wider, pouring her blessing over all the stranded passengers, native and foreign, including Butch and Inés, who sat huddled together under a big rough brown blanket that he had brought along.

Obviously, they had spent last night together at the hotel. She'd even seen Inés slip out of his room at 6 a.m. when Vanessa had gone downstairs for some mate de coca in the lobby and the two women had pretended not to see one another. Inés looked simultaneously startled and happy. Sharing the blanket was their way of announcing a provisional coupledom without actually saying anything about it. Jasper seemed okay with it, or else he was simply mono-focused on getting to Lake Titicaca. Maybe Inés was nervous too about getting back to her mother, and Butch provided a literally enormous shield.

In her mind, Vanessa formed the Yoruba prayer to Shango, who had guided so many through heavy vicissitudes.

Baba Shango, ikawo ilemu funi alaya
    tilanachani nitosi
Ki ko gbamu ni re oro niglati ibinu ki kigbo ni
    na orin

She prayed to the god of thunder, many words, murmuring under her breath, for the protection of all. Yes, she wanted to dissolve into a wayfaring storm, moving into the midst of the huge electrical storm in the sky, without fear of death or harm. A sudden memory came of a close friend of the family, one of those uncles who isn't really an uncle, a man of hearty laughter, prone to bringing small gifts to the house for her and her parents, a man who when left to babysit her—after months of patiently gaining everyone's trust, including hers—did the predictable thing, the disappointing thing, undressing her at bedtime, down to the panties, then removing those as well, kissing her skin tenderly, stroking her hair, calling her beautiful over and over as she lay immobile, waiting for the moment to pass. It did pass, she said nothing, he was not discovered or banished from the family, his jovial laughter continued to fill the house, his thoughtful little presents, but yes, he got cancer soon after and died within six months. She hated to admit it, but Shango probably had something to do with that, but not on her account.

Her mother cried over the loss of a good man on the earth. Vanessa had never wished the man ill, not even in her prayers. She was afraid to, because she knew that prayers were powerful and really did make things happen, so you had to be careful what you wished for. But some part of her felt that Shango or Jesus, or maybe both, had made a pact, as they seemed to do, to get rid of this man. For a while, she felt bad. When the news of his death was announced, she cried tears of relief, tears that felt as big as this Andean storm in which she was enmeshed, and her mother thought it was because she was so sensitive and compassionate and as so often, Vanessa didn't correct her because she was so busy being a good girl.

Now that suppressed rage rose up within her like a gigantic thunderhead, at last ready to be released, all because of a flat tire, and she was afraid, given that she had temporarily become the rain, that the ferocity and sheer mass of her would bring down a series of lightning strikes on this humble restaurant, killing every last person on the verandah, including those she loved.

"Vanessa, honey, what's wrong?" Jasper drew close, putting his arm around her and immediately getting it soaked, as it protruded just past the safety zone provided by the eaves. She was crying her heart out, it felt almost literally as though her heart was leaving her body. She wanted to thrust Jasper away, out of shame that she, too, kept secrets, failed to trust, and she was going to have to get over that shit or it was going to turn into a tumor inside her, so instead she opened her poncho, spread her arms out beneath it and drew him toward her, closer to her body, closer to the rain, as the storm settled into a quieter phase. She could tell that within a few minutes, it would exhaust itself and the man with the tire would return.

"We have to get this all figured out," said Vanessa.

"We will," answered Jasper. "But what, specifically?"

"This isn't a game. We're not just a bunch of tourists on a jaunt."

"What she said," agreed Butch.

Inés was taking Vanessa's measure with her eyes, as if her own fate would be decided in this moment. Yet she added nothing, only preserved the wary expression on her face, the way one carries a pot of boiling water filled to the brim across the floor.

"We are two couples. Let's get that straight. Doesn't matter how or why we got together. Jasper, I'm sorry I passed you off to somebody else. It was execrable."

"I don't care about that, honey."

"Yes! You should care. You just don't do that to somebody. And I want to say it in front of these two witnesses. Our lives are fragile."

"Okay, okay."

"Don't say okay! I'm telling you it's not okay. There are things I should have said to you back then, tendencies that worried me, exasperated me, but I chose never to deal with them. I made you into an eccentric in my mind. In some way, I almost feel responsible for all that money you lost. I left you unattended. Nothing against Geeta, but she doesn't get you. I love you and I get you, that crazy, prolific mind of yours, which can reach the greatest heights if you're supported in the right way. And me too, I want that from you. I'm sick of being a lab researcher. I might as well be a lab rat. I've got to break out of myself. Thank God we came here, so I could start to put things in perspective. I've been living a perfectly wholesome life, by which I mean an early death. And you two, Butch and Inés—there's a connection between you, nobody knows exactly what it is at this point, or understands it, but it was instant, and it might be eternal. I don't want this moment to just pass, like they do sometimes, and we're looking back in ten years and we say, 'Everything was decided on that big sagging porch in the rain, with the warm Coca-Colas that taste different than in the States, I guess it's the water or maybe they just put more sugar in it, but the taste is unique, and the soup that was served lukewarm with too many noodles and not enough chicken, I guess to make it stretch, but weirdly it was satisfying to my soul.'"

Her voice had risen as she spoke, and general applause broke out on the verandah. At the next table, a white man gave her one of those power fists with an upraised arm, ill-advised maybe, but she knew what he meant and she gave him a nod of recognition.

"Still waters," said Inés, reaching for Vanessa's hand. Vanessa had to throw back her poncho to free her arms. They clasped palms, not really knowing what they were agreeing to, but in some way sealing a pact, as warriors do before an impending battle. The rain had indeed quieted, become intermittent and everybody's voices in their own conversations suddenly dropped in volume, because the assembled all at once realized they'd been speaking really loudly over the downpour on the tin roof, as if they were all hard of hearing.

As the tempest finally slacked off to a mere drizzle, the co-pilot returned on foot, holding over his head a tire, by main strength, beaming, as if he had cut off the head of a dragon and were bringing it to a queen as a trophy. The group, already warmed to applause by Vanessa's speech, gave him a standing ovation, possibly the first one of his life. No one knew where he'd secured the fresh, beautiful, unblemished tire, and no one wanted to know. They'd rather let the mystery abide. Soon the passengers paid their bills and filed aboard, ready to face with resolve the many literal bumps in the road ahead, and quite possibly the metaphorical ones as well.

46
LILY

When Butch asked Inés to his hotel room late at night, she assumed they were going to make love. She'd broken up with a girlfriend several weeks before and hadn't had any physical affection since. Inés had been too low in spirits to hook up with someone, which really wasn't her preferred style anyway. She couldn't go home with a semi-anonymous somebody from a club, not anymore. Some days, she had fantasies about moving to Iceland with a snow princess into one of those structures where the walls were all made of glass to let in the sunlight, and you looked out onto a fjord as you sipped your morning cappuccino. But that fantasy vanished as quickly as an icicle in the summer sun.

Other days, the dream was of marriage and children, although it was hard to see herself as any kind of traditional wife, even though she did love to cook for people at the parties she sometimes gave and watch smiles spread over their faces as their mouths discovered her extra spicy ají de gallina. But Butch, she could feel his essential kindness; she'd watched his expressions when he did ayahuasca, and at that moment, she would easily settle for being wrapped in his furry bear arms forever. Once, not so long ago, she hadn't been afraid to express the full range of her emotions, but something had wormed its way into her confidence, and she suddenly found herself utterly alone in the midst of her friends as they continued to party after their full days taking care of tourists, their faces dark from long hours in the sun giving mountain bike tours or traipsing around the Pisaq ruins for the millionth time, explaining a combination of fact and conjecture about the probable origins and use of the archeological sites.

It was hard not to give in to the tourists' desire for exotic explanations that had to do with astrology or human sacrifice, and just say instead, "No, this was probably a bowl they used to wash their faces in, just like you at your sink. The esoteric tourists were the worst, always asking if she was a shaman, wanting her to be a facilitator to their inner traumas, to release their pent-up souls with her authentic ethnicity, as if she were somehow closer to the earth, when in fact, she was more of a rock chick who happened to be born looking like an original settler, in spite of her white-adjacent father. She inherited so many of her mother's genes that she sometimes wondered whether José really was her father. Genetics was chancy and you just came out however you came out.

When Butch invited her to sit on his bed, she wanted to take all of him right then, imbibe his physical force, rut like a bull and a heifer. However, that's not what he had in mind. He played her Mark Knopfler's "Speedway at Nazareth" on his phone, which admittedly evolved into one of the most remarkable guitar solos she'd ever heard. First, he asked her about herself, like a gentleman. When she made it clear she wasn't in much of a conversational mood, he began to talk about a dog he'd adopted. When she asked what breed, he said, "She was all of them. I liked that about her."

He'd found her when he went to a pet store where the local shelters featured adoptable pets. However, he arrived late, and they'd already loaded all the pets in their kennels into the big truck in stacks. Butch requested permission to peruse the truck and the driver said, "Okay, but make it quick." Soon, he spotted a pair of brown eyes at the very back—the eyes were all he could see and they were sad. He asked to squeeze back through the narrow lane between the cages and examine her. She was so thin that all her ribs showed. Her fur, yellow-gold, was scraggly and scruffy, like his beard when he tried to grow one. She had long legs like a cat. Her tag said Lily, and he liked it that someone, at least for a moment, had compared her to a flower because she was beautiful to him. "I'll take her," he said. He had to go to a shelter the next day to claim her, one of those independent ones way out in the desert where the owner was a leathery, lanky broad, with the skin of a chain smoker and a lit cig in her hand, tattoos that felt like last-minute decisions, who probably lost her marriage because she couldn't stop adopting pets, so the husband gave her an ultimatum, "them or me," and suddenly found himself on the outside.

She took Butch into the enclosure with dozens of dogs exercising and he spotted Lily, off to one side, among the many milling mutts. The owner of the shelter told him she'd been found in a feral cat trap, stuck, emaciated, obviously turned out onto the street and wandering around for days. "So she's tough," he said. "I like that." He held out his arms so she would run to him and when she didn't, he went to her and held her in his massive arms like a baby and though nervous, she let him. She peed on him a little but he didn't care. They filled out the paperwork, he paid the fee and took her home to his apartment.

They'd had many adventures together. She got used to hopping in the back of his Jeep as soon as he opened the hatch, knowing they were going fly fishing, hiking to the top of a snowy mountain, off-roading in the desert with her bouncing around, sitting in the front of his canoe while he steered the two of them down Class Two and Three river rapids. Or just sitting at his feet in one the outdoor cafes that allowed dogs while he quaffed a beer, or two, or three, feeding her bread and bits of burger under the table, only not too much, because he worried about her cholesterol. He'd hoped he could train her to be a bird dog. She never quite took to it, running after the bird and sniffing, but never fetching it back to him. But that was alright. Not everybody had bird-dog built into them.

He had her for ten years. Girlfriends came and went, some of whom took to Lily and her shy, skittish ways; others who felt he devoted too much attention to the dog. The second ones didn't last. Meanwhile, Lily grew older until one day, she began to cough out of nowhere. He took her to the vet and was told she was in stage six, end of life, due to an enlarged heart. Butch argued with the veterinarian that she must be mistaken. They put her on multiple medicines, including Lasix, to draw the fluid from her heart. But a few days later, after eighteen hours of body-racking coughs, she passed in her sleep. For weeks, Butch's world felt dull. He lost weight and couldn't focus on anything. He smoked cigarettes without enjoyment. Nor did he even taste them. He couldn't touch weed because it made him break out in crying fits that he couldn't control.

It was right then that he was approached about turning his car mechanic shop into a fence for stolen vehicles. It wasn't really greed that made him do it. He just didn't care. All morality seemed pointless to him right then. Knowing that all creatures are mortal didn't lessen his sense of rage at the injustice of losing Lily, the best dog who had ever walked the earth, so suddenly. That dog had always walked to the right side of him and one step behind; that was her way, and after her departure, he couldn't shake the phantom feeling she was still there. He turned his head a hundred times to see her slightly wary look and how her eyes would soften when she met the eyes of her master. Then she vanished. They gave him a bag of ashes, and he hiked up to the Aztec Cave to scatter them. He had forgotten to write a eulogy, so he made up some bullshit, he couldn't even remember the words he said, but it all boiled down to the fact that she was the best goddamned pooch ever and could run faster than wind off a lake when she wanted to. If she'd had her way, she would have spent about twelve hours a day just running, just because.

47
A CLOSE ENCOUNTER

After telling Inés about his dog, Butch fell into a profound slumber, one where he was shooting ducks out of the sky, somewhere with purple-tinged clouds, it looked a lot like Montana, and for once, Lily was fetching them, bringing them back in her mouth and dropping them at his feet. He awoke with a start, disoriented, sitting up and finally realized that Inés had left the door of his hotel ajar and light was shining through from the hallway. A figure loomed in the doorway, its silhouette looking more like an animal, something with four legs anyway, slender almost like a faun and he wondered whether he'd been in a dream within a dream and now this was the dream closer to the surface, or who knows, he could still be five or six dreams deep. Possibly, he was having an ayahuasca flashback from some residue in his bloodstream. Except he did remember the ticking of the windup old-fashioned clock sitting on the nightstand, a little bit off the beat, like somebody with a heart arrhythmia.

The door to the hallway closed. There was a loud

shoooooffff! and something heavy fell to the floor. It was like the big brown blanket with which he'd covered Inés, or a heavy overcoat. The figure slipped into bed with him and he was about to grab it and wrestle, wring its neck if necessary, but he detected Inés's pleasant scent, but muskier, as if she were aroused, and she was sniffing him also, gently, as if he were a field of clover, nuzzling him gently with her nose, then came soft kisses from her lips, on his chest, belly, everywhere. Butch lay still, naked, the way he almost always slept, even on cold nights because his body was a natural furnace, hoping this wasn't a dream but instead the weirdness of reality.

He felt a deep thrill in his body as she climbed on top of him and as she found his sex and guided it into her. She leaned forward so their naked chests were touching and whispered into his ear, "I'm not a human." Butch had no idea what Inés meant by that, but the truth was, he didn't really care at this point.

"It's okay," he answered. "Sometimes I wonder about myself." Inés had a nimbus around her. Literally, she was casting her own aura of light. Within it, he could see her face was more beautiful than ever, the skin pure, flawless, her prominent cheeks, deep-set eyes and strong brow noble, eternal. Her waist was more slender than he would have imagined with the loose-fitting clothes she tended to wear, the boxy shirts and ripstop pants. Yet his hands palpated the sheer bunched muscle of her torso. She felt powerful to him. Her open excitement made him more excited, which brought her to a keener pitch, and so they continued pushing each other into a fervid, guttural clench, lovers as wrestlers. He heard him telling her he loved her and she echoed his words back. He called her his little colt, and she whispered into his ear again, with a chuckle,

"You're close." At which point he hollered, "I am close, and I hope you are too, little bit!" And he came. And guess what? So did she, right behind.

They lay laughing together, thoroughly sweaty, the sheets ruined. He reached with the free arm she wasn't lying on to click on the night-table lamp and see her better, to ensure that what was happening was real and he wasn't inside a dream within a dream. Sure enough, there was Inés, now quiet, taking in the enormity of him. "You're a beast," she said, tenderly. "A good beast. I like that about you."

"Listen, darlin'. I had a condom in my luggage. Not that I was bird-dogging you. But it's responsible to have one on your person, because you never know."

"You never do. But you don't have to worry. I've had two spontaneous abortions. I'm so fertile that it breaks through the pill, but then my body doesn't want to carry it to term. I think I'm cursed. Nature doesn't want creatures like me to propagate."

"Don't say that. You just haven't had a man with a seed as strong as mine."

"Cocky."

"Damn right. We'll break that curse. I don't know about your Quechua gods and all that, but I reckon they're about the same as the Christian ones, meaning they want us to go around all afraid and shameful."

"Maybe. We do worship Jesus too—not me, but the rest. I'm so messed up, because I say I'm an atheist, but I only believe in the punishment part, not the salvation."

"That's got to change. I want to marry you."

"Butch, it's way too soon to be talking about anything like that. You're carried away because I just gave you a tasty treat. It's sex endorphins, that's all."

"Possible. But I know my mind. I've done things I'm not proud of and I want to get shed of all that. One way or another, I'm going to sell my businesses. I got nothing keeping me in the U.S. of A. I need to enroll in one of those Spanish academies and learn to speak your language. Who knows, maybe you'll teach me some of that Indian talk too. You know, the love words and the cuss words at least."

"We'll see. But you need to get some sleep first. I rudely awakened you in the middle of the night." No sooner than Inés said the words than Butch fell into a deep slumber, as an enchanted person does. When he awoke, the light coming through the half-open curtains told him morning had broken. He was powerful and hungry. Felt like he could eat a horse. As he slid off the bed, he glanced down to see whether Inés had left that long wool overcoat she'd dropped on the floor, but it was gone, along with her.

48

IN THE CAMPO SANTO

The city of Puno was an endless succession of adobe houses with tin roofs set on undulations. In one of those anonymous-looking dwellings was the house of Antuka. Jasper had a slip of paper in his pocket, hotel stationery on which he'd written her address. She'd changed residences at some point over these years—maybe many times, for all he knew. It was in town; that he knew from Googling it, which meant she was no longer raising cows and chickens. Had she remarried? Did she have other children besides him and Inés? Inés claimed not to have seen her in "many years," yet she was young, so what did that mean? Inés didn't really want to talk about the particulars of either a dead father or an estranged mother, but she had found out soon enough this address, only because Jasper had asked her to get it. And she came along with Jasper without making him plead. Now he was stalling for time, for both of them.

He stalled by finding a restaurant, picking one at random, for they all seemed about the same. Puno had no distinctive charm he couldn't identify at first except the familiarity of its apple-cheeked people, who went about their business of carrying burlap bags around on the backs of modified motorcycles or lumber on the tops of cars, giving an impression of an industrious people, except everybody looked poor, exactly as he remembered. They hadn't come during the festive time, so nobody was wearing extravagant costumes sewn with sequins, nor did they sport three-foot high devils masks to make a journey to the cemetery, hundreds of dancers in blue and white satin, little majorette boots, whirling while a series of brass bands dragged over the notes, clashing with one another sonically in the streets.

How well he remembered those processions, ending in troupes entering one by one into the crowded campo santo, a veritable traffic jam of musicians in the streets. One had to leave the cemetery before another could enter, there were just so many, day and night, and entire families hovered around the gravestones, pouring liquor into the earth for the dead, setting out a plate of cold jerky, boiled corn, strips of cheese, fish eggs, for Uncle Demetrio or Aunt Sarita, grandparents and great-grandparents, all of them deceased. He'd never seen as much life as in that cemetery, the long line stretching half a mile down the road, because it was La Virgen de la Candelaria, the fat time, and they didn't have those hang-ups about dead people, because apparently they were still alive and therefore why would you be sad, unless you drank one too many beers with your defunct papa, one sip for you, two for him, three for you, four for him, as towers of fireworks offered their spinning wheels of lavender and green sparks, turquoise and ochre, with little punk kids throwing firecrackers into the middle of a group of women praying with pursed lips, only to watch them scream and run in four different directions before turning in circles looking for who threw that fire-cracker and ending up cursing the air.

Antuka used to take him there. She said it was impor-tant that he see this, that he understood that a cemetery was a place of life and that she knew he was melancholy by nature, but that he had to be sure never to become morbid. Puno was full of misery. And despite his father's noble efforts, because yes, he was doing everything in his power to make their lives better, the situation of the health and welfare of the citizens of Puno was probably going to get worse, much worse. Yet, no matter what, they found a way to be joyful.

"Are you happy?" he had asked her. She didn't answer that question, only popped open for him a bottle of Inca Kola. It tasted like bubble gum, and he didn't love its flavor except she'd given it to him, and he wanted to be apprecia-tive, so he took several gulps with a brave face and forced a too-big smile to show her how much he enjoyed it. He told her he wanted to share sips of it with the dead and, in that way, gradually poured the rest of his drink into the earth. They wandered among the graves, not having one to visit themselves, at least she didn't mention anyone, but rather taking in the expressions of the gathered families as they spoke freely with the dead, catching them up on all the gossip.

After about an hour, she turned to Jasper and said, "You're my happiness." He hugged himself to the rough wool of her skirt, rubbing his face across the fabric while she patted his head. A kid tried to ruin the moment by hurling a firecracker, but she caught it in her bare hand on the fly and threw it at the feet of the startled child, where it exploded, and he ran off screaming and crying for his mommy.

Vanessa, who'd been upstairs brushing her hair and doing facial ablutions, also putting on makeup "for the occasion" came down, plopped next to him, ordered coffee from the waitress and whispered, "Don't be nervous" while squeezing Jasper's leg, a comment he did not dignify by acknowledging it. Jasper said for the waitress to go ahead and bring everybody coffee, even though he had tasted his and it wasn't very good and if on cue, Butch and Inés appeared, holding hands. He and Vanessa gave each other "the look." He squeezed her hand to signal that he was fine with it and she squeezed back to say, "Me too." They tried their best to look serious and casual, but when Butch began to read the breakfast menu out loud with a straight face, all four of them burst out laughing.

"Okay," said Butch. "We're caught." After which, the four of them could speak in a normal way, grateful that this new relationship had in some way taken the pressure off Jasper by becoming the new topic of conversation rather than Antuka. The food was really hot and really greasy but inarguably tasty and everybody chowed down.

49
BANISH MISFORTUNE

Inés had Antuka's supposed address, though she said she couldn't be sure. He didn't really want to know why she hadn't seen her mother in so long. He was already terrified enough on his own without having to carry her feelings. She chatted with Butch and hung on him, as if onto a trapeze high above the ground, and only that bar and her own reflexes would save her from the plummet. Somehow, she had cast a giant, bright soap bubble over the four of them as they walked dingy streets, a bubble formed of glycerin, rainbows sliding over its surface, which could pop at any moment and leave them exposed.

What had always struck Jasper about Puno was its vastness, accentuated by the fact that they lived on the very shore of Lake Titicaca and somehow none of their livestock had ever wandered into those waters and drowned. They had a survival instinct that told them the lake, where they might draw close and drink, beneath its placid surface, held dangerous currents. They could go knee-deep, but no further. Perhaps they felt the undertow, even though they betrayed no visible anxiety.

One sensed the closeness of the sky, the scudding clouds sucked off into space, the mountains crowning rolling fields that undulated off into the four cardinal points as if founding civilization anew on a daily basis. Somehow, among the humble dwellings of adobe and sheet metal, Jasper had been able to experience a sense of mystery and noble grandeur, as though they were abiding amid a cosmic truth that no one had to acknowledge or refer to, because it simply existed. He felt in his bones the sheer fertility of the humans, animals, and even the dirt and living rocks that surrounded him.

Now, as he glanced down at the dust on his shoes as they traversed the unpaved streets, avoiding dog and donkey droppings, Puno seemed like just one more impoverished Andean town, neglected by the government, destined to a perpetual threadbare existence, stripped by history of the magic that had sustained it in its self-conception as the place where human civilization had begun. The sky above, with its striated clouds, looked like one more tin roof, a gigantic one. The mountains seemed like flimsy walls that had been leaned together and could topple with the slightest wind. The incessant barking of the dogs sounded to his ears like an endless, blurred complaint for problems whose origins were now beyond reckoning and whose future was insoluble. His mind strained for myth, for the notes of a distant lullaby Antuka had once sung him, one whose sweet purity was so great that it soothed him to sleep even while he struggled to stay awake just to hear one more note of the song.

Vanessa, intuitive as always, looped one arm around his neck and whispered into his ear, "It's gonna be okay." Jasper realized he was crying without tears or sound, that simply an unlocatable sadness was descending down his being like rain sliding along the outside of a giant picture window through which he looked out onto a green land-scape, its individual contours blurred beyond recognition into a verdant field of sameness, its beauty smeared into sheer color. He didn't want Vanessa to exist here as an appendage of his self-actualization. He wanted her simply to be her, to bring her own sense of self-discovery and deci-sion to whatever was happening at this moment.

But knowing Vanessa, she doubtless wasn't caught up in this same neurotic mind-cycle as him. For her, it was all much simpler, clearer. This visit was one more item to be attended to so that they could sit down like two rational people and discuss their destiny. Yes, destiny was a thing, less an essence than something you could write down on a calendar and schedule a specific day to deal with it. For Vanessa, the future could be foreknown, if you tried hard enough and stayed organized.

"This is the street, I think." Inés was squinting, leaning forward to read a sign that was smudged. Jasper realized that a group of children had been following them down the street, the lost gringos, one enormous, another tall and willowy, a third black, with hair they no doubt wanted to touch, to feel its copious, different texture. Probably they seemed rude to Vanessa, with their mouths hanging open, void of any embarrassment or tact, because their curiosity and sense of wonder were stronger. She surprised Jasper by taking a few steps toward the children, who seemed on the verge of running off, until she stayed them with her hand, squatting before one kid with his own mass of tangled hair, wearing a ripped, striped sweater, more holes than wool, and looking directly into his eyes, said: "You want to touch my hair?" She took his small hand and guided it to her fresh cornrows. With her encouragement, he passed his hand

over them, palpating, watching them be pressed down and
spring up, a live thing. The other four children crowded
around now, touching her all over the head, gently, as if
about to pick their favorite flower, laughing and looking at
each other, excited but not meeting her eyes.

At last, one shyly said, "Your skin is black."

"Yes, and yours is brown. Do you want to touch it?"

"Um," he answered. "May I kiss your cheek?"

"Yes," she said. "Gently."

So he did. And so did the two other boys and two other
girls, literally standing in line as if they were at a carnival
kissing booth. They were now in a state of hilarity, as if they
had gotten away with something. They ran off, the one boy,
no more than seven years old, who had first kissed Vanessa,
blowing her kisses while his friend hit him on the back and
said, "Don't be stupid. Let's go."

By now, Inés had a discussion with a woman who told
her that Antuka's house was the seventh house on the
right. At least that was a lucky number. They reached a
hovel that was undistinguished except that it had window
boxes of flowers. The door was open. Jasper knocked
several times. No one answered. "She might be asleep," he
said. "Maybe we should come back." Vanessa pushed him
through the door. He stumbled into the darkness. Running
his hand along the rough adobe wall, he found a light
switch. The bulb was dim, but he could make out a couch,
two sitting chairs, a coffee table and a picture of Jesus with
a flaming heart on one wall.

This latter surprised Jasper. He'd never known Antuka
to be religious in the Christian sense. She was more attuned
to the mountain gods, the earth-beings. But people did
change when they went through crises. He hadn't seen her
in more than twenty years, so what did he know? "Let's sit

down," said Inés, gesturing to the couch and chairs as if it were her own home. Everybody found a spot and sat, except for Inés, who stood with her back against the wall, as if she expected someone to burst into the room with a rifle and try to shoot her.

Vanessa stood up and went to the shutters facing the street, opening them to let daylight in and make the room less funereal. Now, it just looked like anybody's house and what struck Jasper was how generic it was, how void of signs of Antuka's particular personality. The little dwelling by the lake had been stuffed with endless objects that carried the charge of her special being. It had all been in disarray, one big room, with a tapestry she was weaving; a potato peeler with peelings still stuck in it; a pair of shoes she kept swearing to throw out, yet she would later slip their weary leather on her feet; a shawl she favored, tossed aside, which Jasper liked to use as a lap blanket; a cutting board with a black ring burned into it where she'd once set down a boiling teapot; the bed where she and his father slept, half-made up in a hurry; a bag of wool from a sheared sheep sitting in the corner, adding its faint musk to the smell of cooking, the smell of dried herbs, the smell of love.

Into the room through the still-open front door came Antuka, carrying a pail sloshing with liquid. She stopped cold and surveyed the room with suspicion, as if a group of Jehovah's Witnesses had barged in to convert her. Then her eyes fell on Jasper, and after a moment of misrecognition, she knew it was him and surged forward to embrace him, but then out of the corner of her eye she spied Inés with her back against the wall and Antuka stumbled backward, as if she'd been physically struck with the blow of a hand.

"I went to get chicha," she said, as if apologizing. "Let me go get some glasses for everybody."

"I'll get them," said Jasper, to give himself time to recover from the missed embrace. He should have gone to hug her right then, but the moment had passed and an awkwardness had set up. In he went to the kitchen, opening the cupboard, taking down five glasses, rummaging below for a wooden tray, recognizing it as one she used to have back then. He found a ladle. Carrying the glasses to the living room, he set them on the table. Antuka filled each expertly with the ladle, without spilling a drop. While she did so, Jasper had time to examine her.

She had aged prematurely, as even the most beautiful of Andean women do. The high altitude, the cold, the constant wind burn the cheeks and wither the faces of men and women alike in Puno. Even though her hair remained dark and thick, Antuka was no exception. She looked more like a grandmother than a mother. He felt guilty for even thinking this thought, as he didn't want to be uncharitable. But he couldn't control his train of consciousness. She wasn't the Antuka whose robe had slid off in the half-night, standing naked before his pubescent self, fully aware that he was watching her with a desire he barely understood.

Jasper went to her and removing the ladle from a hand that had begun to tremble, laid it down and embraced her. "Mom, I'm really happy to see you." He was surprised to hear himself saying that word, but that's who she had been to him, in the end. Really, she was the only mother he'd ever had, the only one who had loved him, cared for him, looked out for his welfare, taught him things, led by her example. Their being torn apart had been the great sorrow of both of their existences. They'd had to go on, each down his and her own path, in blank absence and lack of knowledge of one another.

Antuka caressed his cheek with her work-roughened

hand. "But you're okay, son. What's gone is gone. You look good. And this is your partner? She's beautiful. You're a fortunate man."

These were her soothing banalities, the ones she wisely knew were the only ones available to them at that precise moment, the only ones they could bear, for to plunge more deeply into what had been was only to invite a prolonged agony in the view of others who hadn't been there and couldn't fully understand the magnitude of what had been destroyed. She was reminding him both of what was irrevocable and what remained before their eyes, what might be worked with. Antuka wasn't rebuking Jasper, but speaking to him as an adult rather than a wounded boy, she was encouraging him to let go of that half-fantasy that had been clotting his dreams, that had banished him to the place of perpetual first chapters, stories that couldn't be finished, in the vain hope that leaving them open, fortune would supply the occasion for the fantasy to be fulfilled. It was not going to be fulfilled. He had this bald reality and truth in front of him, or nothing. He was wise to embrace it, to have called her his mother, while she was still alive and could maybe do something about that part of it. She was inviting him to swallow his sorrow whole and have done with it. Having said that, without saying any of it, she took a few steps toward Inés, flattened to the wall as if she wished to pass through it, only couldn't remember how. "Daughter," she said soberly.

Inés stepped forward obediently, as if by an incantation, and their palms touched to make flesh that incantation. The others watched in silence, as people watch an improbable occurrence setting up. The very walls seemed to tremble. Jasper saw sparks before his eyes as a wave of deep cold passed through the room, and pinging off the tin roof resounded like heavy hailstones or a comet breaking up and its debris getting deflected rather than burning through and destroying the inhabitants who were either in the wrong place at the wrong time, or else fated to vanish. "It's real," Butch whispered. "What happened to me with her really happened." He didn't elaborate and Jasper didn't ask what he meant, because no one else seemed to have heard him and maybe he hadn't said a word after all.

The room calmed down, the chill was gone. Inés waved everybody off the couch as if they were errant pets who'd climbed up and she and Antuka sat beside each other, staring one at the other in wonder. "How long has it been since you two last saw each other?" Jasper asked.

Antuka sighed. "In my memory, it was forever ago, and it only lasted for one brief moment, then she was gone. For always, I thought."

Inés nodded. "It was as it had to be. But I brought you Jasper, didn't I?"

"Yes, you did, daughter. Thank you for that. And thank you for coming. Please don't disappear again so suddenly."

50
THE DINNER PARTY

Antuka got to work making dinner for her visitors. From a chest, she pulled onions and potatoes, from the cupboard broad beans and rice. She sent Jasper to the corner market for ears of corn and set them to simmer in a huge pot. She gave Inés an apron and set her to work peeling potatoes and onions and instructed her how to make cornbread. If Inés already knew how to make cornbread, she didn't let on, just followed instructions as given. She told Butch to go to the coop in the courtyard and choose a plump chicken. When he brought it back, she began to tell him how to twist a chicken's neck to kill it, but Butch stopped her and said, "I got it." He ratcheted the neck cleanly and Antuka raised her eyebrows approvingly. "I was born in the country," he said.

In a second boiling pot, she singed the chicken and put Vanessa to plucking the feathers. If Vanessa was disgusted by this task, she didn't let on. From under the stove, Antuka snatched up several of the chirping guinea pigs, her chapped hands too fast for their suspicion and banged them against the counter for a clean, quick kill, one thump each. If any of the four onlookers, out of one eye while busy with their assigned tasks, were disgusted by this maneuver, and if they were planning excuses not to eat their assigned rodent after it was roasted in the oven and lay on its side with tiny claws curled and teeth showing, knowing that in the end they'd have to chew its tender flesh anyway, they didn't let on.

Antuka sent Jasper back to the market because now she decided she was going to make rocoto relleno, which meant she'd need chili peppers, cheese, and wakatay. This was turning into a feast, and no one dared stop her. Jasper waved off the money she extracted from a ceramic jar. What had seemed like poverty a couple of hours ago now felt like abundance. Butch went to the corner store for cigarettes and came back with several quarts of beer. After all the guts were thrown away, the chicken boiled and deboned, the vegetable peelings thrown on the dirt floor for the lucky guinea pigs who'd survived to be eaten another day, meat was taken to a wood-burning oven in the patio to cook, smoke curling up above like a flag announcing a successful rescue.

Even though it was clear that they were all going to eat too much, while the potatoes boiled on the kerosene stove, Butch was sent three doors down from the corner store, to knock on the door and ask for Pancha, and bring back a sack full of tamales, so that they could begin eating and drinking beer while waiting for the main meal to be done. And to ask if she had a cake on hand for later, which she did. Butch snapped and went on the errand before she could give him any money. Antuka half-chased him out the front door, but he paid no attention to the bills she was waving, the ones she'd tried to give earlier, and he wouldn't take either.

Before long, they were gathered in the living room, the one that had seemed so depressing and desolate, then chilly, cosmic, and fluctuating, but now appeared as a warm social space, nothing more, in which the quality of the furniture was irrelevant, as long as you had somewhere to sit and hold a plate on your knees. Antuka and Inés kept jumping up in the middle of a story they were telling or listening to, in order to snatch something out of the oven or push another pot onto the stove. They ate and they drank and they ate and they drank. Everything that had come before or was to come after consisted only of words. Misfortune was banished.

When the plates were cleared away and they began to take turns complaining about how full they were and how they would never eat again, while being reminded that there was fresh cake in the kitchen for later to be served with mate de coca, because "it's digestive," Antuka surprised everyone, her children included, the ones who themselves had just admitted to being her children, by going to the cupboard and wrestling out a large box that looked like a boxy suitcase. Out of it, she took a beautiful, shining, deep crimson accordion that looked half as large as her entire being. Spreading out the pleats of her skirt, she settled it on her lap, let it wheeze once or twice, and began to play with skill, her fingers nimble and sure on the hoarse keys, making them cry at will. She sang in a high, keening voice, her words slipping easily between the pulsing notes, as if she'd sung the song many times, whether in a pub among friends, or alone at night in her little house.

> *Khuyakusqan p'asñari,*
> *waqayllañas waqashan*
> *Wayllukusqan p'asñari,*

llakillañas llakishan
punchitullanta qhawaspa,
charangollanta rikuspa,
birritillanta qhawaspa,
qenachallanta rikuspa.

The young maiden who I loved
Spends every day crying.
The young woman I courted
They say she's still suffering.
Take a long look at her poncho
Listen to her charango weep
She pulls her hat over her eyes
See her quena flute moan.

Vanessa was slowly swaying to the music. She stood up, her feet moving side to side. Turning to Jasper, she held her hand out. "You must know how to dance this. What's it called?"

"A carnival," answered Antuka, as she picked up the pace on the accordion. "He knows it. I taught him."

Jasper stood and gave Vanessa his hand, then took her into his arms. He tended to denigrate himself as a dancer, but the truth was, he wasn't bad at all. Sometimes, with the right song and one or two beers imbibed, he got into an absolute rhythm and impressed people, who didn't understand that his intellectual nature and the physical stillness he sometimes projected hid the fact that he was indeed athletic and knew how to use his body. Vanessa didn't look down at her feet. Rather, she stared into his eyes, trusting him to show with his body how it was done. Butch and Inés began to clap, first slowly and then faster, urging the song on. Antuka obliged by picking up the pace even more, so that this song of spurned love became a carnival, suddenly happy, belying its lyrics, which after all are nothing more than the story of humanity, thus not to be taken too seriously.

For a moment, Jasper thought that Vanessa was aroused and was announcing indirectly that after several fallow days, they were going to make love tonight to celebrate his unexpectedly smooth and successful reconciliation with the woman he'd suddenly chosen to call "mom," never once having uttered that name to her, because it would have spoiled the magic he'd imbued in her, the love sorceress, the maker of heaven and earth, keeper of sheep and goats, holder of mysteries she would never divulge, including some deep secret between Inés and her. Some secrets had to be let lie. But then, Jasper sensed that Vanessa was telling him something deeper with the sinuous movement of her body, which was neither chaste nor erotic; rather, it occupied a liminal space. Next, it occurred to him that they were having a silent conversation about whether or not they were going to stay in Peru. They were closing the deal.

He was surprised, even shocked, that she would introduce that topic so boldly and suddenly, that she would be open to leaving her job, even though she had complained briefly about how stuck she was there, how nobody understood her and how she feared that twenty years down the road she'd still be swimming in the same cold, blind channel that led nowhere, except he figured she was blowing off steam, the way everybody does, because she was somebody who liked things to be predictable. She had a mortgage and wanted to make headway on home ownership, which was something you could put your hand on, and not be dragged around by Jasper's mercurial side, espe cially after his inattention had cost him everything. She knew he would be glad to go her way, let her be defined as the stable one.

Yet hadn't she followed him to Peru on a dubious errand? Wasn't she here in a humble, distant house, surrounded by relative strangers who could easily be mistaken at this exact moment for close friends, embracing the strangeness, the very sense of childhood voodoo she'd tried to outrun with her strict, no-nonsense Catholicism? Vanessa leaned into Jasper, not to take the lead, which she could easily do while making it look like he was still leading, because she was that good of a dancer. But no, she was telling him to lead more strongly. This was his native dance, one he was practically born into, and he'd had a good teacher, this woman squeezing the accordion like a goddess who endows vitality into her creations and makes them move, makes them live. Vanessa was telling Jasper to make a decision, to absolve her of the pressure of defining things, because she was physically, emotionally, mentally, and spiritually exhausted. She'd been calling the shots since forever and, for a moment at least, she wanted to be taken care of, to have him act like a provider, a potential husband worthy of the name, a caretaker, a rock, and not get lost in the infinite pathways of his brilliant mind, which, fascinating as it was to be a witness to, could also be a pathway to destruction.

He had survived this onslaught on his life. She hadn't come to rescue him. It was crucial that he understand this point. She had, rather, come to be a compliment. His much-prolonged adolescence was now over. He had to be a man. They could stay here or go back to the U.S. They could marry or string things along with caution for a while. He could probably find a teaching job here, a man who spoke

English and Spanish fluently, and to his own surprise, could have a conversation with Antuka in the kitchen in Quechua.

Who knew what they talked about? It was okay. He didn't have to translate anything for her benefit, because everybody should have a one-to-one relationship, not have to go through anybody else, and not all self-kept knowledge was bad; that was just called good old privacy, having some tact and boundaries to your being, letting the mystery abide, which was exactly what was happening at this very moment, it was like the ayahuasca experience, only now they didn't need that artificial stimulant. They could get by on their hearts and brains alone, which had now been released into the wild universe.

It was scary, this sudden healing that felt like hurt. Yes, it was easy to mistake one thing for another. Death and life manifested so similarly. They were only separated by a millimeter of existence. It was nothing to be afraid of. The universe came pouring down on your head like a cauldron of molten lava, but right before the fusing of your bones, you realized that it was only a summer thundershower, strong, yes, pelting your skin and it stung a bit, but pretty soon you got yourself unclothed because you wanted that rain on every inch of your body. You were all at once a plant, barley, corn, alfalfa, take your pick, waving in the wind, the sheets of rain flattened you to the ground but the stalk didn't break and you became aware within your profoundly green self that you were growing.

All this Vanessa communicated to Jasper through her elbows and knees, hips and stomach, the tilt of her head, the cadence of her feet, and most of all with her steadfast gaze, in this moment where everyone else in the room and in the world ceased to matter, or even to exist.

"Let's get married," he said. "And let's live in Cusco."

"Okay."

Their bodies separated while the others applauded. Antuka unhung the accordion and replaced it in its case, despite the pleas of the others to keep playing. "It's enough," she said. "There will be another time."

51
I SMOKE TO THE RHYTHM OF THE STARS

J asper didn't usually smoke, but he craved a cigarette right then. His body was covered in sweat and he needed to remove to the street to let the night's cool breeze dry his clothes and skin. He bummed a non-filtered cig off Butch, who insisted on joining him. For a moment, they smoked in silence, leaning against the stucco wall, taking in the impossibly clustered stars abiding above them. Jasper was enjoying the brutal bitterness of the cheap tobacco leaving its stain in his mouth. As if reading his mind, Butch said, "Weird. This tobacco tastes like shit but it's good somehow."

"Agreed."

"So what's your deal?"

"With?"

"Vanessa. Your second mom. Inés. Me."

"In what sense?"

"In every sense. I feel like I'm at the Bethlehem Speedway as your support driver. And we've been doing these laps, going faster and faster. And me, I was just driving, like how you go out for a drive to clear your mind.

But all of a sudden, I realize that we're in a race, that maybe we're leading, that we were doing it to do it, but things are getting serious. And we could win or lose. And strategy is starting to become necessary."

"You're a philosopher, Butch. I've begun to understand that."

"I don't know about that. More of a head-scratcher, I'd say. A puzzler."

"Okay, that. So, you tell me. What exactly do you see going on?"

"I met you at a car wash. Looking like a homeless person. Or a schizophrenic. Or an idiot savant. Maybe all three."

"Thank you for that compliment."

"Then, all of a sudden, we're here where that man and woman, god and goddess, you know, those Inca people, walked out of that very god damned lake we strolled past this morning. I feel like if we wandered down there right now, we'd see them walking straight out of it. And I wouldn't believe my eyes, but then again, I would. Because Jasper, there are lots of things in this world I've been ignoring. I'm not saying I'm becoming a hippie, although at this point, I wouldn't care two shits if I was. Just information, is what I'm talking about. Things I don't have the words for and maybe I don't even want to have words for. Either way, they exist."

"I'm with you in the phenomenal cosmos."

"Whatever the fuck that means."

"It means what you just said. In words, ironically. You named the unnameable."

"Well, look at me. You want another cigarette?"

"Sure."

Butch lit it for him and passed it over. "You smoked that first one like it was reefer madness. This time, do the lazy smoke. Let the ash build up. We've got a whole pack of these cheap ass motherfuckers to waste. See, I never told anybody this, but I smoke to the rhythm of the stars. There's another rhythm for a hot, sunny day when it's humid but the wind keeps blowing up. Yet another for when it's cold, like tonight, but I mean in a frozen place, like Chicago in January, and you're on a balcony while everybody else inside is comfortable and warm, drinking wine, you can hear the music muffled through the glass patio door and somebody knocks on the glass, wraps their arms around themselves and makes a pretend shiver, like saying, shouldn't you be inside with us? But you only smile and hold up your cigarette, the wind quiet, to tell them you're okay, that you just needed to be alone for a few minutes to sort things out, or to sort nothing out. In the end, all you're doing is smoking a cigarette."

"You're a fucking poet, Butch."

"Am I a philosopher or a poet?"

"Both."

"This is my night."

"This shitty tobacco is getting better and better. Where are you and Inés in things?"

"I'm almost afraid to say."

"Afraid why?"

"Because if I speak the words, they'll happen."

"That's called an incantation, in my book."

"Okay, that."

"Go ahead. Incant."

"I'm ready to stay here. This place has cast its spell. I know it's going to be complicated. Visas, whatever. That crap gets figured out. But once I get those businesses off my back, I can be a free man. And I want to be with Inés. If that's okay with you."

"You don't need my permission."

"Not permission. Your blessing."

"Of course you have that, future brother-in-law."

"And you?"

"I've got nothing keeping me in the U.S."

"No, no. None of that bullshit. We all know that. What do you *want* to do?"

"This place is calling me back. I don't mean this house. I wasn't raised here. I mean the country. Everything. How it makes me feel."

"You don't have to explain to me."

"I'll see how Vanessa feels."

"She likes it. I can tell."

"If so, maybe marrying. Put an anchor in the ground. She's traditional and I know she wants that. There's a small part of her that fears I will implode and nobody wants to be attached to that."

"Are you going to implode?"

"I don't think so. I feel steady inside. It surprises me. But a great sense of calm is settling over me. I have to be fearless."

"Fearless but not reckless."

"Exactly."

"It's a fine line to walk. I keep falling over on the reckless side."

"But if we weren't afraid? I mean really not afraid?"

"I spend half my time being afraid."

"What are you afraid of, exactly?"

"Only two things. The world and myself."

"Oh, that's all."

A dog came by, sniffed their shoes, and moved on

without making a sound. A piece of paper blew down the alley while the two men watched, as if it might have contained news meant for them. Dogs down the block began to bark, as if the sheet of paper had been a homicidal maniac stumbling along, knocking over trash cans while cursing loudly at no one in particular.

"I don't want to jinx anything, but I feel happy right now. For me, that's saying a lot."

"Amen to that."

Jasper took a long, slow drag off his cigarette and blew a steady flume from his mouth. "I think I'm getting this star-smoking thing."

"You are definitely getting it."

5²
THE WORLD AND MYSELF

Jasper woke early to the crow of a surviving rooster, one exulting perhaps that he hadn't been chosen for the previous night's meal. The sky sported an excessive blue brilliance as if the old sky had been made of glass that shattered into particles and fell to the ground, and this new sheen had taken its place. It hurt his eyes, but he couldn't help but gaze at it in wonder. He found Antuka up early, as was her habit, cleaning up from the previous night's party. Without a word, he fell in to help, scraping burned fat out of the pans, gathering bottles, sweeping the floor with a broom he found behind a door, which is where she always stashed her brooms.

She had become someone who kept a neat house, which maybe was easier when you lived alone. His memory of their shared living space was one of profligacy and abandon, possibly because she had too many things to do and not enough help, yet perhaps there had been a secret order to the mess, for he recalled offering to pick things up and Antuka would say, "Leave it where it is, or I'll lose track of it." And now she had a different order, one related to neatness and what most people think of as organization. She had left off being an artist of disordered space.

He missed that utterly sensual person, who was also able to accomplish a remarkable number of things in one day, with a canny animal strength she knew intuitively how to husband. She spoke to animals, not only simple orders but subtle thoughts and expressions of her current emotional state, as if they actually understood Quechua to the letter and it seemed to affect their behavior positively. Or was it simply the tone of her voice, which contained a broken poetry in its rhythms, unsettling at times but impossible not to listen to? And she had raised him exactly the same as those animals in those years, in the same half-reasoning, half-dreaming spirit that had gotten under his skin, worked all the way down into the core of his being.

As she soaped up the metal pans with her sleeves rolled up, to let them soak for a while before scouring them, exactly the way she'd always done, Jasper had the chance to watch her face out of the corner of his eye while she washed, a face that was focused on a simple task, but relaxed because it was habitual. In that moment, he realized a trait they held in common, a trait that maybe he'd picked up from her, though it could almost be said to be biological. That is, she looked ten years younger today, her features less careworn. His and Inés's arrival and the party had relieved her of years of stress, perhaps guilt, anxiety, or whatever emotions kept cycling through her. Antuka was beautiful again, and while she couldn't shed the erosion of the years entirely, even her skin seemed smoother and brighter. She had passed back over from grandmother to mother.

He had the same tendency, where depending on what was going on in his life, one day he looked in the mirror like a graduate student and the next like a middle-aged man. It was a dramatic swing that many people tactlessly or mindlessly commented on, which didn't bother him because he knew it was the truth. Now, as he gazed with intense curiosity at this woman, he couldn't help but wonder whether she was his biological mother. It would make so much more sense than that alien, pale being who had snatched him away from here and not paid much attention to him after, a person he seldom went to see and only infrequently thought about, because she was distant and seemed to find his presence a distasteful reminder of his father.

In truth, he'd lived alone in that regard. He was seized with an almost uncontrollable urge to rush over to Antuka, take her by the shoulders, and demand that she deliver up the truth of his parentage. But she had begun to smile faintly to herself. She seemed happy, all sadness having flown, humming to herself the same tune she had been playing on the accordion the previous evening. It was catchy, one hard to get out of your mind, he himself would probably be humming it all day. Why bother her with any sort of demand? What did it matter any longer who his blood mother was? He knew what Antuka meant to him and she knew what he meant to her. That was the only truth that could abide, anything else being merely speculative and possibly destructive nostalgia. In a single night, Orpheus-like, he'd gone as far into his past as was permissible. Now it was time to walk uphill out of the depths with his head facing forward.

"Let me scour those pots out for you. The grease looks stubborn."

"It's okay, dear little one. I have my method. All I want is your company beside me this morning. That's the greatest gift you can give. And look how much you've already gotten things looking good while your companions sleep off all that beer." He and Vanessa had made slow, sweet love last night, at whatever o'clock of the morning it was, both having awakened suddenly at the same ungodly hour, as if by prior arrangement. The pleasure of her body was almost agonizing. And he'd given her that deep satisfaction it's not always possible to achieve, in part because she was open and in part because she remained half-tipsy and her drowsy body wanted to be played upon in slow motion.

"Yeah, it sneaked up on them, I think. Butch kept going back for more bottles and I didn't try to stop him." He drew close to Antuka and gave her a kiss on the cheek. She mussed his hair without turning to look into his eyes.

"Jasper, Jasper," she said, as if a whole complex story were implied in those two words which were the same word.

"I'm happy to be here beside you."

"Let's not make a big deal of it. Time passes and then here we are again."

"I'd say it's more than that. It's a reckoning. For all three of us."

"Son, you think too much. You always have. I was always hoping somebody would invent a screwdriver and I could reach in through your ear and slow down that fantastic brain of yours. It was kind of scary at times, if you want to know the truth."

"Look who's talking."

"No, it's not the same. You're smarter than anybody I know. Or that anybody knows. And it's a blessing and a curse. You don't have to use every thought that's inside your head, you know. Some you leave alone."

"I try. It's not easy."

He took her arms and turned her toward him, and she let him. "Antuka, I'm sorry—"

She clapped her hand over his mouth. "For what? For being wrenched out of here when you didn't want to go? And I couldn't do anything about it? I had no power, do you understand? I suffered. I felt horribly guilty. Meanwhile, you went on with your life in a distant country. As you should. You owed me nothing. Yes, you owed me one thing —to survive. Here you are. A beautiful man with kind eyes. You have nothing to apologize for."

He began to cry softly and she wiped his tears with the sleeve of her sweater. He wanted to ask her about what had passed between her and Inés, when was the last time they'd seen each other, under what circumstances, but he knew it was none of his business. They would tell him about it if and when they wanted to.

"I accept that. I'm here now. And I'm going to stay here. We all are, I think. I don't mean in this house, just in the Andes, maybe Cusco, because Inés has her tourist job there and we can probably find work and invest in property."

"Are you sure that's right, to leave your lives and just take off for another part of the world?"

"What are you talking about? This is my home."

"If you say so. But it's not Vanessa's. Her Spanish is okay, but a black woman here on her own? This isn't Lima."

Jasper wanted to get mad, but he found himself laughing. "What are you saying? People here are as dark as her. I'm only getting around to discussing that topic, that and marriage."

"Marriage?" Her expression brightened. She was now interested in the conversation in a new way. "Well, in that case, yes, maybe it's possible. You'll make an honest woman of her."

"She's already honest."

"Your father never married me. Because he was already married. Because I allowed myself to live off and on with a man who belonged to someone else. I was the bad woman."

"Don't say that. You were and are a good woman."

"I didn't feel that way. That's why I let her take you away. You belonged to me, really. We all knew that. I could have prevailed. It's all on me. It's why the gods punished me with Inés. And I didn't know how to handle that. I'm the worst person in the world and I don't even deserve to be visited."

He took her in his arms and held her tightly. "I'm not going to let you talk that way. What was all this about leaving some of the thoughts lying still in your brain?"

She was crying. "I know. I guess they woke up. I left them lying still for a long time."

"I want you to move to Cusco with us. We're selling a hacienda where they found huacas and the government wants to excavate that land. We're going to make a lot of money, Inés says. Butch also wants to invest big. And my guess is we're going to build a house out by Ollantaytambo or Pisaq big enough for all of us to live in. And that includes you."

"I don't know, son. This is all so sudden. You may change your mind."

"I'm not going to change my mind. I'm going to change your mind. Inés and I need you with us."

She separated from him and began to prepare a pot of mate de coca. While the water simmered to a boil, she got the ceramic teapot ready, the blue and white one she still had from way back when. They sat together, staring at it while the tea steeped, as if they expected it to ring. At last, she poured two cups with care and they each took a sip.

"I'm not saying no. I've got animals, I've got longtime friends, I own this house. I have to get used to the idea of actually having children, me, the one they called the barren widow."

In the bedrooms, sleeping bodies stirred awake.

53
THE HACIENDA OWNER'S DAUGHTER

A rich hacienda owner had an only daughter. He hadn't always been rich. He inherited acreage, it's true, but the land was rocky, and he'd had to clear boulders out using oxen and ropes, digging trenches around them, or walking behind a mule filling barrows with stones that he cleared away and used to build outbuildings, a well, and to repair the rock fences his father had let fall down and then the livestock would escape. Thieves came in when they saw how careless this man's father was. The son who inherited the land had run off all the interlopers with a rifle. He'd even shot and wounded a couple and had to fight it out in court, but he won, and after that, nobody dared to bother him. He stationed men on the perimeter of his property until the bad element gave up and moved on, and then it no longer became necessary. Other landowners came to him with their problems, and he tried to help them out and be a good neighbor.

But when the valley fell on hard times, those same men approached, wanting to sell their land. He had never thought of expanding, but he agreed, paying them a fair price and soon he was the biggest landowner in the region. Some wanted to resent him, as success always breeds jealousy, but he made sure to throw feasts regularly, with music and dancing. During those soirees, he would make the rounds, playing the fiddle to raise his neighbors' spirits, asking about everybody's spouses and children, inquiring after what was lacking, or if anybody was sick. He would try to address the situation by sending a doctor or packing them off with a load of fruit from his orchard. In this way, he kept the peace.

The authorities in the distant city didn't care much about the valley or improving it. But the man was smart and cagey and he negotiated water rights with the city, making sure the entire valley had its share. He had to hire more hands as time went on, and he began to wish that his wife would bear him a son to help relieve his growing burdens. Instead, she bore him a daughter. He was ready to be upset at the deity's inattention to his prayers, but when he looked at her darling face, he fell in love with her at once and couldn't imagine any other child holding such a place in his heart. He still hoped to have a male offspring to complement this gift. Eventually, his wife did become pregnant.

The midwife said from her divining that it was most likely a boy, but even then, something told him not to get his hopes up. He'd watched many mares and heifers foal their colts and calves, and he knew that giving birth to a live creature and surviving the ordeal was in itself a miracle. When he prayed at night, on his knees, in silence, it was only for a living baby, whether boy or girl, healthy, and a healthy wife. His wife had stamina, but there was a certain delicacy to her person, and during her pregnancy, she took to bed several times, though the doctor assured them it was nothing to worry about.

When the time came for the labor, he wanted to be in the bedroom next to her, imagining that he might do something to help, or if nothing else, provide comfort to his beloved mate. But the other women folk who'd been called on to aid the delivery shooed him out, acting as if the mere idea of his presence were scandalous. So it was that through the closed doorway, he sat in a straight-backed chair, like a stranger in his own house, folded hands hanging between his legs as he resisted the temptation to cover his ears as she howled and screamed.

She died and her baby, who was in fact a son, also died in the birthing. The rich man wanted to see the bloody mess of it, the physical evidence of his wife and son's passing, the same as the blood and tissue he'd witnessed in the barn on more than one occasion, but the doctor and midwife and attendants had hurried up and cleaned and whisked the evidence all away, as if they'd committed a crime, and all that remained was his wife's cold corpse, looking nothing like the woman he'd once married, more like an effigy mocking the good life he'd possessed only hours before.

Now it was just him and his daughter left. She took on the duties of the wife as far as running the household and attending to their servants, while he tried to recover his sanity by focusing on running the farm and staying atop the farmhands. Those men and women worked doubly hard for a while, as if they were atoning for the loss he'd suffered. As he had sustained them in their various griefs, they now did the same, the women cooking for him and his daughter and the farmhands, wives and widows all up and down the valley bringing loaves and roasts to set on their front porch, and the husbands and single men too showing up for several maintenance projects, such as repairing the barn and chinking walls, that had never seemed to get done.

The daughter turned out to be every bit as capable as the mother, a hard worker, knowing how to preserve, weave a blanket, go down to milk the cows when needed. She grew to be robust in a way her mother had never quite been. She rode horses up and down the valley alongside her father, chased down livestock that wandered away, surprising even the hands as she brought errant animals back into the gates. And she turned out to be a deadeye shot as a hunter, bringing down and helping to skin and butcher prey of a weight and size that any man would have been proud to claim. She'd even skinned a thousand-pound buck before the astonished eyes of the menfolk, none of whom dared to interrupt her peerless separation of skin from muscle with scarcely a nick to the flesh.

The only boast she ever made was her glimmering smile, a smile which along with her soft brown eyes the color of taffy, enamored eligible young men as far as a hundred miles away. Even those who had no business in that part of the valley would ride past alone, or in groups of two or three, making an excuse such as stopping to ask for a drink of water at the well, hoping that this girl would answer the door. Sometimes, they got lucky and would court and spark her for a while, drinking lemonade made from her precious hand. Other times the housekeeper would shoo them away, saying that she knew what they were up to and the girl was not old enough for that sort of foolishness.

Meanwhile, the father grew older. Despite women of the church who'd brought him their best-baked goods after his wife's death, some ready to move in with him right then, others only after the year of mourning was over, and it was right and decorous to aspire to be the rich man's second wife, the father abstained. Some women, unsuccessful in their campaigns, even went so far as to set their daughters upon him, girls of the age of his own daughter, schoolmates and friends of hers. The father handled the situation by playing dumb, assuring his daughter in private that he had married once, for love, and that it was not possible to experience such feelings again. The daughter, in turn, assured him that she wouldn't be against him marrying again, so long as it wasn't one of those little foxes she had used to count as friends. But the father wouldn't budge.

On the contrary, he knew that he himself wasn't as well as he looked on the outside. There was a fatigue that trailed him from the moment he awoke at six a.m. until he finally lay his head upon his pillow, sometimes near midnight, when all the travails of the day had been attended to his satisfaction. He'd been brought up to work hard and now that perhaps the necessity wasn't quite so great and he could have delegated more of his authority to others, it was hard for him to let go of any part of what he'd built.

Yet he knew his strength wasn't going to hold out for many more years. He wanted to see his daughter comfortable; wanted to see a grandson or granddaughter, or both, or several, skittering around on the living room rug, calling him Papa and insisting on crawling into his lap. If he was lucky, and could rest more, he'd still be alive as the grandchildren got old enough to ride and hunt, and he could teach them, as he had his daughter, him still steady at the saddle. He wanted to hold a big dance and have the grand-children milling among the guests, getting their heads patted and told how handsome and beautiful they were and how much they resembled their Papa.

The rich man even secretly hoped that he could teach one of them his particular passion, playing the fiddle. The man had been known to surprise guests at one of his parties with ripping off a few high-stepping fiddle tunes to remind them that he was a human being first, a lover of life, a father second, and a farmer and businessman third. He'd managed to live mostly a decent and moral life against all odds in this wicked world, and he wanted to go out as he had come in, humble and devoted. He didn't mind the idea that someday people would cry at his funeral. He only wanted to give them someone worthy to cry about. If that was pride, well then, that was his sin.

But the girl was happy enough as things stood and in no particular hurry to find a mate. True, she was attracted to this one and that one, and didn't mind flirting or receiving a few kisses on the sly. Still, her intention went no further than that, no matter how much the boys complained. She was intelligent and understood that, in some ways, she was already serving as her father's wife, except in his bed of course, but yes as far as being the mistress of the household, running its economy and having a secure place in the society in which she dwelled. Unlike other girls, who seemed to pair off and get married and pregnant as quickly as possible before their supposed peak of attraction passed, she had no sense that she would become diminished. She possessed in hand most of what those others wanted, all except the romance and the babies. And she was confident that when the right time came, and the right man, it would happen naturally, unforced.

When she looked around at the matrons of the valley, many of them officious and bristling, others even hard and bitter, she asked herself what the fuss was all about. Had she been born only to reproduce? To become one more conniving battleaxe? She had no desire to be like most of the women she was seeing around her. She might in fact stay single forever, if she could. Much of that depended on her father's health. But she also knew that he was more fatigued than he used to be and that death could come suddenly to anyone, as she had been brutally reminded by the deaths of her mother and would-be brother, deaths she had never really stopped to mourn. It was easier to consider that a cosmic fluke, one that had nothing to do with her. But she knew better.

One night, she wanted to go for a ride with a young male friend of hers, one she'd been close to since childhood. There were clouds in the east and darkening skies above the hacienda. Her father didn't think mounting a steed was such a good idea under the circumstances. Yet the young man had come around more often lately and the father suspected there might be a mutual feeling hatching between them. The boy was responsible and had even worked on his farm one summer, so he trusted him, even if his daughter sometimes showed a reckless streak. He gave them permission to go out for an hour, with strict instructions to come back at the first sign of lightning. He'd recently lost a bull to lightning. They agreed and off they rode.

Not long after they were out of sight, the rain began, first softly, then harder and harder still. He imagined that they had gotten off into a barn for shelter and perhaps were necking as young people do when they find a perfect moment where no adults are likely to surprise them. Maybe a few hot kisses on her neck would nudge her to the altar. At first, he decided to leave them alone and trust in their good sense. As the hour slipped by and they didn't return, he decided to saddle up and look for them himself. His chief ranch hand saw his anxiety and offered to go in his stead, and the father let him, as he watched one streak of lightning after another rip through the pure black sky, almost tornado-black.

As he paced and fretted, his heart seized with the thought of losing his daughter. Without her, the farm and all his riches meant nothing. He'd somehow imagined himself earlier in life as the scion of a large family, crowded around his long dining table, but it hadn't happened that way. It was just him and her. Perhaps he had been foolish and a bit arrogant in turning down the many women, beautiful ones, successful ones, responsible ones, loving ones, who'd competed for his widower's hand, dismissing them unfairly as mere fortune hunters. Possibly, he'd so idealized his deceased wife and his daughter that he'd set an impossible standard for femininity to his own detriment. Beneath his daughter's admirable sense of responsibility, perhaps she was covertly spoiled, managing things so she could keep him all to herself. The arrangement, though it had been useful, wasn't natural and wasn't right. She was of marriageable age. It was a conversation they needed to have, if only she'd return home safe first.

Just then, he heard the door to the front porch door open. In came his chief hand, soaked to the underwear, holding his wet hat in a gesture of deference. A shock went through the father. "Is it her? Is she alive?"

"Yes, she's fine but you'd better come outside." On a spotted roan, the boy lay face down across the saddle, unmoving. "Lightning got him." His daughter was sobbing,

The father felt terrible for letting them go out, but his parents didn't cast blame, saying that their son was head-strong and always took risks and nobody could tell him what to do. With time, the incident subsided, after the initial gossip, but not for the daughter. One might think that this accident would have endowed her more keenly with a sense of the passage of time, the suddenness of death, and how you can't postpone things. But on her it had the opposite effect. She had, for once, been seriously sweet on someone, this young man, and his death put her in the same category as her father, idealizing the boy as the only possible suitable mate she ever could have had. With his loss, at eighteen years old, she considered herself out of the marriage market.

Her father didn't know what to do. To insist would only make her more stubborn. He took a softer approach, holding a dinner party for some local couples and their attractive male heirs, for beyond sentiment, the father, a pragmatist, understood that he needed an heir. That's how the laws worked. Yes, he'd left her everything in his will. But if he died, she stood a chance of getting disinherited. Times were threatening to change, but they hadn't yet, and if he were in the grave, he was in no position to defend his daughter or her interests if male cousins showed up to lay a claim on his abundance of wealth and property. Lawyers were lawyers and couldn't be trusted to protect his inter-ests unless he were there to enforce. They were more like the thieves who used to invade his father's property until he ran them off with his steadfast resolve.

But his daughter threatened to not even come to the dinner table to greet the guests. Her father went to his closet and took out his fiddle to alleviate the silence among his visitors. Asking the cook to hold the meal, he pulled his chair back from the dining table, set the fiddle on his elbow and wrist, and played through the set of tunes he was known to feature at the occasional barn dance, when the spirit moved him to show up by surprise and entertain his neighbors. Though none of the invited guests got up to dance, he could hear a couple of feet tapping beneath the table in rhythm to his invention.

The sound of the music lured his daughter down the stairs, so much did she love it, and for a moment, the father believed that the evening would be saved and that his music set would literally be the prelude to her daughter finding a perfect match, or if not that, an adequate one. He imagined that with luck, in a few months, he might be playing this very group of songs, in the same order, at the wedding feast for his daughter and how those present on that blessed occasion would smilingly remember how this fraught moment had been redeemed by melody.

But this fantasy was not to be. When the daughter did come to sit at the foot of the table, opposite her father, in the place her mother used to occupy, her back as straight as her straight-backed chair, her manner came across as aloof and somewhat supercilious. She didn't make a favorable impression on the parents or the sons, try though they might to hide their disappointment and anger. They departed with feigned courtesy, no longer impressed with the rich man's fortune. If they came back a second time, it would be out of sheer calculation.

That winter, after a hard storm that required all hands, including him, to clear the debris from felled trees that had to be cut up into firewood and lumber and stored in the barn, the temperature below freezing, the father fell ill with pneumonia. He'd never gotten seriously sick in his life, so his being reduced to coughing in bed all day and night, with sweats and fever and water sounds coming from his lungs, came as a shock to the daughter. Unwittingly, she believed in his permanence because she had to. She began to regret her high-handedness, her depression that had turned to stubborn cussedness, not fitting for her age and station in life. Sitting by her father's side, as he wheezed and made pained faces, too weak even to reach for his water glass, she renounced her mulish ways. She prayed within his earshot to a God she had long neglected as a turgid if comforting misbelief for weak-minded people, for the full recovery of her father, at which point she would subscribe to the virtues of marriage and do her best to find a suitable and worthy mate.

Things got so bad, despite her fervent prayer, that a minister was called for, in case the father had sins he wanted to confess. While they waited for him to arrive, she went to a closet and took out her father's cherished fiddle. In secret, she had practiced, when her father was out in the fields and her left alone in the house where nobody would hear. Scraping across the strings, she'd tried to teach herself to play as her father did, the same way she'd imitated him in learning how to ride horses and shoot a gun. The task frustrated her, for she was used to doing everything well and picking it up easily. Her ear wasn't bad and she was a decent singer in church, joining the choir when duties allowed her. At last, just before he got sick, she had perfected, so she thought, his favorite song, the one he was most asked to play at parties.

Putting bow to string, her head cocked as if listening for instructions from the fiddle, she began to play. The first few notes were sweet, pure, and the father's breathing quieted down as he listened. But her hands began to shake. She put too much pressure on the strings to keep them steady, making the notes come out sour and sharp. When she tried to ease off, the bow began to slide, as she had feared, making a sonic mess of the one song she had spent many weeks practicing in private.

Angered, she hurled the fiddle to the ground. Immediately, she was horrified as it hit the floor, expecting it to splinter into a hundred pieces, before her gravely sick father's eyes. But the thick rug perhaps cushioned the blow enough, for the fiddle simply bounced, making one final yelp, before settling on the carpet. Filled with shame, she picked the instrument up gently as she would an infant, returned it to its case as to a cradle, and shut it back into the closet where it would live in silence.

The minister came and did what he could to urge words of contrition from a sick man. The father confessed nothing, for he was too busy sleeping and sweating. But after the minister's departure, the father's fever broke. It took weeks afterward for him to regain even a modicum of strength. In that time, the coughing and hacking lessened until it disappeared. His color came back and he walked about the house in regular clothes, even sitting on the porch one mild afternoon when the sun broke through.

The daughter stayed close by his side. And they began to talk about life and how he'd have to depart this world sometime; how he'd have to die; how he'd have to leave his daughter alone; how she could make someone fall in love with her. He told all these things to his daughter; everything she needed to know, things he'd always spoken to her but she hadn't listened, and other things that she was now enough of an adult, however protected she'd been, to understand. It wasn't hard for her to listen intently or make promises, because she saw him gaining strength every day, and her search for a mate, even if it were to begin in earnest, didn't have to be rushed.

But fate had another plan. One night, as she slept with the door open to the hallway, as had been her custom ever since her father had fallen sick, she heard a brief cry that made her start up in her bed, followed by silence. Into her father's room she rushed, only to find him with eyes and mouth open in a rictus. She fell to her knees, only allowing herself to scream inside, where every nerve was now singing a song of sorrow. She took care of all the details—ordering the coffin, arranging the invitations to the funeral, writing a eulogy for her father that she gave without breaking down, all while encased in a leaden sense of paths not taken and time that couldn't be clawed back. She had nightmares in which she relived the electrocution of the boy brave and foolish enough to go out riding in a storm with her. He was the one she would have married, if events had only gone the other way. He was the one who knew how to get around her sometimes petulance and reach the woman in her, the one who really did want to break free of her prolonged girlhood under her benevolent father's protective dome.

But something strange happened. She was prepared to sink into a prolonged depressive state, while the household gradually sank into ruin and the once-virtuous farmhands who had surrounded her father became lazy, selfish, deceptive and tried to take advantage of her. In two years, she predicted, neighbors would pass by shaking their heads at the weathered façade of the hacienda, and the tumbled-down rock fences that her grandfather had once let go to ruin, until her father restored them, and now she would let them fall into disgrace again.

Yet after a brief, intense, desolate stretch of a few weeks succeeding the funeral, during which she found herself crawling under her blankets several times a day, her head thick and eyes swollen, she pulled herself together, drank a shot of liquor at 6 a.m., prepared herself an omelet of cheese, sausage and eggs, polished her favorite muddy boots, pulled them on, buttoned up her jacket and went out to seek the farmhands, who were gabbing by the barn when they should have been out in the field. Their supposed boss stood by, watching them, as if not knowing how to act. "We have work to do," she said to the chief hand.

"Let's get started, boys," said the chief hand.

The others looked at one another in mild surprise, picked up their implements, and marched to their stations. She told the chief hand that his new title was farm manager. If he accepted, he would have a lot more duties but make significantly more money. He and she had to form a partnership. Until she found a suitable mate to help her run the farm, she would rely on his wisdom, long experience in the family, his honesty, and his ability to motivate anyone else on the payroll who didn't share his natural sense of hard work. He agreed. Soon, alfalfa and barley that had gone uncut were mowed, baled and stored.

In the meantime, she went to her vanity, inspected her aging makeup, so long unused, and decided to throw it out and get fresh cosmetics. Likewise, she inspected her so-called wardrobe and found it utterly lacking. It was time to go to the stores for fabric and find a good seamstress and create enough feminine outfits to set off what she'd long been told were her natural good looks.

The aspirants began to visit her on Sundays, the respectable day to begin courting, after church. Several young men would attempt to walk her to her carriage. She let them, evaluating the words of each for sincerity and wit. Finally, one stood apart from the rest, tall and lanky like her father, of a good family with whom they'd always had respectful relations. His father was of a similar age, his mother still living, warm but tactful. The daughter liked it that the young man was daring enough to give her the nickname Pepper. It suited her and made her laugh. Feeling daring, she nicknamed him right back, Sugar Cane, or just Cane for short. After two visits, Cane made his intentions clear.

"I want us to marry, me and you."

After so much time lost, she wasted no words. "Charmed. I accept."

"Cross your heart?"

"And hope to die."

"We'll get married?"

"Yes, let's get married."

But Pepper warned him: "Where I go to stay, you have to go too. We go together. Whatever I eat, we'll eat together." That was their understanding. They began to walk down the road together, like fiancés. Out in the fields, the moon was shining as if it were day. Pepper had gotten all dressed up and put on her fresh-bought makeup.

Cane was walking by her side. And they reached the edge of town. They arrived at the cemetery, the same one where her father had been recently buried. The branches of oaks brushed against the mausoleum of the town's founder, as if wanting to awaken him. They had not gotten more than a few yards into the cemetery, when Sugar Cane let out a holler and ran away. He left Pepper all alone with her nickname.

To the next contestant, she didn't give a spoken nickname, except in her mind, she called him Lips, because during a walk in her nasturtium-strewn lane, he grabbed Pepper and gave her a kiss that lasted a full minute, breaking down into multiple smaller kisses, but in the end, it was a single kiss, like a series of notes that accrue into a symphony. In short, he was a good kisser.

In a niche in the cemetery, she had prepared roast lamb, spiced to perfection, juicy lamb. And whenever someone proposed to her, she had the meat prepared and put inside the niche. She had a little key to the niche.

Lips and Pepper dismounted from his coach. His family was even richer than hers, which was probably why he thought he could take physical and verbal liberties. If they wed and matched resources, they would control most of the valley. Lips was brazen, so he had pitched that fact of their mutual strength to her as a selling point. She didn't care about power or influence, but she liked his confidence, which had turned out to have been so lacking in Sugar Cane. He was several years older than Pepper, and that suited her.

It had begun to rain just as they set foot on the ground and Lips opened his big black umbrella, the kind you take to funerals, to cover her precious head while they ventured inside. Lips asked Pepper whether maybe they oughtn't call off the promenade, given that the weather had grown inclement. That was the kind of word he liked to use, to show off his pricey university education. Just then, forked lightning ripped through the sky, followed by a viciously long roll of thunder.

The storm was approaching. All the drama of the death of her first love came back to Pepper, how foolhardy they had been, how she had insisted on galloping when he wanted to go back. She still had not lived down entirely the guilt of how she'd wanted to get to the far barn so that they could shed their wet clothes and make love. Her passion ran high at this very moment as well, though, and although she had grown less reckless overall, she wanted Lips to kiss her naked skin all over while droplets covered it, as if he were drinking her, and make love to her right on the wet ground in front of the niche where the roast lamb was kept. A girl-friend had advised her never to wed a man without trying him on first, to see what kind of lover he was. She had a feeling that Lips would be a good one, and that prospect overrode all caution.

She thanked him for being so protective, but declared that onto the niche they would go. Just as Lips opened the cemetery gate, a streak of lightning hit one of the oaks that had been scraping the town founder's mausoleum and the branches caught fire. Lips hollered and ran away as fast as he could.

And so it went. Soon it was four suitors down, then five down. None of them could face her afterward. On the contrary, Lips, as befitted his name, gossiped about how she'd exposed him wantonly to danger and though his friends mocked his cowardice, they too feared walking alongside her into the cemetery. They all knew from repu-tation about the dead boy with whom she'd ridden fear-lessly and foolishly into a massive storm and they didn't want to be the next victim. Behind her back, they criticized this singular, strange demand of visiting the pantheon at midnight, and took their courting skills to other, lesser, safer girls' houses.

Thus, Pepper remained alone. Until the chief hand's son got sweet on her. She didn't think about him often, but whenever she happened to spy his happy countenance, she remembered him as one of the first to show up to repair the well after the death of her mother and infant brother. This hand, with cornflower blue eyes, had a shy smile he was prone to flashing whenever she passed. Given his reticent nature, Pepper was surprised when he suddenly came forward, almost as if on a dare. One day, as she walked by where he was repairing a harness, he said, without looking up, "I'm in love with you."

"Charmed," she replied, exactly as she'd replied to all the suitors who had dared to profess their intention. At this point, she had no reason to turn him down, even though others might see his attentions as perverse, given the differ-ence in their social stations. Yet she hadn't been raised to see people as high or low. Her father, rich as he was, had taught her that property and money mean nothing unless you have the right mate. "Wherever I go, we'll go together," she said, looking into his kind eyes. "Whatever I eat, you eat. Then we'll get married in the morning." His name was Darien. She decided not to give him a nickname, not yet. That would come later, naturally, if things worked out. Though in truth, she just liked his name Darien, how it sounded.

Darien rubbed his skin with alcohol. He was going in high spirits. They arrived at the cemetery, him right there by her side. It was a moonlit night, though he wouldn't have cared if it was rain, storm and lightning. She opened the cemetery gate with her key. He was at her side and didn't let go of her hand. That tiny little key was right in her purse. And with it, she opened the iron gate covering the funerary niche.

After she opened it, she pulled out a big platter of roast lamb. She gave the young man a big old chunk of it, right into his hands. Pepper began to eat. Darien also ate his fill with gusto, of lamb and many other things, on a blanket for a pleasurable hour in the cemetery in the middle of the night. In the morning, they went back to the village, hand in hand.

She married the least expected one, the chief hand's son. And for the marriage feast, they slaughtered sheep by the dozens. The whole town feasted for days and three fiddlers were brought to town to keep everybody dancing.

ABOUT THE AUTHOR

Johnny Payne is the author of many novels, including *Confessions of a Gentleman Killer* and *The Hard Side of the River*. His poetry collections include *Ostraca* and *Midnight Sutra*. His book of short stories, *Fish Head*, is forthcoming from Bright House. He is also a playwright and an essayist for Merion West Magazine.

At Silent Clamor Press, we seek to illuminate the human experience with excitement, elegance, and unflinching honesty. If this work has resonated with you—offering a profound journey or a new way of seeing the world—consider sharing your reflections with others. Your voice enriches the ongoing conversation that keeps literature vital and transformative.

www.ingramcontent.com/pod-product-compliance
Lightning Source LLC
Chambersburg PA
CBHW050025120726
47903CB00006B/1907